I0819051

## Praise for *The Creek, the Crone, and the Crow*

"*The Creek, the Crone, and the Crow* begins with an ending, the loss of a way of life that forces change. With this change is the start of an enchanting, mystical journey, where deeply held secrets lead to intrigue and self-discovery. Weiss leans into the folklore of the beloved Appalachian region, allowing those secrets to unfurl like the petals of a blooming flower. Reading *The Creek, the Crone, and the Crow* is an immersive exploration of a distinctive setting and the alluring people who inhabit it. A divine and captivating story, it's one I hope readers will enjoy as much as I did."

—Donna Everhart, *USA Today* bestselling author of *When the Jessamine Grows*

"*The Creek, the Crone, and the Crow* is an impressive blend of history, folklore, and imagination. Kate Shaw and Lydia Brown are memorable characters who are courageous and persevering in their fight against injustice."

—Ron Rash, *New York Times* bestselling author

"I was captivated from the first page of this beautifully crafted story. With rich prose, an evocative setting, and intriguing characters, Leah Weiss had me completely engaged in a world where the people are mysterious and the land holds its secrets close."

—Diane Chamberlain, *New York Times* bestselling author of *The Last House on the Street*

"Thanks to Leah Weiss for writing the women of Appalachia back into history. Filled with folklore, folk remedies, and mountain wisdom, *The Creek, the Crone, and the Crow* is a beautiful tribute to a fading piece of unique Americana. This is a novel for book clubs to savor."

—Pamela Klinger-Horn, Valley Bookseller (Stillwater, MN)

"Leah Weiss has masterfully captured the magic of Appalachia and the soul of her people. Through strength and sisterhood, the healing power of mountain folklore is revealed—and maybe, just maybe, some secrets are meant to stay buried."

—Rose Martin, host, *Write Around the Corner*, Blue Ridge PBS

## Praise for *All the Little Hopes*

"Like all great Southern writers, Leah Weiss's magic turns the local into the universal. *All the Little Hopes* is both a deep dive into the life of a North Carolina town during WWII and a national portrait of an era with all of its attendant glories and pains. I love this coming-of-age novel—its portrayal of friendship, the complications of family, the threats that outsiders can bring. Lucy Brown and Allie Bert Tucker will break your heart, but Leah Weiss's beautiful writing will sew it back together again."

—Wiley Cash, *New York Times* bestselling author of *A Land More Kind Than Home* and *When Ghosts Come Home*

"Wrapped in hope and mystery, this beautifully crafted story, set under a warm North Carolina sun, is full of heart. You won't want to miss this one."

—Kathleen Grissom, *New York Times* bestselling author of *The Kitchen House* and *Glory Over Everything*

"With her latest novel, *All the Little Hopes*, Leah Weiss confirms the place she's earned among top-notch historical fiction writers. Her thrilling coming-of-age story of two young girls in the tobacco country of the Carolinas, growing up in the shadow of World War II, is compelling, alarming, and heartbreakingly satisfying. It grippingly explores the mysteries of one of my favorite themes: Who can really be trusted when the chips are down?"

—David R. Gillham, *New York Times* bestselling author of *City of Women* and *Annelies*

"Leah Weiss has done it again. Another powerful, masterfully observed story. This time, firmly setting us down in tobacco land North Carolina with two teenage girls at its heart and told in language that is uniquely Leah's. I read the novel with my jaw dropped open. For Leah's fans, prepare to be thrilled again. For future ones, get set to be."

—Bren McClain, author of *One Good Mama Bone*

"*All the Little Hopes* is the kind of wise, compassionate, and deeply empathetic novel that we all need right now. In this heartening and heartrending book, Leah Weiss embodies a whole world in her affecting portrait of a small North Carolina tobacco farming community turned upside down by the loss and hardship visited upon its inhabitants during World War II. It's a novel with an irresistible emotional momentum, as we follow all the ways its characters cope with a war come home. Weiss's lyrical sentences are in themselves little wonders, tugging us along, delivering us to one surprising place after another, and in so doing, somehow restoring us to ourselves."

—Tommy Hays, author of *The Pleasure Was Mine* and *In the Family Way*, retired director of the Great Smokies Writing Program, and lecturer emeritus at the University of North Carolina Asheville

"I fell in love with Leah Weiss's debut, *If the Creek Don't Rise*, and have been waiting with toe-tapping anticipation for the release of *All the Little Hopes.* Set deep in tobacco country in North Carolina, Lucy Brown and Allie Bert Tucker capture readers' hearts and won't let go. Weiss richly draws characters so vivid readers feel they are walking the tobacco fields of Riverton, North Carolina. We taste the deliciously rare purple honey, sing along with Glenn Miller, and cheer as Lucy and Bert piece together clues and solve a mystery fit for the pages of a Nancy Drew novel."

—Renea Winchester, author of *Outbound Train*

"*All the Little Hopes* is as warmhearted as the sun that beats down on Lu's family's tobacco fields. With feisty heroines and a fascinating yet little-known piece of American history as a backdrop, this is a coming-of-age story with a mystery at its heart. Yet the novel's crowning achievement is Weiss's creation of the Browns—a family that, in keeping with the best literary traditions, every reader will long to be a part of."

—Kate Moore, *New York Times* bestselling author of *The Radium Girls* and *The Woman They Could Not Silence*

"Small town North Carolina during WWII is brought vividly to life with German prisoners, missing husbands, and hidden stories. *All the Little Hopes* is abuzz with fascinating characters—Aunt Fanniebelle, Trula Freed, and especially Bert and Lu, two very different girls on the cusp of adulthood, learning about life's mysteries as they play Nancy Drew and investigate three puzzling disappearances. Lush, poetic prose, characters you'll not forget, and immersion in a past that has lessons for today make this a compelling read."

—Vicki Lane, author of *And the Crows Took Their Eyes* and the Elizabeth Goodweather Appalachian Mysteries

"Leah Weiss is a beautiful writer. She writes about women and Appalachia with such heart and soul it often takes your breath away. Weiss has a knack for weaving together stories of love, friendship, and family (those we're born to and those we create) against the stark backdrops of hardship and war. The world she has built here, and the characters she has created, are vivid and so real that you will miss them the second you close the book. If you love *Where the Crawdads Sing* or the work of writers like Elizabeth Strout and Ron Rash, you will love this book."

—Ericka McIntyre, editor-at-large at *Writer's Digest*, writer, and fiction editor

## Praise for *If the Creek Don't Rise*

"The 1970s Appalachia of Weiss's brilliant first novel has a culture of moonshining, clan feuding, and enduring poverty that has kept an iron grip on generations of inhabitants... Writing with a deep knowledge of the enduring myths of Appalachia, Weiss vividly portrays real people and sorrows. A strong, formidable novel for readers of William Faulkner and Cormac McCarthy."

—*Library Journal*, Starred Review

"In this tender but powerful debut, Weiss paints both the bright and the dark in the lives of her fictional Appalachian community's denizens."

—*Publishers Weekly*

"Weiss catches and weaves together compelling voices from the haunted and haunting interstices of America. Each chapter is told from a different character's perspective, and they all add new pieces to the puzzle of Roy's dark soul, Sadie's bittersweet hope, and Darlene's mysterious disappearance. Part gothic, part romance, part heartbreaking Loretta Lynn ballad—Weiss's tale is a beguiling, compelling read."

—*Kirkus Reviews*

"An engaging page-turner...the characters who populate those pages [are] realistic enough for readers to passionately connect with, whether through an empathetic enjoyment, a delightful fascination, or a raging disdain. With its bewitching residents and rugged landscape, a journey to Baines Creek is a trip worth taking."

—*Shelf Awareness*

"This one nearly broke my heart. With deeply human characters I will not easily forget, Weiss captures the fierce pull of desperation and the formidable power of hope. An impressive debut from a talent to watch."

—Kathleen Grissom, *New York Times* bestselling author of *The Kitchen House* and *Glory Over Everything*

"Every page of Leah Weiss's debut, *If the Creek Don't Rise*, has a pulse as fierce and unyielding as its Appalachian setting. Told through an ensemble of narrators, men and women of all ages bound by the inescapable power of place and belonging, it is a lush exploration of the darkest rooms in the human heart and the brightest fires of the human spirit. Weiss's remarkable gift for language left me breathless, and her characters, distinctive and unapologetically human, will haunt me for some time."

—Erika Marks, author of *The Last Treasure*

"Leah Weiss brings Appalachia to life in Sadie Blue's story. The setting becomes a richly developed character, and the hardscrabble tale satisfied this reader to the very last page."

—Ann Hite, award-winning author of *Ghost on Black Mountain* and *Sleeping Above Chaos*

"This is for fans of Ron Rash, Wiley Cash, or Nick Butler. Simply fabulous writing topped by breathtaking characters who you will think about long after you close the pages of this stunning novel."

—Jessilynn Norcross, McLean & Eakin (Petoskey, MI)

"*If the Creek Don't Rise* by Leah Weiss will give readers reason to laugh, to cry, to whoop for joy, and to scream with anger... This story of pluck and courage will energize that acquiescent core in many of us."

—Nancy Simpson-Brice, Book Vault (Oskaloosa, IA)

"Leah Weiss pulls on your heartstrings with characters that are unforgettable! Each voice in this town creates its unique attitude...and yes, it has ATTITUDE! You'll love the sweet and sassy, root against the nastiness, and cheer on those open to change. What a fun read!"

—Lori Fazio, RJ Julia Booksellers (Madison, CT)

"Each of the characters will touch the heart of the reader in some way, and you will cheer for their victories!"

—Elizabeth Merritt, Titcomb's Bookshop (East Sandwich, MA)

# ALSO BY LEAH WEISS

*All the Little Hopes*
*If the Creek Don't Rise*

# *the* CREEK, *the* CRONE, *and the* CROW

***A NOVEL***

LEAH WEISS

sourcebooks landmark

Cover design by Nicole Hower
Cover images © Thomas Szadziuk/Trevillion Images, tajborg/Getty Images
Map images © Kalistratova/Getty Images, paladin13/Getty Images, bogdanserban/Getty Images, Pimpay/Getty Images



Published by Sourcebooks Landmark, an imprint of Sourcebooks
1935 Brookdale RD, Naperville, IL 60563-2773
(630) 961-3900
sourcebooks.com

Cataloging-in-Publication Data is on file with the Library of Congress.

Printed and bound in the United States of America.
KP 10 9 8 7 6 5 4 3 2 1

*For Fran and Joe at Finally There—*
*a destination and a state of mind.*

For most of history, Anonymous was a woman.

—Adapted from Virginia Woolf

The one-room schoolhouse still exists in the United States. There were 190,000 in 1919, but today they've dwindled to 400.

# BIRDIE'S REALM

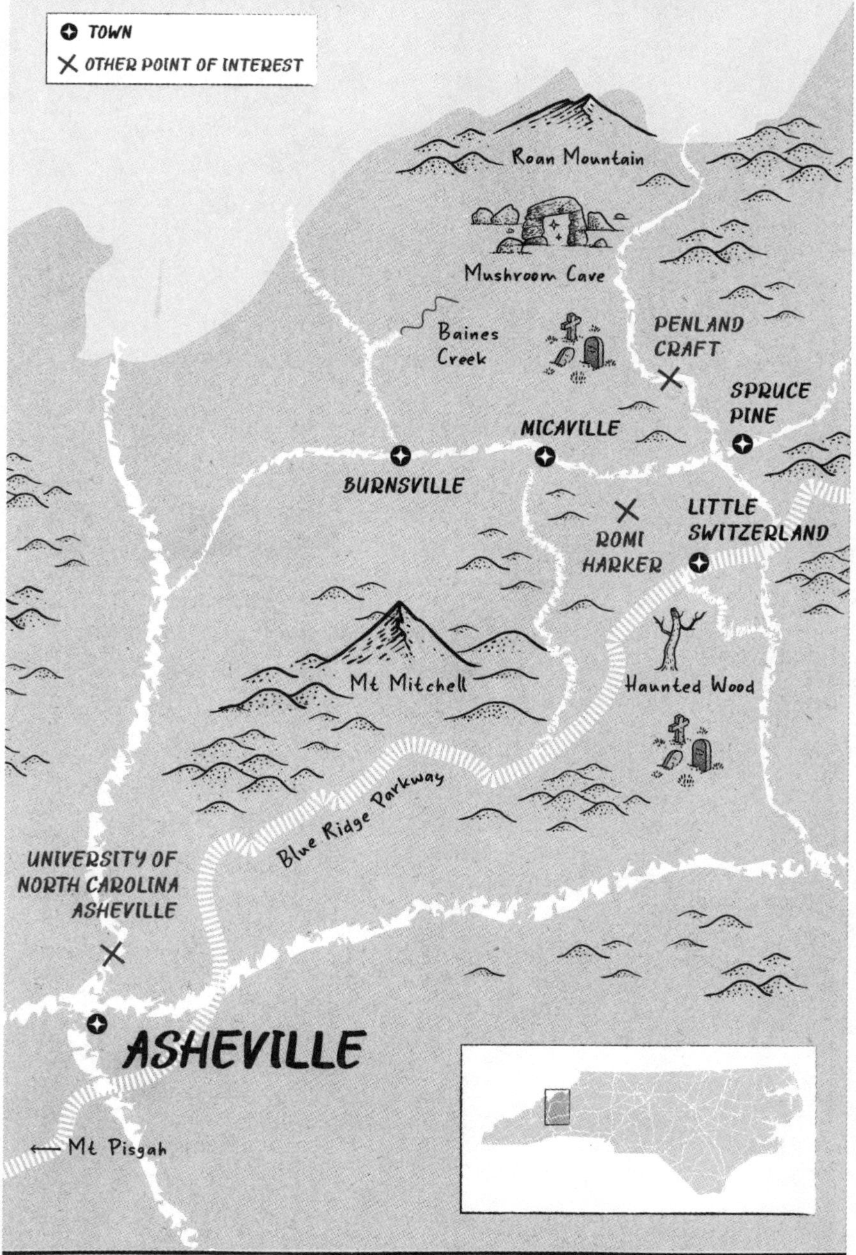

TOWN
OTHER POINT OF INTEREST

Roan Mountain
Mushroom Cave
Baines Creek
PENLAND CRAFT
SPRUCE PINE
MICAVILLE
BURNSVILLE
LITTLE SWITZERLAND
ROMI HARKER
Mt Mitchell
Haunted Wood
Blue Ridge Parkway
UNIVERSITY OF NORTH CAROLINA ASHEVILLE
ASHEVILLE
← Mt Pisgah

# Chapter 1

## THE END

**Kate Shaw**

It is the night that will change everything, and we wait unsettled, restless, picking lint from faded overalls, pulling hangnails on tough hands and threads from frayed dresses. We're in church but not on Sunday, so we don't know if we need to keep quiet out of respect. Is church sanctified every day of the week? We keep mostly quiet out of good manners. Reed-thin men lean forward with elbows on knees and spin dusty hats between calloused fingers, then sit back, sigh, and slouch. Some clear their throats, needing their thirst quenched. Women hold empty hands in their laps or the youngest child, slicking wayward hair down with spit, checking behind ears for grime.

I'm the teacher who stands in back and studies bare necks scrubbed clean and hair turned gray before its time. For ten years I've been the outsider hoping to make a difference for these children. Trying to make a place for myself that mattered. A tenderness engulfs me for these people who will never be my people, such is the truth of belonging or not, and I don't belong.

Preacher Eli announced last Sunday that good news was

coming on this last Friday in May. Every school day I sent home reminders, so here we are—mamas, daddies, and grannies of schoolchildren and the teacher all asked to leave what we'd been doing and meet at five o'clock. The preacher and I've done our parts, and everyone complied out of obedience or curiosity—but the surprise is late, so we wait.

Luke, nine, and Jimbo Walker, ten, wearing outgrown coveralls and holey T-shirts, stand watch at the door, proud to have the task of lookout. One of them poots, and the rude sound causes giggles, and Jimbo points an accusing finger at shy Luke, who blushes. That's when we hear a car strain up the hill and enter the clearing. The boys yell, *They comin', they comin'* and rush to sit with their mama and daddy. Preacher Eli steps out to greet the visitors.

The stranger speaks outside the door. "Where in the Sam Hill are we, Eli? We still in North Carolina, for Christ's sake?" He snickers in a cynical way. He doesn't know his voice carries in the high air. That his taking the Lord's name in vain precedes him as a sign of poor character among these believers. His disdain sours the air with more than flatulence.

The two jaspers and Eli enter church and walk past me, though my hand is out to shake theirs. My cheeks flush at the insult. They follow Eli the ten steps to the front and turn to face us. One is short and the other tall, like runty Eli and six-foot me. But unlike Eli, these men wear blue suits that fit and matching ties not worn to a shine. The preacher introduces them with respect that curdles my stomach.

"Friends, this here is Mr. Clooney, the superintendent for all schools in Yancey County. And Mr. Jessup, the assistant superintendent. They oversee seven public schools in Burnsville, and they come all the way up here to deliver good news bout a change coming to Baines Creek."

Eli grins extra wide like he's a barker at a carnival selling snake oil. Maybe he's making the best of a bad situation. I try to be patient with him because he's the reason I'm here. His plea for a teacher for this settlement was written on an index card and posted on a bulletin board in an Asheville church. I sought cover from a thunderstorm and found my next calling.

We are friends who spar over everything. Eli is faith-filled and blindly trusts the unprovable; I'm the pragmatist who requires tangible proof. He is ruled by the narrow teachings of seminary; I'm educated in the liberal arts. His devil has horns and can be exorcised with words from his Bible; my devil is called Mother. The one thing we agree upon is our hope for the children in this high place. If only Eli's prayers and my jar of penny candy could guarantee a brighter future.

"Gentlemen—" Eli starts with a flourish of his arm, then sits in front, resting that arm on the back of the pew. He turns an admiring face up to the men, and I stay standing in back, worried. How are folks going to take this change that didn't come in an official letter addressed to me? It was delivered by Eli sitting in my cabin, sipping a cup of tea, casually dropping the news like a lethal bomb.

Mr. Clooney pinches his thin lips over buck teeth and stares at a blank spot on the back wall to the left of me, as if poverty is catching if gazed upon. His nose twitches at the smell of honest sweat. He reminds me of the pitiful Ichabod Crane character who interviewed me for this position ten years back. That overcrowded Asheville office reeked of nicotine and despair. Any scraps of hope I had to bring with me, and that precious hope dissipates today.

"Like Preacher Perkins said," he starts with an air of pomposity too big for this plain place. "I am the superintendent of seven schools in Yancey County. We have over two thousand students enrolled in traditional schooling. We take their education seriously with a regimented routine and testable outcomes as governed by the National Board of Education."

He looks up at the ceiling before delivering the surprise.

"Now this here settlement is the last one-room schoolhouse in all of North Carolina, and we've been ordered to absorb your children into our county schools."

*Ordered to absorb?* Is he being intentionally cruel? He ends with "Come Friday, June thirteenth of this year nineteen and eighty, this one-room schoolhouse is gonna close. And come late August, your children are gonna go down the mountain to regular school."

From the looks on people's faces, it doesn't feel like Mr. Clooney brought good news at all. It's met by a stilted silence, and it settles uneasy on worn shoulders.

Buck Dillard, sitting next to his wife Sadie Blue and their three children, says what's on everybody's mind. "What's wrong with our one-room schoolhouse? All us families up here got schooled here and done fine. And how you figure they can travel them roads twelve miles to school and twelve miles back in bad weather when we cain't do it ourselves?"

Mr. Clooney smiles for the first time, but the chilled smile doesn't reach his eyes. His oversize teeth make him look like the jackass he is. "We aim to fix that blasted road, that's how. We bout broke an axle coming up here tonight driving those last miles, and fording that creek was plum scary. The Department of Transportation is gonna start hauling gravel to fill in them gall dang potholes and shore up shoulders. Then we gonna build a bridge over that dern creek so nobody's got to drive through deep water."

"Then what?" Buck continues as our spokesman. "You gonna give us gas for our trucks? Tires that ain't bald so we can git to our kids' lives off the mountain?"

"Course not. We're doing this so we can send a school bus every morning and afternoon. Your kids are gonna get picked up and dropped off at the old schoolhouse."

"What for?" Buck asks earnestly.

"*What for?*" Mr. Clooney snaps back with a slap. He

grows rigid from being questioned. "So they're educated in the real world, that's what for. So they got a fighting chance to rise above ignorance."

*Oh mercy.* This is not going well at all.

Folks stand in quiet rebellion. They begin to herd their families toward the door when Eli intercedes in a rising voice. "Hold your horses, everybody. Please stay. *Please.* We're talking about your children's future." His plea turns to a whine as tired bodies continue to flow toward the door.

Buck sees me standing in back and halts the exodus with the rise of his hand. The hand thickly scarred by fire ten years back, connected to a gentle body damaged in a coal mining accident. He came home a living hero whom folks worried about and fretted over. The crowd stops.

"Miz Shaw," Buck says with respect. "What you got to say bout this change for our babies?"

Eyes are on me, their last resort after the teacher's house burned down. Me, who had been fired for helping a student who was pregnant. Me, who came to this remote place to teach without enough books or desks. Where in winter, ice forms inside tall windows but potatoes cook in the woodstove for the hungry. The blackboard is cracked but not the spirit of folks who manage with scraps and hold tight to tradition. Electricity came awhile back so there is puny light on overcast days in a handful of places, but it remains a dark place with long shadows.

"Miz Shaw." Preacher Eli's voice is desperate behind the wall of people. "Why don't you come up here so folks can sit comfortable and hear better?"

I slowly walk to the front wondering what to say that will matter. Little is in my control now except the anger I hold in check. Even the most basic courtesy has not been extended to me, but I choose not to address the visitors' rudeness. The heart of this story isn't about me. I knew this schoolhouse couldn't stay off the education radar forever, but I'd hoped we would be forgotten for longer. Hoped that the road to get here was too steep. Hoped the cost too high to herd a dozen children into the standardized world.

It sounds so simple on paper. Bureaucratic decisions always do. But in truth, the one-room schoolhouse has become obsolete. Inside the confines of our four walls, I bend rules or ignore them. I understand my students' struggles. I am tender when the school system is tough. Being told at the end of school speaks volumes about the disrespect being shown to these people: We are an afterthought.

I get to the front and Misters Clooney and Jessup don't acknowledge me. They hold tight to their center spot. In their eyes, I'm a babysitter who wears trousers and boots and whose hair is cut too short. A woman with degrees brought to her knees and relegated to the fringes. But I doubt they checked my résumé.

I do know this: These are limited men ruled by limited laws, and it's the first time anyone from the Department of Education has come to Baines Creek. Shame on them. Families still stand and I say, "Please sit." Their skittish eyes hold fear because they are at a crossroads: To stay in the backwoods and fight a never-ending battle or to venture into the modern world that's coming—ready or not.

I wait in front of these people who humble me. I look upon each face and wait till the brink of embarrassment because I don't know what to say. Families wait, too, and the respect they show in waiting is noticed by the visitors. For the first time, they glance at me.

Finally, I begin and confess. "Last weekend I heard about this change coming for your children."

Bodies squirm, disappointed that I kept this secret from them.

"Heard it from Preacher Eli. He asked me to keep it to

myself, which was hard to do. He wanted you to hear the news from strangers instead of us." I watch Eli squirm. My emotions build, and I clear my throat to keep the swell of tears away.

"No one from the education office told me directly. They gave me no warning."

The strangers' faces stay blank.

"I was as surprised as you that we have at last been recognized as important. And why now, you ask. *Why now*, when we've got our daily routine down and your children can read, write, and do figures. Some of you are learning right along with them."

A few bodies scoot up straighter.

"Why now, when we finally have enough secondhand books for everybody to study for their grade level?"

Heads begin to nod.

"Why now, when we've printed ten issues of *Creekrise*. That newsletter printed in Burnsville highlights your traditions and talents. You see your names and your children's stories in print and are rightly proud."

They're all nodding now, but those are our successes earned against staggering odds. We've clawed our way to some semblance of literacy. Everyone here is supreme at making do with little, but they're not trained to follow the structure and regulations of the modern world. Their children can't compete for good-paying jobs.

I look with gentle eyes upon my friends whose lives always wear a tinge of gray, and I say what I must. "We have two weeks left, but your children deserve more than this one-room schoolhouse and me. Send them to town."

# Chapter 2

## BLESSED

**Lydia Brown**

I was born in 1938 in the quiet time between the Great Depression and the Second World War. I was the last child in a long line of Brown children living on a farm in eastern North Carolina, and the family declared me the best of the lot. As proof, there was a peculiar birthmark at the base of my middle finger on my right palm: a trigon. Being the best of the lot was the kind of thing my people could proclaim without envy, for they were tenderhearted and inclined to be benevolent.

In the flatlands of North Carolina, we raised tobacco and tended a hundred beehives in white boxes lined up like soldiers. My people planted and worked an orderly garden that bore a bounty of food, and for generations this rich patch of land yielded more than enough. Then, while the good countries of the world fought to save democracy to the west and to the east, the Browns created a haven that was safe. Even when two German POWs came to work our tobacco fields and bees, they became changed men because of their time with the Browns.

Summertime was the season that stretched the longest in

my childhood, and it was mostly lived outside. Our hundred-year-old witch elm was an imposing presence in the front yard, and it spread its arms over the tin roof of our porch which ran the length of the house. As if by magic, on the hottest of days, that tree could conjure a breeze and bring relief from sticky heat. In the evenings, a line of rocking chairs held tired bodies and creaked on warped boards while we listened to adventure stories and fairy tales, and snapped beans and made butter from clabber in mason jars. The population of my world was ten, and it was a mighty universe.

In the weight of oppressive heat that started in April and stayed through October, we watched to the west for the coming of the rain. When that happened, everybody paused to pray that the wall of wet would cross our property line and quench parched fields. That silent plea was granted so often that I believed the power of prayer was our birthright. I believed there was an unbreakable tenet between heaven on high and the Brown family below. Back then, God answered our prayers.

Once there came fierce clouds that brought a deluge of rain that fell for days, and that flood lay on our land like a wide lake. Everything looked off-kilter, like the barn and the house and the witch elm had up and moved somewhere different. When the storm clouds left and a billion stars came out of hiding, Daddy took us outside to stand at the edge of that still water that had swallowed our field. In place of dirt was a vast bowl of brittle stars in perfect reflection. I was scared that if I stepped forward I'd fall into space, so I clutched Daddy's hand and he didn't let go. After, while we slept, the world righted itself again.

Being born into the Brown family was a safe and solid thing. It was winning the gold ring at the State Fair. Being born last in a line of bright and promising children was proof that luck isn't made but bestowed. When I was single-digits old and untested, I thought I would live forever in the bosom of my family's protection where I wanted for nothing and feared even less. I thought it was how life was meant to be.

But even the best of the lot can get it wrong.

# Chapter 3

## WOUNDED

**Kate Shaw**

I walk the short aisle and leave the church and the rising voices. Outside in the dusk waits a witch, a medicine woman, my mentor and friend. She leans against the fender of the outsiders' car, puffs on her corncob pipe, and squints through purple smoke. During the decade I've known Birdie Rocas, little has changed. She's still a squatty woman with cotton-fuzz hair piled high on her head and layers of long skirts. Her crow Samuel usually rides on her head, which elevates her stumpy stature, but tonight he's absent. She wears a long necklace of beads, bones, and feathers that hangs to her waist and a belt made of braided leather.

When I was new to mountain life and walked past her abode going and coming, it was entering that rusty trailer that I feared the most. Would I understand her speech? Would her smell be too ripe? And if I was repelled, would I become an enemy of someone I needed to befriend?

But the witch's dwelling place wasn't foul. It was a mystical room with potent herbs and moss, with colored stones and delicate skeletons of tiny creatures that lined the window ledges. It was a place of comfort. In those first months it was where I learned the rules of nature, because up here the rules are different, and I was only book smart.

Tonight I say, "Evening, Birdie," and we leave the settlement together because we've heard enough *good news*. We head up the creek trail to our homes spaced a half mile apart. After a hundred paces, the worn path narrows, and I step behind the crone and we follow the rise into the darkening woods. As always, her hips lumber from side to side like an ancient metronome. Her skirts swish the ground, and her walking stick beats to a primitive drum. She is the leader and I follow.

I always imagined I would leave Baines Creek when I was physically unable to live this life. When old age and aching joints and a mind that had grown feeble would help me make the right decision. But not now. Not yet. Not with someone making the decision for me.

The niggling question that haunts me at this time in my tenure is *what's the point of it all*. After teaching for forty years I'm at a place where opportunities grow thin and purpose should be defined. But I fear Judgment Day when the students take unfamiliar tests and the outcome, not my good intentions, will be the determinator. I fear my students will fail and it will be my fault because I was lax.

We come to Birdie's weathered trailer set back from the creek and up an incline. She lights an oil lamp hanging from a low branch where Samuel perches, and we sit in the lamp's glow on tree stumps in the dirt yard. I haven't been inside in years. We've become close neighbors, not close friends. But tonight, she rests her gnarly hands on her knees covered in layers of fabric and she's quiet. Minutes build and then I chuckle wearily at the end of this arduous day. "What do you want me to say?"

She is blunt. "You took it," she says, and hurts me.

"What do you mean?"

"You took it," she repeats with greater disdain.

"What did you expect me to do?" My hackles rise in defense. "Shout? Lash out? Make a scene? Start a war with the education department?"

"Ya know what's comin, don't chu?" she goes on with a bitter drag on her pipe and hard exhale. "When down *there* come up here inside our chil'ren's heads and scramble thinkin."

"I have an inkling," I mumble.

Birdie goes on. "All the hard livin we do ain't gonna be good nuff. They don't get no good mark for huntin and whittlin, for weavin and quiltin. For foragin in these woods and tellin the difference between killin and healin plants. They ain't taught our ways in county school. That world's a store-bought world our chil'ren ain't ready for."

She sucks deeper on her pipe and I think she's through with her rant, but she starts up again. "Them do-gooders is all messed up. They think they know best when they don't know us a'tall, but that don't stop change from rootin us out."

Birdie reaches a crooked stick into the fire pit to poke ashes to life. "They like busybodies who got nothin better to do but stir up trouble and change things." The flames flare to reveal a wizened face that belongs here. Her DNA is pure Appalachia. A weathered survivor. A solid body at home in this wild place. A place in danger of morphing into something it's not meant to be.

"What can we do, Birdie? Aren't we helpless to fight back? Isn't the law on their side?" I run my fingers through cropped hair. "Are you really prepared to take a stand? To build a wall around this place to ward off outsiders?" I press fingertips against my temples and switch tactics. "I'd like to think there's some merit in all this. Some benefit that could lead to a broader life for some of the children, especially for the likes of Eddie Dillard and Sassy Wright. They're bright and courageous and curious enough. My hope is that they'll fit in and find a bright future."

Birdie is puffed up like a toad till the heat leaves her, and her tone turns different. Her face is still and her eyes like bits of coal that glow.

"A kinship violation be crawlin outta the grave, Kate Shaw."

I stop kneading my temples. She's not talking about county schools and a bridge that spans a creek. She's talking about something else the way she's apt to do at odd times.

I whisper, "What kinship violation?" Her eyes have turned black as tar and don't reflect firelight. "How do you know what you know?" I ask as I've asked a hundred times about dangers out of sight. A death, a season of drought, a wildfire, a traveling sickness, a blight. And now *a kinship violation is crawling outta the grave*? What a strange string of words. We don't need another worry added to the pile.

She doesn't explain and the drone of the night insects ratchets up and we look over each other's shoulder having run out of steam, knowing we'll soon run out of time.

"Will you write about this in your Books of Truth?"

"Done wrote it down," she says wearily.

Of course she did. Birdie's homemade books are at the heart of her days, and they've accumulated in her trailer over a lifetime. They are precariously stacked around the inside perimeter of her space. She writes with homemade quills and ink, then binds them in leather she cures. Nobody reads them except by invitation, so their overarching purpose is unclear. I've read sections she picked for me to understand, and my favorite is the mystical tale of the crows. Especially the coming of the loyal corvid Samuel.

When Birdie was in her prime and out hunting, she wore the bearskin that her Cherokee mentor gifted her. Mistaken for a bear by young hunters on that snowy day turning to sleet, she was shot in the back and left for dead. She crawled beneath an evergreen prepared to die, but crows found her. They brought her berries for sustenance and lured a passing mountain man to rescue her. Against odds, Birdie was saved and healed, and one of the crows came home with her. It's an unusual union the likes of which I've never witnessed. It's as though the crow is Birdie's appointed guardian. Or they are a pair that together make a whole.

Birdie likely knew about the county's decision as soon as I did, when Eli heard and delivered the news to the witch on the way to see me. It's not only the challenge of getting the children to town every weekday. It's the way that this isolated place will have to absorb outside thinking. I am a lifelong advocate for education, but it is the clash of mountain traditions with the modern world that is the sorrow I carry tonight. Not for the end of my teaching career which spans nursery rhymes to Greek classics, but for the end of this community's cloistered uniqueness unified over generations. Much as the Appalachian Mountains were transformed when the continental plates shifted three hundred million years ago, today's world is coming for them. Such a disruption could end the old ways entirely.

She repeats, "Done wrote down the kinship thang too," and I feel a jagged chill pass through me, and I'll have to wait to understand more. The medicine woman takes pity on my headache and reaches deep in her skirt pocket for a tiny bag of herbs. "Make tea, eat food, get sleep. This ain't done," she warns, then collects the oil lamp from the branch, lumbers up the two cinder blocks, touches the eight-sided star on the trailer wall, then shuts the door, leaving embers to illuminate the space.

I stare at the coals and wonder. Should I have done more to protect my students? Should I have known sooner that this day would come? Is there an alternative to following orders? Is there middle ground that straddles precious tradition and the modern world where one doesn't cancel out the other? Misters Clooney and Jessup are now on their way back to their safe homes with their creature comforts and conveniences, but they left behind fault lines. Fresh fractures that run deep in the hollers where ginseng grows, moonshine is brewed, and hunting traps are set. On any given day that is to come, that fissure will crack and split and swallow the place whole. But by then I'll be somewhere different because I have to go.

I stand and reach in my pocket for my penlight, but it's not there. In my anxiety over the meeting, I left it in the cabin or at school. When I step away from the dying fire, my heart flutters with familiar fear. It's more immediate than the worry Birdie declared tonight. I've never grown used to the dark in this untamed place. A whispering, growling place, and me without my torch.

My pride prevents me from knocking on Birdie's door and asking for help. It would be one more barb she'd fling at me. I stubbornly move through the black as quickly as I dare, my heart racing, my breath quickening, my ears on alert. I move with my arms outstretched like a blind man groping through the dark. I keep the creek on my left and work to calm my ragged breathing. The cacophony of tree frogs and cicadas and katydids is mind-numbing.

That's when I see them. Lights on the ridge, moving out of rhythm. They're not lanterns and the orbs are too large for insects, too small for humans. They move independently until they sense me watching them. Then they come together in a line and *watch me*.

I run. I run through the dark with brambles and low branches clawing at my arms and face. I stumble over roots like a drunkard, fall to my knees and struggle to my feet. I gasp for mercy while racing away from the alien lights. I'm overly frightened like a silly child with my heart thudding thick. I break into my clearing and Rachel steps out of the shadows, my comfort on four legs. I'm relieved and crying and calmed all at once when my dog nuzzles me and licks my wounds.

This tender mongrel dog I named Rachel is a boy dog, not a girl dog. He's named for my love, *Rachel.* It was that Johnny Cash song, "A Boy Named Sue," that gave me courage. I heard it playing on Sadie Blue's transistor radio, a clever song about acceptance and gender struggles. My boy dog doesn't mind a girl's name, and I gain relief when I say *Rachel* out loud and confide my struggles to his attentive ear.

My breathing slows, and Rachel and I enter the cabin. I light the lantern to see the damage done by my dash through the woods. Blood runs down my arms, but they're only surface cuts. I wash the scratches with a clean cloth and add a layer of witch-hazel ointment Birdie gave me. My trousers are muddy, and blood has seeped through at the knees. My headache has ratcheted into a blinding pain. It's a dismal end to a dismal day.

I now stand in a plain place that looks the same as it did a decade ago: a saggy sofa the color of mold, a bowed table, a thin mattress in a sleeping loft. The roof still leaks when it rains. There are no frills except the line of *Creekrise* newsletters tacked to the wall like celebration flags. The arsonist who set fire to the teacher's cottage beside the school was never apprehended and it was never rebuilt. This empty cabin was to be temporary, but it became permanent when I didn't complain. The message upon my arrival in 1970 was clear: Teachers aren't welcome up here. Yet I came and stayed because I had nowhere else to go.

I feed Rachel from the bag of dog food that I haul up the trail every month. I'm criticized for letting him stay inside at night and in harsh weather. I don't require he hunt or guard to earn his keep. Practical mountain neighbors say I spoil him too much to make him any good, but Rachel serves a mighty purpose. He is my sounding board. My confidant. My comfort.

I stoke the fire in the woodstove to boil water for Birdie's tea. I'm ignorant about what medicine from the forest will provide tonight's relief, only grateful. Where she learned all she knows is a mystery I don't question. Was there a granny healer who taught her? Or her mother long gone? She told me once about an old Cherokee who had gone to the woods to die but delayed his leaving to pass his wisdom on to her. He gave her the truths of the forest and Birdie became a revered medicine woman. She was called a Skinwalker by the Natives. Everyone in these parts has heard of Birdie Rocas. She is a puzzle that I can't solve, so I don't try.

Tonight, after a demanding day that became tolerable only when I reached the safety of home, I eat day-old corn bread with my hip propped against the butcher block and sip hot, bitter tea. For the moment I ignore the disappointing church meeting and think about those peculiar lights I've never seen before. If I'd had my flashlight, I would have been watching my boots and missed them altogether, so maybe they aren't new. Only new to me.

Now that I'm safe within my cabin, they seem benign compared to the callous strangers who delivered hard news to people I admire. Was Birdie suggesting we fight the system? Or is she hoping we can hold on to the old ways and not have deep roots ripped from sacred ground? Whatever happens, the good and the bad, come two weeks from now my time here will be over.

Exhausted, I climb to the loft and step out of my trousers. Both knees are bruised and bloodied, and there is a ragged hole in my favorite pants. I punch my flat pillow before I lay my weary head. I'm angry at worries that followed families home tonight. Some older children will play hide-and-seek with truant officers until they turn eighteen. Some families will retreat deeper into the hollers and cross the Tennessee border. Others will be carefully taught to fear change. And those who flourish might become outcasts for thinking differently.

Birdie's tea begins to work. Tense muscles let loose. Throbbing wounds are dulled. I am pulled under into a dreamless void. My last thoughts are this: None of it is as simple as dropping gravel on a steep road and building a bridge over a creek to bind disparate people.

Misters Clooney and Jessup stirred up a hornet's nest.

# Chapter 4

## LOST GIFT

**Lydia Brown**

I became the odd child at five when dead people came calling in the night. I'd feel their breath in my ear. Smell their chewing gum or pipe tobacco or cooking spice. Feel the heat of the triangle on my palm that pronounced me different from my siblings. By the time I was seventeen, I was living comfortably with this dream gift that came when it was needed to find lost things, warn of danger, or advise folks in matters of the heart. I got used to looks of worry or wonder on the faces of neighbors. Then I got careless.

I slept in that April Saturday because I was feeling poorly. I didn't work market like I was supposed to, and Daddy took my place. Midmorning, Cora and I were making sugar water for our honeybees when a car pulled in the driveway. Through the window we saw the sheriff get out and put on his official hat. I went to the door and stepped back when I saw his face. Trouble was here for sure, but whose? Was it Aunt Fanniebelle or Uncle Nigel? Was it my sister Helen down the road? What brought him out this morning?

Cora came up behind me, and my brothers Everett and

Grady made their way in from the field. It was the four of us at home, too young for the news the sheriff came to deliver. From a lifetime of practice he said, "Can we sit at the kitchen table?" and we shuffled from the parlor down the hall to the pine table with long benches on each side. The same table that brought the Brown family together mornings and evenings with Mama at one end and Daddy at the other. Today, the four of us lined up on one side and the sheriff sat on the other, his shoulders slumped. Then he spoke words I wished he would take back.

"Your mama and daddy are gone."

"Gone where?" Cora asked.

"It was a car accident. They were crossing the bridge. A stranger coming the other way had an episode. A heart attack, we think. His car swerved and ran your parents' truck into the river."

Cora looked at me and said, "But Mama and Daddy can swim, c'aint they?"

I looked at the sheriff. "Not if they got hurt."

He nodded.

We sat there trying to process impossible thoughts, then I pleaded, "Are you sure?"

He played with the rim of his hat but finally met my eyes and nodded.

My first stupid thought was to find Mama and Daddy and tell them this god-awful tragedy. They would know what to do, how to act, what comes next. Seconds ticked by and I felt myself getting madder. Felt anger curdle in my belly like spoiled milk. I hadn't dreamed a single damn warning about this abomination. Didn't feel Mama and Daddy leave this earth and pass over. Wasn't washed in the smell of Vicks that Daddy believed held healing powers. Had no hint that death came and took our parents while I stirred stupid sugar water for the bees.

"What's his name?" I asked.

"The stranger?"

The sheriff took out his notebook he carried in his khaki shirt pocket. "Wilford Gentry from Tarboro way. Sells vacuum cleaners."

I hissed, "I hope he's burning in hell."

We became untethered. Helen and her husband were summoned from down the road. Lucy and her husband and son living north of Asheville came home. Irene and Byron drove from Lynchburg across the state line. Bert Tucker, now a secretary in Washington, DC, already married and divorced, came home alone. All of them returned to the farm of our youth to mourn with Everett, Grady, Cora, and me. And they cried till they were wrung out.

But not me. My eyes were dry from anger and guilt I couldn't release.

My siblings knew the dead talked to me. They had witnessed my uninvited testimonies to friends and neighbors, but they had never spoken to me about it—not until our parents died. My oldest sister Irene started first. "What have Mama and Daddy told you? Are they safe with Oma? Did they see Daddy's people? Tell me they don't hurt." I turned away as Irene ugly cried.

Lucy, pregnant with her second child, said, "If it's a little girl I'm gonna call her Minnie. Would you tell Mama that? It would be a comfort to say Mama's name out loud every day," and she cried quiet tears. It was spooky how no sound came out.

I couldn't eat at the kitchen table because of the crushing pressure to tell them what I could not. Nobody yearned for answers more than me, but I had no comfort to offer. Not at the wake. Not afterwards in the kitchen walled in by acres of covered dishes. I stayed in my room and listened as hard as I could, though listening hard was not how the gift worked.

My failure grew more crippling the next year because no one shared my burden or eased my guilt. Even Trula Freed, the clairvoyant who lived in the nearby cottage with the red door, looked at me with pity. After graduation, I left Everett and Grady and Cora to tend bees and put in tobacco, and I never went back. Home became Asheville-Buncombe Community College, the alma mater of Lucy and Bert. And then came the magnetic mystery of Appalachia and my library work, and a man named Jack Reynolds who looked like my daddy. Jack loved books and wrote poems and took soulful photographs of a land I already loved. In 1963, I married him and kept my maiden name as women of the times were beginning to do. To the man I married I confessed my failures and my quest for the spirit world, and Jack Reynolds loved me still.

# Chapter 5

## WARRIOR

**Kate Shaw**

Saturday morning at the schoolhouse, I'm reworking the final lesson plans but struggling, when in walks a welcome respite: Sadie Blue and her middle child Mary Harris.

"Figured you was here," she says. "Loretty gone to be with Birdie, Baby Blue be with Granny Jolene, and me and Mary Harris bake a batch a scones with you in mind. We brung em with lemonade."

Sadie is my oldest friend in Baines Creek. On that first morning ten years back when she was seventeen and pregnant, she waited on the school steps with an offer to help and a hunger to read and a reprehensible husband as her albatross. Those first months were a worrisome time till fate turned kind for the girl and salvation was delivered in a hunting accident.

"Scones will lift my spirit for certain. Hope you'll join me."

"Mind us interruptin?"

"I got time for you."

I get jelly jars near the water bucket for the lemonade and pull two desks close to mine so we face each other. Mary Harris unfolds the gingham cloth and with pride reveals three lopsided scones. She places one before each of us and bows her head, mumbles a little prayer I can't understand, and commences to eat in tiny bites around the burnt edges then the soft center.

Sadie declares, "Me and Buck gonna obey the law but we ain't happy one bit."

"I understand," I say, and that concludes talk about last night's tough topic that neither of us can change. Mary Harris goes to the bookshelf for a coloring book of flowers and a tin can of broken crayons. I look at Sadie with her hair going gray, and she looks back, understanding that our days sharing scones, lemonade, and talk are coming to an end.

"Ten years—" she says.

"Ten years," I say.

"I ain't sure I'd be here if it won't for you saying I got *possibility*." She fishes for a compliment that's easy to give.

"I knew you were a warrior, Sadie Blue. Right from the start. And an *awfully good* mama," I add, and she grins at the oxymoron. It was our first mind game she easily mastered.

"Where you gonna go?"

"When it's over? I don't know, but not knowing is okay."

"What's that place you go to in summer?"

"Ocracoke. On the other side of the state. It's on an island." I reach for the globe that spins and point a pencil tip to this side of North Carolina and then the coast on the other against an expanse of blue. A place Sadie Blue will likely never see. For comfort's sake, in my desk drawer I keep two black-and-white photographs, a vial of fine white sand, and a conch shell with pink innards.

"Did I ever show you a picture of my sister, Rachel?"

"You might've but I don't recollect right off."

I hand Sadie a photo of two tall women standing on the steps of a weathered bungalow shaded by stunted Southern live oaks. Rachel and I are in our thirties and are the same height and build. Our suntanned arms are casually thrown around each other's shoulders. I say, "That's me on the right."

"Y'all sure look alike."

"We do," I say and hand her the second photograph. "And here we are on the beach waiting out a storm with the churning ocean at our backs." Our short hair is blown wild, and our shirts and shorts billow and we're laughing carefree in a glorious moment. Sadie's seen pictures of the ocean and beaches in *National Geographic* magazines but not one with me in it. She looks closer at the roiling water stilled by the snap of a camera yet powerful all the same.

"It's scary, ain't it? Water that wide."

"The ocean can be scary, especially in a storm when the force of nature is unleashed. But it's magnificent, too. It's nothing to be feared. It's to be admired." I sweep scone crumbs off my desk and drop them in the basket. "There's a poem by Kahlil Gibran, a man born a hundred years ago in a land far across that ocean and beyond the horizon you see. It's a poem called "Fear," and it begins, *It is said that before entering the sea / a river trembles with fear. / She looks back at the path she has traveled / from the peaks of the mountains...*" I finish reciting the poem I know by heart, and Sadie is the usual attentive student and intuitive beyond her upbringing. Even Mary Harris looks up from coloring, lured by magnetic words.

Sadie says, "So fear ain't all bad."

"It sure feels like it when you're dealing with it. But no, it isn't all bad. I guess you walk through it like you do any storm, and you'll come out the other side changed. At least that's the plan."

Looking at the photo of Rachel and me on the steps of the beach house surrounded by gnarly oaks, she says, "You look different, Miz Kate."

I laugh. "Of course I do. I was young and only mildly tested."

"So that's Rachel, your sister."

"Yes." I speak the lie easily and take back the precious photos.

I open Sadie's palm and pour a thimbleful of sand from a vial I refill each year. She feels its fine grittiness that is the beach. I hold the shell to her ear. "That's what the ocean waves sound like, crashing on the shore, breaking shells like this one into tiny pieces and turning them to sand."

Holding tight to the sand in her palm, she takes the shell to her daughter. "Listen here, Mary Harris." The girl has heard the ocean in my shell before, but she listens again. Sadie hands me the shell with great care but holds on to the sand.

"And your dog be called Rachel."

"Yes. After my sister…who died seven years back."

"It was a sickness that got her, won't it?"

"It was a sickness that got her."

I'm always private about my last summer with Rachel. I don't say to my oldest friend here that when I came to Baines Creek, banished for my criminal actions that got me fired, two years later my love was diagnosed with breast cancer. It was the swift and virulent kind that showed no mercy. That following summer we went to our beach house for the last time and stayed out of the sun under a beach umbrella or in the faded rocking chairs on the shady porch or in the hammock when she grew too weak to sit. Early August of '73, we left Ocracoke and took the ferry to the mainland, back to the hospital for medicine to make her dying easier. I was with her till the end because we called ourselves sisters.

I put away the sand and the shell and the photographs in the drawer. We fall silent lost in thoughts until Sadie says, "I be a fool back when you come."

"You were young."

"And a fool," she repeats. "My girls won't be bringing

home no Roy Tupkin, Miz Kate. His kind won't be getting his sorry self in our door or in them hearts." Her jaw is set tight as she looks at her six-year-old daughter on her knees coloring, her flaxen hair hanging over her eyes, her lips clinched in concentration.

"You and Buck will stand between your girls and anything harmful in this world. Your girls are protected. They're safe from harm's way," I say carelessly.

Buck Dillard is Sadie's second husband, a kind man who does the right thing. They are united in faith and family.

"You didn't have anyone to protect you back then, Sadie. You weren't prepared for the likes of Roy Tupkin's cunning and greasy charm. You thought your love could change a bad man—"

"—love and my baby," she adds. Then she nods over and over and whispers, "You know what I done that day, don't chu?"

Mary Harris now colors outside the lines using mustard yellow and a streak of violet.

I know she's talking about the dying day that came after she lost her first baby because Roy beat her. She went back to him after, and I wanted to steal her away but didn't have the right. Three weeks later on Halloween, two hunters went into the woods and only one came out alive.

"What did you do?" I ask because Sadie wants to say.

She watches Mary Harris with an aching tenderness then raises hard eyes. "My blood runs through my chil'ren's bodies, Miz Kate, and I knowd what they made of. My babies be warriors, too."

# Chapter 6

## WITCH

### Lydia Brown

I first saw the name Birdie Rocas three years ago. It was in a stack of papers where it didn't belong. I was finishing my library science degree at UNC Asheville in '77 and assisting in the newly formed Special Collections alongside my husband, Jack Reynolds. He had been named the first head of that department, which was created to preserve the diverse culture and history of Asheville and the surrounding areas. His workspace was cobbled together from several rooms on the lower level of Ramsey Library. One room served as his office and workspace, and the second adjoining room held shelves for the collections that he was starting to amass. Both rooms opened to a public area in the library where Jack would oversee people using the collections for their research. Jen Williams was the second student assistant, and Jack called us his treasure hunters.

Our task was to process papers, scrapbooks, journals, and a plethora of photographs. Some collections we anticipated, like the one from Congressman Roy A. Taylor, Asheville's representative from 1959 to 1977. Then there was the Lucy S. Herring Collection by a prominent black educator in

Asheville, and the Congregation Beth MaTephila history, holding papers from the oldest Jewish congregation. Some collections were staggering, like the E. W. Ball Collection of more than fifteen thousand photographs, negatives, and glass slides of Asheville and surrounding areas taken between 1918 and 1965. The dizzying donations filled boxes and boxes and boxes, waiting to be classified and referenced and typed in duplicate and entered in a notebook in the public area. Every day, the notebook grew into something greater. Jack's new department was a beehive of activities.

In one stack of random papers, I found a note on an index card that read *by Birdie Rocas, medicine woman, found in family bible*. The card was paper-clipped to a single sheet of handmade paper but there was no Bible or family name or donor attributed to it. The writing on that handmade paper was made with a quill, but the sheet didn't hold a medicine woman's herbal remedy or recipe as I expected. It was a cryptic sheet that began with the partial sentence *meadow of our ancestors* and ended with the fragment *Made with lapis lazuli from*, and there was a paragraph written in the Celtic language I couldn't discern. But it was the illustration of a hand with a mark on the palm that drew me in. It was a triangle exactly like my birthmark. Beneath it was the word *KEEPER*. I was puzzled. Why would Birdie Rocas draw a picture of my palm?

I turned the page front and back looking for more about the donor while my palm began to itch. Why was this piece of paper even in Special Collections? In the bits that came before and after in the donated stack, Birdie Rocas wasn't mentioned again. I wondered where she lived or if she was alive. And if she was, could she explain her drawing of my palm?

I made a Xeroxed copy of the index card and note, and in the coming months I worked Birdie's name into conversations. At the university and farmers' markets. On field trips to pick up collections, I asked about the medicine woman. When Jack and I bought an abandoned cottage and guesthouse in the wood that was said to be haunted, I spoke Birdie's name at lumberyards and the café and the post office, but the witch remained an enigma.

Every weekend for the next year we worked to make our dilapidated places livable. We replaced broken windows and rotten boards and leaky roofs. Repointed the fireplaces, removed stains from stones, and updated wiring. In the summer of '78, there remained only one step to complete the transformation: to bring Jack's framed photographs of Roan Mountain's flaming azaleas, Mount Mitchell's moss forest, and Mount Pisgah in the mystic gloom. I added to the stack the photo I took of Jack standing at our bluff while an eagle with the sun on his wings hovered just out of reach. Then I waited for Jack to come home.

It was Friday, June 17, the start of summer break. The framed favorites were wrapped in old army blankets when there came a knock at the door. It was Bob MacDonald and Jen Williams from Ramsey Library. They looked grief-stricken.

I'd seen that look before.

Without preamble, Bob said, "Jack is gone," and he reached out to keep me from sliding to the floor. He had likely labored over what to say on the drive over, drawing the short straw, asking for consensus, choosing to be direct.

"He had a heart attack at his desk, Lydia. Bout an hour ago. We called 911. They came quickly but there was nothing they could do for him. We're so sorry for your loss," Bob said. "We'll take you to see him."

The numbing grief that came was heavier than my childhood grief. My bones were thicker at forty than when I was seventeen. My spine less pliable. The metallic thud of my older heart was duller in my ears, and like before, color leached from the world. After the necessary work of a funeral that I barely recollect, I left Asheville and the university because without Jack there, I no longer fit. I went to Little Switzerland with its solitary line of shops. I burrowed into the solitude of my haunted wood that regrettably wasn't haunted but where memories with Jack were most vivid and the cottage was filled with his oxygen. I washed with his Irish Spring soap. I lit cherry tobacco in a bowl for the fragrance. I wore his flannel shirts and hung his soulful photographs on the walls that stared back at me. Over and over, I read the compilation of Jack's poetry I bound for his last birthday, and over and over repeated an opening line I wanted desperately to believe. *I should hope to pray like the trees, roots running deep, limbs singing above.* Those words gave me weak solace and a goal.

The truth was, I was angry with God. I believed my anger was righteous and that I had been wronged yet again. I nurtured that burning coal of anger as though my breath depended on it. Not the expansive view from the porch nor the cooling calm of the wood nor the skill of our joint labors gave me respite. I roamed our cottage like a trapped animal. I wallowed for months, sleeping days away and spending nights by the cliff looking into the void. At the start, the phone rang and rang, then after weeks of ignoring it, the phone went silent.

Until one day the phone rang and I answered.

"Hello?" My voice sounded broken, out of practice.

"Lydia, it's Jim Baylor in Special Collections. I hope you're doing better."

"I'm okay," I lied.

"Do you have a minute to hear a proposition?"

"A proposition?"

"Yes. There is fieldwork to do in your area for Special Collections, and I could use your expertise."

"Doing what?" I felt a pinprick of light pierce my grief. I smelled my unwashed body. My scalp itched.

"There are collections in Mitchell and Yancey counties that have been offered to us. One is compiling the unique history of Penland School of Craft. There's the oral history, architectural renderings, maps, and publications as well as photographs and films that need preserving and documenting. Another is the life's work of Judge Heriot Clarkson, who founded Little Switzerland where you now reside. Would you be willing to do fieldwork for us?"

"What day is it?"

"Tuesday." He said, then added gently, "October seventeenth. Jack died four months ago."

"Oh," I said, only mildly surprised. I thought it had been longer.

At Jim's suggestion, I rented a workroom at the top of the stairs at the bookstore two miles from home. It was a whitewashed room with a long porch across the back that reminded me of my family farmhouse. The smell of coffee and the hum of voices and footsteps below were a comfort and helped me return to the land of the living. It became my healing place.

This Friday morning in May, the phone rings in my office; it's librarian Jen Williams who stuns me. "Lydia, I found your Birdie Rocas."

My heart skips a beat. "Where?"

"In a remote place called Baines Creek, north of Burnsville. My source says it's hard to get to."

"So, she's alive?"

"He thinks so. Would you like the directions?"

The next day it's raining, and I deliberate the wisdom of looking for a place *hard to get to*. I have a convenient ploy that will help my visit make sense: an article I owe *Appalachian Folklore* magazine. I called the editor last night with the idea about medicine women, and he gave me the go-ahead. At the Diamondback Café, for lunch I eat basil tomato soup and homemade crackers and watch heavy rain turn the slanted blacktop into a scurrying river, and feel an urgency I can't tamp down. It's been three years since I found that card and saw that sketch and read that name. Answers are long overdue.

I drive through hard rain into Spruce Pine with my wipers on high, and turn west across the valley, past the road to Penland, through Micaville and into Burnsville where I review Jen's directions. I turn north into hills and follow winding roads that climb. The final miles are brutal and the road narrows and turns muddy, and there are switchbacks with potholes and steep drop-offs. If I meet another vehicle, there's no room to pass. I lean forward over my steering wheel tense, trying to see around blind curves. I come to a stop at the edge of a violent creek but see the road continues on the other side. Determined, I drive onward with water up to my floorboards that threatens to float me over the edge. Thankfully my tires find purchase and I round the curve into a clearing.

Here unpainted buildings stand as sentinels to guard a virgin forest. The secluded settlement carries few signs of the modern world. I step out of my Jeep into the wet chill that is Baines Creek at the end of May. My watch reads two-thirty but it feels like evening because of looming mountain walls and low clouds soggy as cotton balls. The small church on the hillside is marked by a cross of two-by-fours. The Rusty Nickel is closed, but through dirty windows I see mostly bare shelves. There are the charred remains of a house beside a square building that could be a school. Lastly is a two-story house that leans to the left, with a faded, hand-lettered sign that proclaims *rooms to let*. There's not a lick of paint on the buildings. The bleached boards curl at the edges and the raised grain is raw.

This is not a pampered place.

I am forty miles from home yet I have arrived somewhere outside time. It's 1980 but it could be 1880 except for a rusty Edsel parked in the weeds and a single power line that connects five buildings. A curious someone in the boardinghouse peeks out the limp-curtained window. I knock on the door and step back. The floorboards creak, but the door doesn't open.

"Hello?" I call out. "Can you help me please?"

The door remains closed.

"My name is Lydia Brown. I'm looking for Birdie Rocas."

Moments tick by and I wonder if I'm in the right place and I turn to leave when I hear a woman's muffled words, "What chu wont wid'de witch?"

Relieved Birdie is known, I lean closer to the door. "I'd like to talk to her, that's all. Can you tell me where she lives?"

I think she says *up de creek*. Boldly I ask, "Would you mind opening the door so I can hear you better?" and she surprises me when she does. I introduce myself again and she stands there blankly. I ask her name.

"I'm'a Jolly," she mumbles, though there's little that is jolly about this woman clad in a loose housedress the color of mud. Her untrusting eyes take in my long, smooth hair parted in the middle and my bohemian dress in shades of turquoise, wrapped in a braided leather belt. In this plain place I'm too bright. A butterfly in the land of moths.

"Ms. Jolly, I'm writing an article for *Appalachian Folklore* magazine about medicine women and want to include Birdie Rocas. Can you tell me where she lives?"

"She won't talk to the likes'a you." The corners of her

mouth turn down in disdain. "She don't take kindly to jaspers."

"Jaspers. Oh, you mean strangers."

She gives a quick nod.

"Could you at least point me in the right direction?" I ask.

"Won't do no good." Unflinching, the woman shuts the door with a soft click. I glance around, unsure what to do next, when a tall woman comes out of the square building. Her hair is cropped short, and she wears trousers and a man's shirt with sleeves rolled up. Her arms and face are covered in scratches. She sees me and calls out. "May I help you?"

I hurry toward her, skirting mud puddles. "You certainly may." I offer my hand. "My name is Lydia Brown, and I'm looking for Birdie Rocas. Do you know her?"

The woman is six inches taller than me, with an air of worry burdening her. Her handshake is firm, and she says, "Yes, I know Birdie."

"Oh, thank goodness," I say. "And you are—"

"Kate Shaw, the teacher here—at least for two more weeks."

"Then what happens?"

"School will close for good. Come fall, students will go to county schools. We got the news last night."

"They didn't tell you sooner?"

Kate shakes her head and says, "No, and I think we're in a pickle. I take an easier view to the class day. I don't stick to the state syllabus or tests, and that's gonna be a problem."

"What do you think will happen to the children?" I ask.

"They'll feel overwhelmed and confused. I wish I could sit beside each child those first weeks and tell them it will get better if they hold on."

"Big change is coming, isn't it? I had a devil of a time making that drive up here, so nobody comes here by accident, do they? How will they even get to school?"

"The men from the education department say they're gonna build a bridge over that creek. Lay down gravel in the potholes. Shore up the shoulders. Seems like a lotta work over one summer for a handful of children. And why go to all that trouble? I don't think the education department expects them to succeed, but we have to comply."

Kate rubs the scratches on her forearms, and they start to bleed. She dabs at the blood with a man's cotton handkerchief.

"What happened?" I nod to her arms.

She chuckles cynically, rolls down her sleeves, and buttons the cuffs. "Was my own foolishness. Forgot my flashlight last night and had to stumble through the dark partway to get home." She reaches in her other pocket and pulls out a penlight. "Won't happen again," she says and puts it back. "How do you know Birdie Rocas?"

"I don't know her, but awhile back I saw a page from a journal thought to be written by her. It was at the university library in Asheville. I was hoping to talk to her about a magazine article, but she doesn't know I'm coming. What do you suggest?"

"I go by her trailer on the walk home, but I don't know if she's there. You can follow if you'd like, but you're gonna get wet and muddy." She looks at my long dress and sandals. "You need boots and a slicker. This morning's rain might not be over."

"They're in the car. Give me a minute," I say, relieved to find someone to guide me and give me an introduction. I hurry to my car, step into boots, and drop my sandals on the floorboard. I hitch my long skirt higher under my belt and slip on a red hooded raincoat. In the glove box I find my flashlight, a pen and notebook and grab a copy of the magazine to leave with Birdie. Lastly, I bring my walking stick with its steel point for defense.

"I'm ready," I say and follow this wounded Amazon into gray woods on a furrowed trail lined with water-laden fiddleheads. The way is steep and rocky and a fitting path to the truth I seek. I struggle to keep up.

# Chapter 7

## FUTILITY

**KATE SHAW**

The woman following me looks familiar, but where would I have seen her? Up here, other than wildflowers, monarchs, and evergreens, the colors of this place are earthy and raw. They speak to folks who scrape by. People up here make something out of nothing, but the relentless effort grinds them down, and the colors reflect that. This woman carries a refined light.

I go slower than I usually do so Lydia Brown can keep up. "What is it you're writing?"

"An article for *Appalachian Folklore*. A magazine out of Asheville. The stories are about the magic of this place. I suggested one about medicine women. They liked the idea."

Lydia struggles to catch her breath, so I go slower. I don't have the heart to tell her that after the strain of this climb, it's possible Birdie might not be there, and if she is, she might not talk to her. She isn't generous with her words. But Lydia will have to find out for herself. I doubt she'll take my word for it.

"Known her long?" she asks, winded, and I stop to give her a rest, turn, and look down on the woman whose flushed face is damp with sweat. She reminds me of myself when I first came here out of shape and out of luck. This steep climb beat me down day after day, until one day it didn't.

"Ten years."

"But you're not from here," she says, clearly trying to buy more resting time, swatting at gnats, slapping a mosquito on her calf.

"I come from Tennessee."

"We're not far from the state line, are we?"

"No. Where do you come from?"

"A few hundred miles east of here, but still in Carolina. Grew up on a tobacco farm. Daddy tended bees. My parents died twenty-five years ago. I haven't been back in a long time. There's nothing there. Home is gone."

I know that plight. Home is a place you belong until the person who is *home* is gone.

We continue our climb, and I think about the private sorrows she and I carry, dropping tiny pieces of ourselves like puzzle pieces to collect until we might have a picture worth seeing. I wouldn't think that Lydia Brown had private sorrows and no home to go to, what with her polished exterior, but I'd be wrong.

"What are you going to do when it's all over?" she says.

"I'm not sure. I have a place on Ocracoke so I won't go homeless."

"That's not far from where I was born."

"It's lovely to visit but I don't know what I'd do for employment. Maybe it's time to retire."

"Or maybe something wonderful is right around the corner for you," says the optimist.

The climb has been tediously slow and the sun has dipped below the highest ridge when we near Birdie's place. The crows are settling on the branches when we enter the clearing and see young Loretty Dillard sitting beside Birdie at the yard table. They face away from us, sorting herbs into bundles and tying them with twine. Loretty points and names the herbs: blood root, Solomon seal root, Indian pipe, wild ginger. There's a pile of morel mushrooms. A fire burns beneath a simmering pot of rabbit stew. There's blood and fur on the flat rock by the creek.

"Afternoon, Birdie. Hello, Loretty."

Lydia studies the totem pole, the wind chimes, the painted rocks laid in a circle with a red bowl in the center. Birdie stands and turns to face us. She's the perfect picture of a witch from a primeval forest. Her scowling face is not welcoming to the stranger.

"Birdie, this is Lydia Brown. She writes for a magazine and wants to include you in a story about medicine women. Could she have some of your minutes?"

Lydia starts to step forward, but I hold out an arm to stop her. Birdie will let her know if the distance between them gets closed. Or not.

"Hello, Birdie Rocas. It's a genuine pleasure to meet you," she says respectfully. There's a touch of awe in her voice. She's a more pitiful outsider than I am.

Birdie stays standing, puffing on her pipe, contemplating the jasper. Lydia takes a magazine out of her coat pocket and holds it up but doesn't step forward. She wants the witch to see she's on a legitimate business. "This is a copy of *Appalachian Folklore*, a magazine dedicated to mountain ways, like what you're doing at the table. My article will be about medicine women. What you know is a source of great interest for readers."

I tap Lydia's arm to stop her talking. She's spouting too many words. Any second the crone will go inside and close the door. Lydia takes the hint and turns quiet. The light from the ridge dims, and Birdie is now masked in shadows. Only her pipe smoke swirls around her fuzzy head and her eyes hold the glint of a feral night creature.

Birdie rests a knotty hand on Loretty's thin shoulder and, like she is sometimes inclined, speaks peculiar words. "Y'all watch over this marked child. She be a Keeper," she says and holds up the girl's right hand for no reason I can speculate except that it is as tiny as a doll's hand. With a nod of the old woman's head, Loretty leaves us, crosses the creek, and without a backward glance is gone. She's a child at peace in this wild place, and she'll be safely inside her house with Sadie Blue and her family before dark fully falls. The witch pockets a handful of morels from the table then goes to the stew. She uses her wool skirt to take the hot handle and lift it off the fire, then carries it inside her trailer and shuts the door.

"Oh," Lydia says surprised. "So that's it. She won't come back out, will she?"

"No. That was your one chance."

She whispers in reverence. "Did she call the girl a Keeper?"

"She does that sometimes. Speaks things that don't make sense, then later they might."

"And could you see what was on her hand?"

"No."

"At least I know Birdie's alive." Lydia works to make something positive out of her failure. "And I saw books inside that look homemade." She still holds the magazine. "I'll leave this on her table so she sees it's an important publication that values the life she lives. In case she changes her mind."

"You're brave, Lydia Brown," I say, but I think she's also foolish. "Do you go to this much trouble for all your stories?"

"I'm only a journalist part-time, mostly for fun. But this story and Birdie Rocas are special, and I don't quite know why." Lydia stares at the closed door and speaks as if in a trance. "I've never met her till today, of course—"

"But you said you'd heard of her," I say.

"No. I saw her name on a card at the library three years

ago. It was paper-clipped to a piece of paper and was intriguing. I'm glad I came today."

Lydia hands me a business card with her name and phone numbers on it and *Books and Beans and Special Collections* in italics across the bottom. "My home number is on the back. I'm not far away. I'll drop everything to return if the opportunity arises to talk to her. Please call me if she changes her mind."

I turn to leave when she says, "Can I ask you something?"

"What?"

"Were those homemade books I saw stacked inside?"

"Yes. Birdie calls them her Books of Truth." I speak softly in case Birdie's listening.

"What are they about?"

I grin and say, "Truth of course." Then add, "Stories, recipes, odds and ends, I guess."

"So you've read them?"

"Bits and pieces. I read what Birdie wants me to read."

Lydia nods and holds out her hand to shake mine, then surprises me when she says, "I'd like to stay here a little longer."

"In Birdie's yard? But it's growing dark, and she sent you away."

"I know. I'll respect her privacy, but I'd like to sit here among her things and think."

"But it's scary in the dark."

"I'm not afraid."

"How will you get back to your car?"

She pulls a penlight out of her pocket and clicks it on and off then holds up her walking stick with the metal tip. Lydia Brown is prepared. "It's a straight shot following the creek, isn't it? There are no forks so I can't get lost. Thank you for your time, Kate. I hope our paths cross again. Good luck with your end of school and your students' transition.

And like I said—maybe something wonderful will come from all this."

Reluctantly, I leave her outside Birdie's trailer, sitting at the yard table as the dark arrives. The embers in the fire pit are dying and she throws another log on the coals, comfortable being where she's not wanted.

I'm halfway up the trail to my cabin when I remember who she looks like: Gloria Steinem. The advocate for women's rights. The woman who inspires those of us standing in the wings, waiting, doing little but wanting more.

# Chapter 8

## REBUKE

**Lydia Brown**

I was in the presence of a powerful being when I faced Birdie, and I don't want to leave. From the sharp gaze in her eyes, the raised chin, and ease of her stance, Birdie Rocas knows important things. Things that matter to me.

I moved to Appalachia twenty-five years ago because of my status as orphan and because of an intricately carved bear. My middle sister Lucy bought the bear from a mountain craftsman for my sixteenth birthday, and from that carving grew a fascination for story quilts, folk art, and pottery. Those kinds of handmade treasures first crowded my room at the boardinghouse near college that I shared with two roommates. I had followed in the footsteps of my sisters Lucy and Bert, and at that *College in the Sky* I received my first degree in library science. It was a bonus that Asheville was on the edge of Appalachia, the spiritual place that began to heal the hole in my soul.

I was a witchy girl—until I wasn't. But Birdie Rocas is a bona fide witch. Her rusty trailer high on a mountain is as close to a portal to the other side as I've found. The triangle on my palm burns with knowing, and I touch it and feel it throb. To my way of thinking, it would be foolish for me to walk away tonight, so I stay and wait outside her door, sitting at her yard table while the cicadas and click beetles and frogs ratchet up their racket.

*Help me understand why my gift has forsaken me, Birdie. There's a long line of ghosts on the other side that I long to hear from. For comfort I often list them in their leaving order. My grandmother Oma, my sister's husband Wade Sully, sweet Mama and Daddy, and Trula Freed, Aunt—*

—The trailer door flies open and startles me.

"You gots to stop yor yammerins," Birdie declares with her hands on her hips in reprimand, her anger palpable, her outline electrified.

"But I haven't said a word," I stammer in defense.

"But you thinking hard, Lydia Brown, and you gotta let me be. It ain't time for you to know my secrets." She slams the door and leaves me stunned. The trigon is swollen like a bee sting.

I am baffled that Birdie remembered my name, then I'm perplexed. Why would she say I'm thinking hard? Why would she link me to her secrets? Why did she say the time isn't right? I have no choice but to leave her clearing and take my mental *yammerins* with me, but the thoughts inside my head sounded like words to her. I know this witch is important to me.

With every step I wish I didn't have to leave, but I follow the creek with my penlight at my feet and my walking stick in hand. These dark woods alive with chittering night sounds don't frighten me like they did Kate. Her wounds were excessive for someone who has lived in this wild place for ten years. But I know to be on high alert. Being in the woods after dark is dangerous, and old-timers would call it pure foolishness.

These hills are home to many predators: black bears,

coyotes, and ghost cougars, but I listen for a different sound. I listen for the snort of the wild boar who also inhabits these hills. In the early 1900s, they were brought to the Lodge of Hooper Bald for a rich man's sport. That sprawling preserve is a hundred and fifty miles southwest as the crow flies, and once tired of the folly, the owners turned the boars loose. The hogs scattered and multiply to this day. Its lethal tusks can gore and gut a man in seconds. That's a fact.

I was ten years old when I saw one. I had a warning dream about my friend Yancy Mayhew, and in that vision Yancy was killed by a big hog with tusks. Daddy said I'd described a wild boar. Nobody I knew had even seen a boar, so I felt foolish speaking about something that seemed more horror story than real. But all the same I told him. Days went by, then a week, then Yancy's truck pulled in the yard and I walked to the tailgate, drawn by dark energy.

And there he lay: a massive, muscular, hairy monster with evil tusks. Shot square between the eyes, it still wore the shock of surprise. My warning dream had saved Yancy's life. Long after, he died from something else but not the gore of a wild boar. That's how my spirit dreams were supposed to work. And here I am in Yancey County in the dark, thinking about Yancy Mayhew, who is long gone.

Tonight, without incident, I enter the clearing. It's a ghost town without a soul stirring. At my car I take off muddy boots and stash them in back in a paper bag, slip on sandals, and unloop my skirt so it falls to my ankles. My Timex reads 7:52. A faint light shines from the back room in the boardinghouse and smoke curls from a skinny chimney. I'm tempted to knock on Miz Jolly's door and ask to rent a room. Would I be forgiven if I showed up at Birdie's place at daybreak? Would she reward my tenacity? But while I contemplate, the light winks out.

That's when I see them.

Up in the hills.

White lights bob above the trees, and if my bearings are right, they dance above Birdie's place. I watch them float into a straight line. They're luminous and lovely and radiate peace. They give me delicious goose bumps. I watch till they fade into the trees.

Reluctantly, I start the Jeep and the motor is obnoxiously loud. My glaring headlights sweep the small enclave of buildings—and in front of the schoolhouse I spot a child. The girl I saw at Birdie's. The one they called Loretty. But what is she doing standing in the dark? Why isn't she home with her family? I drive toward her and roll down my window to ask if she needs help—

But no one's there.

# Chapter 9
## COUNTDOWN

**Kate Shaw**

The first Monday in June feels different from any that came before. For one thing, fewer students come to school. Three of the Mayhew girls have been attending, but now only two are here. Crystal tells me that Peggy, the oldest at fourteen, won't be going to school in Burnsville come fall. She's needed at home to help with the new baby coming. She could have attended school here while doing that, but now she can't be so far away. For Peggy there's no more book learning, so she stops now. Her family won't be following North Carolina school laws—they follow the code for survival.

Harlan Biddle, the twelve-year-old nephew of Jerome Biddle, won't be back either. After hearing the *good news* at church last Friday, he told the preacher he'd rather play hide-and-seek with that dern gov'ment man than miss hunting and helping at the still. He declared he's already got more learning than he needs.

Two children down and ten sitting here with fear in their eyes. I don't tell them it's against the law to drop out of school before they're eighteen. That their parents or grannies or aunts will be breaking the law if they don't comply.

To say that sounds like the police-state nobody appreciates. Besides, the last time anyone saw an officer of the law up here was last year when Sheriff Sykes led a raid on a still that had already been moved to a different hiding place. Up here, folks take matters in their own hands. I doubt they'd believe that something like skipping school would get the sheriff to ford the creek on official duty. Maybe we didn't need a full school year to ponder the closing. Maybe in that span of time I would have lost every student.

All these years my jar of penny candy has been used as a bribe for answers, so it's nothing new for the children when I set it on my desk. They don't even smile. But this time, I surprise them when I say, "Take a handful. Take two if you're extra hungry." This isn't the time to be stingy; plus I'll have little need for penny candy in two weeks.

I pull my chair in front of my desk and watch them grin at their good fortune. They become children again with loose shoulders and a twinkle in their eyes all because of a dime's worth of sweets.

"Who wants to go first?" I say without explanation because I want to hear what folks have been talking about since Friday's meeting. Sassy Wright starts first, fiddling with the Tootsie Roll paper she unwrapped, the candy a bulge in her jaw. At twelve, she lives up to her sassy name, and I'm going to miss her forthright speaking.

"Aunt Fleta say she don't want me to look like a ragamuffin and a scalawag so I need me some new clothes. I don't wanna look different from the townies. I ain't never rode a bus, neither. Think it's gonna fall off the edge and we get kilt?"

Before I can answer, Mary Harris, the usually shy middle child of Sadie Blue and Buck Dillard, speaks up bravely. "Cain't I be with Loretty? Mama says we ain't gonna be together cause I'm behind."

"You're not behind, Mary Harris. You're younger than Loretty, that's all. It's your age that decides what grade you're in."

I need to start at the beginning because these children are confused. "Does everybody know the difference between our one-room schoolhouse and the Burnsville school?" The only time the children saw the county school was when Eli and I took them to town for October Festival to get free candy. They didn't see the classrooms. They didn't see neat rows of desks and chalkboards that aren't cracked, and hallways with posters and glass-fronted display cases holding trophies and sports jerseys.

Eddie Dillard, age fourteen and uncle to Mary Harris and Loretty, answers. "County school's got a lotta kids." He looks at Mary Harris and winks. "More than you can count on your ten little fingers."

I nod. "That's right. And where you're going there will be more children the same age as you. You might have twenty-five boys and girls in your class, all the same age, all studying from the same books, doing the same figures, and reading the same stories. And every boy and girl will be a chance to make new friends," I lie, knowing all it will take is one outbreak of head lice and deep lines will be drawn in the dirt.

While they munch on candy and chew wads of bubble gum, I go to the blackboard and write their names from the youngest to the oldest. Beside their name I write the grade they will be going into, at least in theory. I draw lines between elementary and middle and high school. This is a new way of looking at each other, not alphabetized or grouped by family or gender.

Eddie is the brightest of the lot. He's Buck's youngest brother, mannerly, reliable and smart, so doors in the new world will open more easily for him than for others. But he is tender-hearted and a champion for the weak. He will be tested.

The child who concerns me most is eight-year-old Loretta Lynn Dillard, who doesn't belong anywhere but here. She was born old and odd.

Once I witnessed that oddness when she sat by her great-granny's sick bed. I'd come to visit Sadie Blue and bring her a book in the Narnia series, *Prince Caspian*. The winter before, the Dillards had moved into the broken-down farmhouse to give a dying woman a modicum of peace. Gladys Hicks lay in the parlor by the heat of the woodstove while Buck replaced rotten stair treads and broken windows, patched holes in walls and leaks in the roof.

Loretty sat by the old woman's side in the darkened room while Gladys mumbled on and on. I sat at the kitchen table with Sadie and saw shades of the tender girl I first met who collected oxymorons like *bittersweet*, *old news*, and *awfully good* and glowed with a hunger for book learning. But that day, her face was etched with gravity.

"Loretty don't leave her side," Sadie whispered, while laying a piece of muslin on the table and smoothing it over and over, then folding it precisely with the corners lined up. "When she ain't got school or chores or church, she sit by my dying granny," she said. "You know what she doin'?"

I shook my head because, in part, I couldn't fathom kindness or patience being given to such a spiteful person. I'd never heard one good deed Gladys Hicks had done, and her greatest cruelty had been inflicted on her granddaughter, Sadie Blue, who is more forgiving than I am.

"She pulling Granny's sins into her own little heart. Pulling out them black sins what come from living long."

I'm only partially confused. I've come to expect preposterous statements from simple folks. Still I say, "How can that be?"

"It be her divine gift from God," Sadie replied, as easily as a mother would talk about a child's lovely singing voice or a talent with figuring numbers.

Eli had told me Loretty's birth was special. That she was born encased in a bubble that held her birth fluid intact. With a straight face, he said that birthing veil declared the girl was protected from malevolent forces and it came with a rare gift: She was a sin-eater. I'd come across that archaic term in Greek mythology once in graduate school. Eons ago, every village had a sin-eater who did necessary work to help sinners cross over. Whether I believe it's true or not, that need persists in dark hollers today.

I sipped weak coffee and nibbled on a day-old scone, unsure how to participate in this bizarre conversation without crossing the line that divided common sense and fairy tales. But curiosity got the best of me.

"What does she do with their sins?"

Sadie gazed out the back window and up to the ridge. "They be a laurel hell up that'away called Peavine Gap. Don't nobody go on purpose partly cause a wild boars and that laurel hell. When a hunter be fool enough to shoot a boar, it knowed to worm its way inside that thicket. A hunter goes in to git it, but gets turned around and c'aint git out."

"What do you mean? He dies there?"

Sadie didn't answer, but said, "Folks know to stay away, but my girl listen and take 'em to that laurel hell at Peavine. She dig a hole and hurl them sins in, covers 'em up and tamps 'em down. That laurel hell holds pain as good as a bear trap clamps a paw. Folks be at peace cause they sins be left behind."

I didn't dispute Sadie's story because to argue was pointless. I tried to offer sympathy. "Aren't you frightened for her?"

"Naw. Angels watch over my girl," said Sadie Blue with a beatific smile—but I was never sure angels were enough.

Today, at the start of our two final weeks, Loretty stares out the window. She is disconnected from our conversation about class size and grades and the last *Creekrise* newsletter. Besides the story about a taxidermist that Eli arranged, each child is to write a paragraph about their greatest talent.

"Like what, Miz Shaw?" Luke asks, puzzled.

"Can anybody help Luke?"

Eddie says *singing good* and *wood carving*, then Sassy adds *playing the fiddle and banjo*. Pretty soon our options are substantial with the addition of storytelling, basket weaving, and quilting. I want to emphasize the mountain gifts these students will bring to their expanded community.

I watch Loretty take three suckers from the candy jar when it reaches her, but she doesn't eat them. She's not as easily tempted as the other children. She places them on her desk in the shape of a triangle. This isn't the first time I've seen her make the trigon shape. It's a common doodle in the margin of her papers. Sometimes it's an outline. Sometimes it's filled in. I worry that the girl will only feel at home in Baines Creek. If any of her uniqueness comes to light in town they will call her terrible names. They might do terrible things. Loretty Dillard doesn't belong off this mountain, but I don't know how to stop her from leaving. Sadie and Buck are law-abiding people who want more for their children. But *more* can be a dangerous thing.

At the close of the day, when she's leaving school with the suckers in her pocket, she speaks for the first time. Through bangs of limp hair, her hazel eyes glint and she says, "A kinship sorrow gotta be undone, Miz Kate, and it's me what gotta fix it."

"What do you mean?" I call after her, "What kinship sorrow? And why do you have to be the one to fix it?"

But she's walking away, holding Mary Harris's tiny hand, their delicate bodies heading home, and I think, *What are we to do with this odd child who lives in a world apart?*

# Chapter 10

## FOLKLORE

**Lydia Brown**

I'd counted on Birdie Rocas being the crux of the *Folklore* article. Counted on the start of a friendship that would allow me to return. She sees we're tied together in some mystical way I can't understand yet. Otherwise, why did she remember my name, read my mind, and say it wasn't time for me to know her secrets? But Birdie and I will meet again. Saturday was the beginning, not the end. For now, she's unwilling to participate, I've procrastinated long enough, the Friday deadline looms, and I must settle for another subject for my article.

I choose a different healer for the article, one who lives closer to the haunted wood. One suggested by Professor Covey at the bookstore. He said Romi Harker is a recluse who follows the old apothecary ways and is not tainted by the modern world. She tends to the hill folks we never see. But there's no map to Romi's door. Nothing as easy as driving narrow dirt roads and crossing swift water to enter a clearing, then walking a marked path.

At sunrise Monday morning, I meet a guide named Tonto outside the bookstore. He, too, was recommended by the professor. My canvas backpack holds a recorder, notebooks, pens, a camera, and extra rolls of film. I've thrown in chocolate bars because I heard Romi's partial to dark chocolate. We start driving south on the Blue Ridge Parkway, then take a narrow fire trail to the end and beyond. His truck fords two streams before it can go no further and we hike the final stretch, me struggling while Tonto watches the ridge, looking for signs.

When we pause for a rest, I say, "If she's willing to speak to me, I'll want to stay."

"I ain't staying."

"Then how will I get home?"

"Tell me when to fetch you and I'll come back—but I ain't staying on this here mountain."

He is emphatic about an unnamed danger. I ask, "Do I have anything to fear? Is where we're going safe?"

"Depends."

"On what?"

"If she takes a likin' to you."

We continue around an outcropping of rocks and past massive laurels. I'm pondering this worrisome conversation when Tonto stops and points to smoke that's different from regular. It's rose-colored like Professor Covey said we'd find. I feel a rush of excitement. Tonto covers his nose with his bandanna, distrustful of the smoke.

I'd feared that Romi Harker might not be alive, but the woman I find in the clearing commands a royal presence. When I step forward, the intoxicating smoke embraces me and I drop my guard. Her eyes meet mine, and the shock of the familiar sparks between us.

*She looks like Trula Freed! My dear childhood friend.* Silver hair, simple caftan on a straight frame. A smooth arm full of gold bangles. I am disassociated for a moment, almost expecting to see a red door with a brass lock and an old yellow dog named Biscuit lying across the threshold. She looks the same as she did twenty-five years ago, and that's the clear warning that this vision is not real. Trula is long dead. My brother Emmett called me with the news. But today I am drawn to a past I suddenly miss with a primal ache. I long to be a child again and enter Mama's fragrant kitchen and eat at the long table with my brothers and sisters and walk the dirt path between Daddy's tobacco fields and enter the pines to Trula Freed's place, which always felt perfect and safe. I shake my head to scatter those dead memories, but they cling to me like the rose-colored smoke.

Romi's homestead holds four perfect apple trees and four beehives. The bee boxes are painted with an artist's hand, like a mosaic glass, and the honeybees' legs are thick with pollen. Jars of honey are lined up on a ledge. They glow golden. A small corral confines a handsome horse, a plump milk cow, and two goats. Fancy chickens peck for grub and their plumage is fit for hats in France. Romi's lean-to perches at the mouth of a cave, and although that sounds common, the whole of the space is regal and faces east overlooking a verdant valley. This is a rich and healthy place.

I glance back at Tonto, who trembles inside the tree line, then I walk toward this woman hoping she won't turn me away like Birdie did. I think history will want to remember Romi Harker. I want to remember her.

"Welcome, Lydia Brown," she says as though I arrived at the appointed hour instead of showing up unannounced. Behind me Tonto mumbles *godamighty, godamighty* and stumbles deeper into the tree line. If he leaves and doesn't return, I'll struggle to find my way home, but I'll take that risk.

"Would you come back for me, Tonto?" I ask over my shoulder, without acknowledging the oddity of the witch knowing my name.

"When?" His voice quivers.

"Tomorrow," I say, though I've had no invitation to stay.

"You gonna stay *here*?" His tone is incredulous, as though I've lost my mind, but he says, "I be back," and off he goes, slipping and sliding through the brush till the sound of him is swallowed by the forest.

Having invited myself overnight, I say lamely, "You look like a friend I used to have." Me, the brazen stranger who has barged into her domain. I take a step closer. "Her name was Trula Freed." I have rarely said that name out loud over the decades, yet it rolls off my tongue like a comfort. "She could read minds and tell the future. She was a healer who saved my family from a killing sickness. She counseled me about my spirit gift. She was kind when I didn't deserve it. But she's dead now. I didn't go to her funeral." The trigon on my palm burns.

A stew simmers in an iron pot over the fire. Romi spoons a ladleful into a crafted burl bowl and offers it to me. I come forward and drop my backpack full of questions on the ground and take a seat on a stool. I'm ravenous, and the stew is delicious. Romi Harker has only spoken my name, but I'm at peace in her presence.

That afternoon we walk the virgin forest to collect botanicals for her apothecary, me with pen and paper, the healer with her gathering bag. Garlic mustard, columbine, nettle, goldenseal. We gather colorful mushrooms and drink from pure springs. I think my questions, and she reads my mind like Birdie did, but unlike Birdie, this witch answers me. Those answers fill cassette tapes, and I take copious notes and only occasionally feel the presence of something ominous lurking underneath.

My notes are extensive, and that night I sleep as close to heaven as I've ever been, competing with the majesty of Mount Mitchell's elevation of over sixty-six hundred feet. In my dream I dance with a coven of women in a clearing. We wear gossamer gowns in shades of lavender and gold. Romi is in the coven, and all the women have the same birthmark on their right palms they raise to the moon. Their faces morph between fresh maiden and haggard crone. After a night of celebrating, I wake refreshed under a crystal sky of lapis glass.

Too soon, Tonto comes for me as he said he would, and he calls from within the tree line. Once more, he is careful not to breathe the witch's smoke. Before I leave, I hug Romi deeply. She has been generous to me. She is the sweet childhood I've lost and today miss desperately. Little of the last twenty-four hours makes sense. I want to stay. *Please let me stay.* But I leave because Romi says it's time to go.

After we get back to his truck, Tonto says, "That witchy woman scared me somethin' terrible with her warts and black gums and that bald, spotted head. Her old hag of a horse was bout bent in two, and them scrawny chickens scratching in the dirt was painful to look upon. I almost didn't come for you, but a promise is a promise, and I promised."

Romi didn't appear to me as she did to Tonto. I believe he speaks his truth because in my time with her, there were crippled shadows and sour smells that didn't fit the perfection I saw. When I listen later to our conversations on cassette tapes, they unnerve me. The scratchy voice is not what I heard spoken by the gracious woman I saw. And when the rolls of color film are developed, the pictures show watery forms in shades of dirty gray. There is no discernible person. There is no beauty to behold. There are only disturbing fragments.

Romi must possess great magic to shift into someone else. Maybe Trula Freed offered to be that someone. Maybe Trula wanted to remind me that, once upon a time, when I was innocent, I had a guide and a friend. Maybe this is a sign that I can have those things again.

I complete my article, but I withhold much of what

Romi Harker revealed. Some things are too fantastical to put on paper. Readers grounded in the modern world can stretch their thinking only so far.

But Romi's story isn't Birdie's story.

# Chapter 11

## SUNDAY

### KATE SHAW

Over the following days, I think of Lydia Brown and her bravery. The magazine article was a pretense; the crone meant more to her than a story. There was a hungry look on her face when she saw Birdie, a look reserved for idols and heroes. But who in their right mind chooses to stay in the dark outside a witch's place when the witch doesn't want you there? It was hard for me to leave her, but I wasn't going to fight Lydia's battle. I know not to push back against Birdie. I'd say Lydia was crazy, but I don't think that's it. There's more to that woman than beauty and polish and nerve. She's keeping a secret.

On a misty Friday morning, one week after the good news was delivered by heartless strangers, three boys leave school to conduct their final interview for *Creekrise*. The assignment is simple: For our newsletter they are to interview Mr. Curtis Sunday, an animal stuffer who specializes in black bears, wild boars, and ghost cat cougars. It's said he makes dead animals look alive. The boys have their list of questions. Eli made the arrangements.

Curtis Sunday lives where the hermit Pharrell Moody

used to live. Pharrell was the legendary man said to have been possessed by the devil fifty years back but who was exorcised by Eli's preacher daddy and granddaddy. It was one of the first stories Eli told me when I came, and I believed little of it. What I do believe is that with every retelling, the story grows more far-fetched, with Pharrell prancing naked on the mossy roof of his hut, his skin coated in mud, and howling to the moon while his fingernails turned into claws. Unlike Pharrell who died, his story never will.

The morning passes routinely. Students help each other with multiplication tables and vocabulary tests and begin writing about their best talent. After lunch, I read the next chapter of *Tom Sawyer* where Tom has misbehaved and will have to whitewash the fence. This is a confusing image since there are no whitewashed fences up here. It reminds me of how many simple things will confound these children when they go to town. We're debating Aunt Polly's punishment for Tom when Eddie, Luke, and Jimbo crash through the school door. Their clothes are tattered, voices hoarse, arms scratched, and eyes glossed with fright. Luke trembles and Eddie sputters, *Git the sheriff, Miz Kate*, and they sink to their knees.

"Hold your horses and let me see if y'all are hurt," I say, and a quick scan shows no serious wounds. "Loretty, get the boys water, and Sassy, my first aid kit." The boys take turns gulping water from the ladle and get their wind back enough to tell the story that ends with the shocker: Curtis Sunday is dead.

I call the sheriff and the day drags into late afternoon before he arrives, takes the boys' statements, and they leave with their parents. Tomorrow the sheriff will go to Sunday's place with his deputy. I carry the weight of this unsettling incident up the path, slogging through the wet woods, exhausted more than usual. When I pass Birdie's trailer, she stands in the doorway backlit by her oil lamp. Her unkempt hair is piled off-kilter on her head.

I call out, "Got a minute?"

"I got some minutes."

I need to repeat the story to understand it. It's too surreal. "Three boys found Curtis Sunday dead. They went to interview him. That's tragic enough, but I want to tell you the bits that don't make sense."

Her face stays in the shadow.

"Eddie, Luke, and Jimbo agreed that he was sitting in a rocking chair with his body starting to spoil. They didn't see wounds or blood. The old man was surrounded by his creatures mounted in scary poses. Some of the animals' eye sockets were set with dull green stones instead of resin. Jimbo used his pocketknife to pry the stone out of the panther's eye socket. The boys say they're raw emeralds but I've never seen one, so I don't know. But he stole it and he knows better—but that's when the story turns stranger."

I clear my throat. "After he plucked out the stone, the chair holding dead Mr. Sunday started to rock."

Birdie stays mute, so I go on.

"The boys got scared, even Eddie, and they ran out of the hut with Jimbo still clutching that stone. All three said they were chased by phantom animals. Could hear wild animals crashing through the underbrush. Even Eddie, who's the most trustworthy boy I know, said he could feel their hot breath on his neck, they were that close." I take a deep breath and add, "They sounded convincing."

I don't mention the three ghosts with red eyes that swirled through the treetops.

Birdie puffs on her pipe, like I'm supposed to read smoke signals. She waits so long I'm ready to leave, when she says, "You believe 'em?"

*That's* her first comment? To cast suspicion on *my* doubts?

"Some of it. Not all."

I'm miffed that my voice sounds defensive. Birdie and I have been at this crossroads a hundred times. She never offers an explanation that I can understand.

"How come you think that'a way?" she adds.

"*Me?*" I strike back. "A chair doesn't rock on its own. Dead, stuffed animals don't chase boys. Curtis Sunday *is* dead. Jimbo *did* steal a green rock, but for the rest I think their fear got the best of them. That's all."

She pauses again and I turn to leave when her cutting words stop me. "You so gall dang sure a yourself, Kate Shaw. So gall dang sure..." Birdie uses the condescending tone I despise: the superior adult calling out the weak child.

"No, I'm not sure at all. In fact, I'm rarely sure of anything."

She snickers. "You be that teacher woman hearin somethin she cain't 'splain, so she boil it down to nothin. That the best yor educated brain got?" She blows one last stream of pipe smoke and leaves the open doorway. The smoke hangs in the air. I'm so mad I could spit darts. I am ready to leave this place.

Holding my flashlight at my feet, I continue the trudge up the path, muttering. *I didn't stop to argue, old woman. I wanted your opinion, for Pete's sake. Wanted you to explain so I could understand. But, no, you had to put me in my place. Had to criticize me for wanting logic instead of a damn Grimms' fairy tale.*

As I near my clearing, I let go of my anger before I see Rachel. He moves slower these days since the killing snow that almost took our lives last February. I let go of the anger because this creature only gives kindness. I light the lamp on the counter, hang my slicker and satchel on pegs, fill his bowl, and wish I had something better to give him than dry food. He gulps the nuggets in three swallows while I flop on the sofa. He comes and lays his head on my belly and studies me.

I confess, "I know you're tired of hearing this, but I'm not made for this place. Not the pushback, not the judgment, not the mystical mumbo jumbo that everybody swallows without question. Maybe it's good that the end is here and we get to go somewhere else—but where shall we go, my friend?" I rub his velvet ears, and he loves it.

"We'll go somewhere far away. Somewhere that doesn't have steep hills to tax my knees. Someplace that doesn't keep me twisted out of sorts. A place with soft sunshine. One grounded in common sense and defendable science. A place where the magician performs tricks but understands it's only an illusion."

# Chapter 12

## LIGHTS

### Lydia Brown

You have to believe in magic to write for *Appalachian Folklore*. It's an unwritten rule. The stories tell readers about supernatural happenings witnessed in Appalachia. About old-timey traditions that need to be preserved. About the ways of the forest that blend Christian beliefs with paganism and Native American practices. Foxfire glows green in these forests, as do luminescent mushrooms named bitter oyster and dripping bonnets. And there are elusive blue ghost fireflies that appear in mating season in a few places only in western North Carolina. The stories within the pages of *Folklore* marvel at the unexplainable and the mystery of Appalachia.

I'm the occasional contributor who comes up with an idea the editor likes, and he gives me permission and a deadline. I've not managed my time well for this requested assignment, and it's too late to mail my draft, so I hand-deliver it to Rudy at his unpretentious, bustling office in Asheville. Paperwork and photographs are piled high on his scarred desk. The wide table in the middle holds sequential pages ready for review. The whole scene is ordered chaos repeated every thirty days.

I'm only partly pleased with today's story because of what's missing—Birdie Rocas and her perplexing world. But I made my deadline.

"Look forward to reading your article, Lydia," Rudy says, removing his reading glasses. He holds out his ink-stained fingers to add my paperwork to the pile awaiting his red pen.

I nod to Rudy but don't make excuses. Instead, I say, "Do you remember the article about lights north of Burnsville?"

"I do." He scratches his scraggly beard. "Got a lotta mail bout that story. Specially from witnesses who had seen them. It's a hard line between those who believe those lights are supernatural and those who don't. The town officials like to point to electricity coming to remote areas or headlights winking through trees on back roads, but these lights go way back before electricity or even cars. Why'd you ask?"

"I saw something when I was researching my story. I wanted to read the article to compare. I'll check archives."

"If you uncover something more, let me know." Rudy slips on his reading glasses, back into editor mode. "We might do a follow-up article. Everybody loves a mystery that keeps expanding. We could include new stories the first article generated."

I climb the narrow stairs to the second floor and find the cramped room where back issues are stacked by date on shelves. There's a small desk and chair for researchers. I can't remember what the cover looks like, but it won't take long to begin a year ago and go back from there. I check the index and resist rereading my favorite articles about a revered maker of banjos and fiddles, and how mountain foods get their odd names—like red-eye gravy, which doesn't contain red eyes, and leather britches, which would flummox anyone outside a ten-county range. In ten minutes, I've flipped through thirty back issues when I find what I'm looking for. The article is titled "Mysterious Lights in Yancey County." I'm surprised to see that the writer is Professor Terrence Covey, retired history professor from UNC Asheville. Now owner of Books and Beans, and my landlord and friend.

I reread the five-page article, study the photos, and take notes. Professor Covey has presented both sides of the story, and he quotes the mayor of Burnsville giving fair warning that the lights aren't a mystery at all but rather harmless flashes, nothing but trouble leading people to a dangerous pastime.

*Folks got no business heading up into hollers at night, sticking their noses in where they don't belong. We won't take kindly to trespassers, and neither will landowners. They protect their own. It's best to stay away.*

This was the mayor's way of warding off liability. Those winding roads that spin off from the town square are treacherous on a good day with only slow local traffic. A curious crowd on a mission after dark is another threat entirely.

In rebuttal, Professor Covey spoke with six witnesses who described *white lights high in the trees*. The interview with an elderly man living with his granddaughter was the most convincing. He said the bobbing lights date back to before the Civil War. *Long before electricity and cars and modern thingamajigs*. He remembers his great-granddaddy talking about those lights. Nowhere does anyone report danger or injury inflicted by the orbs. They are a benign occurrence that at worst are baffling and at best are beautiful.

I wonder if Birdie ever wrote about the lights in her books. That could put a historic slant on the phenomenon, and it could give me a reason to see her again. But she isn't a woman to be coerced or sweet-talked. She could see through my fabricated ruse. Though she could read my thoughts last Saturday and knows my eagerness to befriend her, I must tread lightly. Of all my virtues, patience is my weakest.

# Chapter 13

## MOURNFUL

**KATE SHAW**

There are five days left before this school closes forever. The hourglass is running out of sand, and my affirmations to the remaining students sound hollow even to my ears. Up here, hunting and trapping are revered skills. So are foraging and preserving food. Even the mountain language is quaint, and words like *poke sallet*, *jasper*, and *airish* will set the children apart in a disparaging way.

Today, Saturday, with rain beating on the cabin's roof and buckets strategically placed to catch familiar leaks, I'm reviewing the paragraphs the children wrote for *Creekrise* about their best talents. Some miss the point of the exercise entirely. Luke brags that he can hold his breath the longest of anybody in these parts, and Jimbo counters with the fact he can stuff more acorns in his mouth than his brother—thirty-nine. Some entries hold an air of humility, like Eddie, who writes that he believes reliability is his greatest talent, while Sassy Wright thinks she is the best at everything and is having a hard time choosing. I'm chuckling at these declarations when I hear a shout outside my cabin.

"Kate, you in there?"

I glance out the window and see Eli standing in the rain like a numbskull and I wave him in. He's crying and throws his head back and wails, "Burley's red!" which doesn't make a lick a sense. I open the door to this waterlogged gnome in his brown bucket hat and macintosh, looking more forlorn than I've ever seen him.

"What's red?" I yell above the drumming rain. "And who's Burley?"

He shakes his head over and over. "Dead, Kate. Birdie's dead."

The shock of his words sinks me to my knees. *What?*

Eli shuffles over to me and we hold each other and cry over the end of the world. He's half in the rain and I'm on the threshold. I sob, "I am sick… How can this be? I talked to her only last night."

"Death comes quick."

I gather my senses. "Let's get out of this rain and you start at the beginning."

Eli rises with difficulty and plops in the kitchen chair. I pull mine closer. Rachel licks the water dripping from his slicker.

"How'd she die? Did she fall or get hurt?"

"No. She's in her bed looking peaceful. Got the quilt pulled up neat. Hands are folded on her chest. I couldn't find a reason for it, but she's dead all the same. I came for a visit…" he stops. This shocking tragedy has unsettled him. He starts again.

"I come see her most Saturdays, you know. I come before I head over the ridge on my rounds to visit the infirm. Her door was open, and you know that means she's home, but she didn't answer my knock but I went inside anyway."

This gentle man, who has seen everything from dead babies and lost limbs to mangled bodies and lost minds, chokes up again.

"What now?" I ask.

"I need you to go sit with her while I set the wake in motion."

I shake my head *no no no.*

"Why wouldn't you go?"

"She hates me…or hated me. Or at least didn't approve of me."

"What in tarnation are you talking bout, Kate Shaw? Birdie was grateful for you. She saw you for the gift you are. You're talking nonsense. She even left you a note."

"A note?" The childish me hopes for forgiveness. "What'd it say?"

"I didn't read it cause it had your name on it. Get your slicker and come on."

Eli opens the door and steps back into a damp world where the rain has stopped. He doesn't have his walking stick and I grab one for him. "Hold your horses," I holler in concern he will slip on these slick trails. I catch up with him on a path I've walked every day for the past ten years. A path on which many problems have been solved, but this time it feels different. Empty. It no longer leads to my protector and most critical teacher.

In a dozen minutes, we're at the empty doorway. Leaves have blown inside that weren't there last night. It's a place missing its heartbeat. *You that teacher what needs new learning* were Birdie's first words to me, as though she knew everything about me that mattered. Despite my ill fit back then, the witch didn't give up on me. She saw a troubled woman who wanted to bring hope to children. But maybe it was hope for my soul I sought. Maybe I was in search of my own salvation.

Pewter clouds bunch overhead as Eli and I face the open door. We hear a ruffle of feathers and look up to see Samuel surrounded by the comfort of crows. I have no doubt that he grieves an unfathomable loss, and he stares forlorn into the distance. Shoulder to shoulder, crows line the branches of the hemlock tree, their feet clinched in place, their sleek blackness sharp against the milky sky. Out of respect for the day, they are silent.

Without another word, Eli heads down the trail. I reach for the crooked nail holding a scrap of paper to the narrow doorframe. The paper with my name on it flutters like an agitated moth pinned against its will. With trembling fingers I unfold the sheet.

*Books go to teacher.*

I gasp and clutch my chest. How did Birdie know death would come last night? How did she have the wherewithal to write this note? Why would she entrust her precious books to skeptical, inadequate me?

The boughs of the hemlocks and pines begin to whip into a frenzy as rain returns. I signal Rachel inside and close the door, half-expecting Eli to be wrong. Hoping this is a cruel hoax, a test of obedience, proof of loyalty. Hoping to hear Birdie chastise me for entering without an invitation, I close the flimsy door.

A clap of thunder has Rachel cower under Birdie's desk in a space that is cold as a cave. I haven't been inside in years. I've taken to standing in the yard for a quick exchange caught on the fly. But those first years I sat before her on a low stool and was instructed like the pupil in a master class. The long room has grown narrower since I was inside. More books line the walls.

The sections I've read were because she ordered me to, but I've caught glimpses of others. Folklore, mountain history, and healing recipes, some with foreign words. And there are sketches of herbs and wildflowers and insects. Whatever Birdie deemed important she's been putting down on paper and binding in leather for three-quarters of a century. She knew *truth* was fickle and got skewed in remembering. She wanted to tie it down so it couldn't morph into a variation. But she died, and the burden of what to do with that collection passes to me.

Where do I begin?

How long will it take?

What should I do with Birdie's truths?

I stand in gray shadows and listen, but my friend doesn't call out. Her body lies on her narrow cot with a faded quilt spread neat, like Eli said. Her gnarly fingers used to *doing* rest on her chest, which doesn't rise. With trepidation, I stoop and inch forward till I loom over her. A woman with a face that looks like a dried apple-head doll with creases and crevices and a fat wart on her chin. On a block of wood beside the cot sits a chipped teacup with moist dregs in the bottom. I lift it and sniff, curious. What did it contain? What does it matter?

I need the stool I always sat on, so with knees bent to keep from bumping my head on hanging herbs, I shuffle to the other end of the trailer. Rachel is asleep under the table. He doesn't stir as I clomp and bump down and back. I set the three-legged stool beside the cot and drop low, a tall girl in a small world with knees bent high and shoulders curved inward. The drizzle that started when I entered now falls harder. The wind buffets Birdie's home from side to side, and I want to be anywhere but here. I wish I could unhear Birdie's disappointment in me last night. Wish I'd simply asked to better understand the boys' story. Wish I'd listened with an open mind and not reservation.

I touch her wrist for warmth, and her skin is cold. I feel desolate. Birdie was my sense of this place. She grounded me. There's a book closest to her cot. I open the page she marked with an indigo bunting feather. My favorite bird whose blue is an impossible shade of blue. Like an Impossible Dream that came with me to Baines Creek. I begin to hum the *Man of La Mancha* from the album I play in music class, then softly sing words that are made for this aching moment—*to bear with unbearable sorrow, to run where the brave dare not go*. And I cry gulping sobs for the death of my friend.

What will this place do without Birdie Rocas? She knew the mysteries of the woods and had a cure for every ailment. She was midwife to every child born in these parts. How will Baines Creek cope?

My hand lies flat over the marked page as I look at it in the weak light from a high window. I hesitate before reading the words, mildly afraid. Will I see a cryptic message? Wisdom for the ages? The prophecy of her death?

Tentatively I raise my hand.

*BUTT BOILS.*

I blink twice and look again.

There it is. In all caps. I cover my mouth to suppress a giggle and feel a loosening in my tight chest. It's been a long while since I laughed, and in today's grave situation it really doesn't feel right, so I try not to picture butt boils or body parts. They creep in anyway and a silly smile stays as I read the list of herbs for the compress: tea tree oil, castor oil, neem-oil. There is a footnote in small print that tea tree oil is poisonous and should not be consumed.

A disturbing thought enters my mind. Suicide. Is that what happened? If so, that would trouble me to no end. It would mean we'd failed Birdie, which is nonsense since we were never her keeper or her equal. She was *our* keeper. But is it a possibility? I turn the pages of this book and wonder why this recipe, this page was singled out. Close to the front are pressed leaves I can't identify, insect wings, berry stains. Near the back is a tender entry: *I knowd me a blind dog when*

*I was but a girl. He licked my feet and I give him a drink of my branch water.*

*Oh, Birdie,* I whisper. *I am a blind dog sitting beside a wise woman who has passed on to somewhere else. At least I hope there is somewhere else you've gone, and I wish I knew for certain.* I cry messy gulps while the rain mimics my heartache. I bravely take her right hand and rub my thumb over her stony skin, feel a callous on the palm, and turn it over to see it's not a callus at all. At the base of her middle finger is a raised mark, discolored but distinctly shaped like a slice of pie all puffed up.

I place her hand back on her chest and lean my head against the wall. I must have dozed because I jump when I hear my name, *Kate*, and turn toward the doorway. My neck is stiff, the light inside the trailer almost gone.

"Kate?" the voice calls again from the doorway. The day has drifted away, and I turn to see a stumpy shadow.

"Eli, is that you?"

"It's me," he calls out.

"Let me get out of your way."

I shuffle to the door, still holding the book about butt boils. Annie Walker and Sue Sorrels have come with Eli to prepare Birdie for burial. Though Birdie helped birth Annie's Luke and Jimbo, she's never been inside this place. I know from the squint of her eyes that she's scared. This trailer is a witch's world peppered with pagan symbols. Today is a test of Annie and Sue's faith. Eli may have assured them that the healer was a believer, but they wonder what they'll find under all those layers of clothing. Possibly a butt boil.

While Tattler builds her a short coffin and will deliver it when it's ready, Annie Walker and Sue Sorrels will bathe, dress, and tie the old woman to a cooling board to keep her from sitting upright when rigor mortis sets in. Her quilt will line the coffin, coins will rest on her eyelids and a soda cloth on her face. Brave believers will take turns and sit through the night until she's buried so the devil can't steal her soul. Eli has explained these steps as I stand outside useless while their faith ritual begins. The rain has stopped.

"When will she be buried?" I speak low.

"Tomorrow after church."

"Where will she go?"

"You mean heaven or hell?"

I scoff. "That's not what I meant, Eli, and you know it. I meant where will she be buried."

"Her family graveyard."

"Birdie has a graveyard?"

"Behind her trailer. Not far."

I look beyond the trailer to a place I never ventured. It's overgrown with a tangle of thick vines. "Who else is buried there?"

"Her family gone before, I think."

"Oh," I say, surprised to hear that Birdie had family. I know she didn't spring from the earth or drop from the stars to walk among mortals. I glance through the open door at her oppressive legacy of books and feel overwhelmed. I itch to leave, but my plans changed today. If I accept her request, I won't be going anywhere soon.

# Chapter 14

## BOOKS AND BEANS

**Lydia Brown**

For the past seven days and nights, Birdie Rocas has tugged at my heart, and I've stayed away for fear of offending her. The next time our paths cross we won't be strangers. Conversation will be easier. Answers may be forthcoming. In the meantime, on Saturday I pursue two mysteries that need tending.

Books and Beans in Little Switzerland has enough creaky steps and hidden niches to be a bona fide destination for bibliophiles and explorers. Its eclectic shelves hold some new but mostly vintage books on three rambling floors. The curious will also find compasses, sextants, old pocket watches, magnifying glasses, binoculars, spyglasses, and weather instruments to satisfy anyone finding their own way in life. It smells of rich coffee, endless mystery, and ancient ink, and it sits at the end of a line of board-and-batten buildings with stone foundations and wandering vines that burrow their way inside. It's where I have my office, which legitimizes my work for Special Collections and gives focus to my weekdays. But today I don't go up the stairs to my rented room.

"Is Professor Covey in?" I ask Nancy behind the counter.

She looks at me over her reading glasses, annoyed that I interrupted *The Lion, the Witch and the Wardrobe* in the Chronicles of Narnia. "I've got that one on my bedside table," I say.

She doesn't react but says facetiously, "He's in his office," for the proprietor's wooden desk is wedged in a slice of space beneath steep stairs. On his scarred desk are a black telephone, a cracked mug holding pens, and a green banker's lamp. Boxes of used books line the hallway to be recorded and classified.

I knock on the wall. "Professor?"

He turns stiffly, takes off his readers, and smooths back thinning white hair.

"Lydia Brown." His voice is gracious as he rises, shuffles from under the soffit, and extends his veined, slender hand. "A delight to see you again. Have you found that old graveyard on your property? Was the family named Morrison or was it Morrigan?"

"I'm not sure. Morrison, I think, though it's been a long time since Jack and I stumbled upon it. One day soon I'll find it again and take rubbings of the headstones. But today I bring two fascinating topics for us to discuss: shapeshifters and the night lights near Burnsville."

His eyes light up. "Excellent topics that go well with a rich cup of coffee, don't you agree?" He heads down the hallway with a bounce in his step, and I follow. At the coffee station he grinds fragrant beans for the two-mug French press, pours in boiling water, and hands me two oversized cups with thick handles and a small pitcher of cream. We settle at a round table beside the stone fireplace where hot coals have worn down to embers. At this elevation, there's always a chill in the air that needs chasing. Even in June. He throws on a fresh log and it catches flame. The coffee steeps.

"Let's start with shapeshifters, shall we?" Professor Covey's voice compels me like a seasoned actor on stage.

"It's an idea as old as mankind. Proteus is the Greek god who was a shapeshifter. His name has come to mean 'capable of changing form between man, animal and spirit.' It's referenced in Homer's epic poems. There's also an article I recently read that described a twelve-hundred-year-old Coptic text discovered in a cave. Controversially, the text referred to Jesus as a shapeshifter because he appeared to different people in different ways. It's completely refuted by religious scholars, of course, but it made for interesting reading."

He pushes the plunger in the French press then fills our mugs. He cocks his head to the side while studying me. "And you've seen one."

"I have."

"How marvelous," he exclaims with a flush of joy to his craggy face.

I say, "Romi Harker is a shapeshifter."

"I'm not surprised. Please go on." He adds a dollop of rich cream to his coffee then leans back in the chair, settling in for a good tale.

"I went to see her at your suggestion for an article I was writing for *Folklore*. I couldn't have found her without the guide you recommended. We drove as far as we could then walked another hour, and when we arrived, Romi appeared to me as someone I used to know. I think it was the rose-colored smoke from her fire that cast a spell. It was strangely enchanting.

"My guide, Tonto, stayed back in the tree line and didn't risk getting close. He was afraid of her magic. At my request, he left me there overnight and came back the next day, but it was the twenty-four hours I was with Romi Harker that make no sense. What appeared to me was a dear friend from my past living in an enchanted place; Tonto saw a frightening hag."

Professor Covey listens intently to my retelling, including the odd dream of women dancing in a meadow, each with a trigon mark on their right palm. When my story ends, he says, "Interesting, the triangle. It's sometimes called a psychic triangle, and in palm reading, it symbolizes good luck."

I hold out my right hand, palm up. "Like this one?" He reaches out and gently rubs the raised mark.

"Usually the triangle is made by lines in the palm. This one is special. It appears that you might belong in Romi Harker's world, and if so, does that frighten you?"

I shake my head. "It was a strange comfort."

"Lydia, will your magazine article include the details you told me?"

"No. I withheld much of it."

"Good, good." He pats the back of my hand. "Some readers of the supernatural think they understand what it is to be a witch or seer or psychic, but they haven't a clue. And the curious reader, in his hunger to possess more knowledge than he's entitled to, could plunder her sacred world. I'm glad you protected Romi's way of life—"

"Which leads to the lights north of Burnsville," I say.

He gazes out the window with woeful eyes and surprises me when he says, "I wish I'd never written that story."

"Why? Rudy says it's the most popular article ever printed."

"That's precisely why. Some things are meant to stay a mystery, to exist in peace, to be left alone."

"Professor, you talk like those lights are living things that could be hurt."

"Regrettably, I didn't see them, but I heard enough from witnesses who could not have coordinated their stories. They all said similar things. That there was something alive in the way the lights responded and connected to their presence. After swirling in a dervish dance, their movements looked intentional, and they lined up to watch the watchers. The people back in those hollers are either used to them or afraid of them, but either way they leave them alone. I wish I'd done the same."

He drains the last of his coffee, then looks at me and stops, prepared to ask the question he should have asked first. "But you've seen those as well?"

"Yes."

"When?"

"Saturday, the 31st of May, at 7:52 in the evening." I grin.

His face once more lights with joy. "Last Saturday. Where?"

"In Baines Creek. When I went to interview the medicine woman, Birdie Rocas. We only said a few words before she turned me away. The lights lived above her place."

He holds up his hand and impishly grins. "Hold the story there, my dear. Let me fix a fresh pot of French roast in hopes you will tell me everything."

And I do. Including the part where I behaved poorly and overstayed my welcome, until I was dismissed for thinking too loudly and disturbing her rest. What I don't confide is the assurance I felt in her presence that I was where I belonged. That Birdie's ways and wisdom held answers specifically for me. That the lights were signs and I'll return at the first excuse I can muster.

# Chapter 15

## THE BURIAL

**Kate Shaw**

"Am I obligated? Is Birdie's note binding in some legal world?"

I pour mint tea in two mugs, open my tin of oatmeal cookies, and place it on the roughhewn bench I use as a coffee table. On this heartbreaking Saturday, Eli has come to my cabin a second time. He sits in the middle of the lumpy sofa where the ends of the cushion rise like thick wings. Grief envelops my friend who can be annoying at times but who is mostly kind.

At my question, he stops the cookie halfway to his mouth. "I thought you'd be honored." He eats the first cookie in two bites, hardly tasting it, then reaches for a second.

"I'm not honored and I'm not worthy. I don't feel excited or even hope I can make sense of them." My tone is hard like a stale biscuit. "What good will Birdie's books do me or anyone?" My hand trembles from emotion so I put down my mug.

"Aren't you curious?" He slurps his tea noisily. "Curious what would pique Birdie's interest enough to write it down?"

"You mean like butt boils?" I say cynically.

"Why'd you say that?" He looks up with interest.

"It was in the book beside her cot, the page marked with a blue feather." I point to the book on the table, and he reaches for it and thumbs through it. Maybe butt boils are of more concern around here than I can imagine.

"Take it with you. I glanced through it hoping she left a clue about what happened last night, but I didn't find anything helpful."

My eyes wander to the window and the bright sunshine that now speckles the forest floor. After two days of rain, the leaves move in the breeze like broken marionettes.

"You asked if I was curious, and I am a tiny bit," I admit. "But this is happening so fast. I'm still struggling with the shock that she's dead."

What I don't confide is my sadness that I'll never have another chance to prove myself to the mountain woman. She was my compass in this high place, and without her I'm not sure which direction to turn. Today I fit more poorly here than I did when I came. Maybe it's a good thing my job is ending. But now there are those blasted books…

"She's gone, Kate, and those books will be left unattended after her funeral tomorrow. They'll be in danger from the elements and nosy souls or the frightened who want to destroy them. Surely you agree that they were too precious to Birdie to risk being damaged. You and I are the logical caretakers—"

I interrupt, flooded with relief. "You'll help me?"

"Of course I'll help." His enthusiasm ratchets up. "When school is over on Friday, we can use that space. We'll move student desks and put up sheets of plywood on sawhorses for worktables. Bring in extra light so we can see better. In the meantime, after the funeral, we'll take them to the school storage closet and lock them in for safekeeping and hope nobody goes looking for them."

"Thank you, Eli," I say, genuinely relieved to know he'll help determine what to do with all these pages that mattered to Birdie. But will they matter to anyone else?

Eli stands and moves to my cabin door. He puts on his raincoat he doesn't need now that the sky has cleared. I follow him outside. "See you at the funeral. Should start around one." He tips his hat and limps down the mountain.

How will this ceremony work? Is there neutral ground between Birdie's beliefs and Eli's faith? Was her funeral something she discussed with Eli? Or is a funeral to comfort the living left behind? I see Eli left behind the butt boil book, and I feel mean-hearted the way I've handled this bizarre day. It's been about *my* feelings, *my* shortcomings and *my* losses. I feel my usual guilt.

The mystery of her perfectly planned death is the real puzzle. How does a person do that? Was her destiny written in one of her books, to die in the early morn of June 6, 1980? Did she live life on a different plane with different rules?

Under blazing clouds of orange and gold with blunt slashes of red, I listen to a bizarre chorus. It's coming from a half mile off, outside Birdie's old trailer. Crows cry. While the sun's brilliance drains from the sky, I listen to their lament until it's dark. Even when I go inside and close my door, I hear them. The next morning, it's silent.

At one o'clock, I walk to her trailer and join the gathering crowd. Buck and Sadie Dillard are there with their three children. Little Loretty looks lost. She stands beside the totem pole and runs her finger over the carved snake that winds around the core. Birdie told me that snakes stand for rebirth, that they are the gateway to new beginnings, but I've killed two copperheads in my woodpile without a drop of remorse.

Mooney's here from the Rusty Nickel, and Irma Jolly from the boarding house with her brother-in-law Lester rumored to grow the best corn for moonshine. Mr. Turner the mailman, and Harlan and his Uncle Jerome stand in a line beside Tattler, who built her coffin. Luke and Jimbo are with their parents Annie and Montel. Folks stand warily beneath wind chimes and dream catchers interwoven with bleached bones and mirrors.

More people keep coming through the woods. Silent strangers who knew Birdie least stand on the far side of the creek or further back in the trees. At Eli's signal, the pine casket is carried by Tattler, Buck, Jerome, and Harlen, and they head around back of the trailer to a trail that's been cleared through the kudzu. We shuffle past a shell of a cabin brought down by determined trees rising up.

Birdie left a note for Eli asking to be buried outside the stone wall. She even marked the spot, and men dug the hole on Saturday as superstition dictates. To dig a grave on Sunday would mean another grave would be needed the coming week. Why take chances on dark folklore when a witch is involved?

A wall two feet high surrounds the ancient burial site. Lichen and moss and old candle wax lay on the flat top stones, likely from ceremonies during the full moon or the solstice. Birdie would celebrate such bizarre things. Three worn headstones poke up from the ground inside the wall, with unreadable names and dates. That ground has heaved, and tree roots have riddled the soil. Eli waits beside Birdie's grave outside the wall. He holds his worn Bible against his chest like a shield. He signals everyone to come closer.

Absent today, as every other day in recent years, is Prudence Perkins, Eli's bitter sister. She has cut herself off from the living and has become a recluse to be pitied or forgotten. That sour woman was the first Baines Creek resident

I laid eyes on ten years back. I remember thinking it was the hard living of this place that had damaged Prudence Perkins. Now I know her damage is self-inflicted. Also missing is Marris Jones, Sadie's aunt, who's become infirm yet still does good deeds. Two sides of the same hardscrabble coin.

Eli announces a reading from the Song of David, Psalm 18: *My God is my rock in whom I take refuge, my shield and the horn of my salvation.* All heads are bowed with eyes closed except mine. I watch Eli in his well-practiced role as comforter. Across the clearing of wild grasses, Samuel the crow sits in the midst of other crows at the edge of the woods. The field is scattered with upright boulders that today look strangely human, shoulders curved, rounded tops bowed in respect. A family of deer watches inside the distant shadow line.

And then I see them. Ten lights, floating deep in the leafy dark where daylight doesn't reach. They are the angel lights I first saw a week back, but today they don't look dangerous, not when I'm in a crowd and the sun is shining. They shimmer like a mirage in a desert. Standing among the lights is a wisp of a girl with red hair surrounded by black-cloaked figures. When Eli says *Amen* and heads are raised and eyes opened, the lights and the images vanish. Everyone leaves, and Eli asks Harlan, Tattler, and Eddie to help us move Birdie's books. He saw fear in some folks' eyes over Birdie's written words she left behind. More than one person asked could spells be let loose if the covers of her books were opened. Eli fears someone may torch her life's work to be rid of her magic. The books will be safer in the locked closet at school.

"Her eight-sided star is missing," I say. "The one that hangs beside her door. The one she touches every time she enters. When did that happen?"

Eli says wearily. "Maybe the storm blew it off."

"No, that nail was bent to keep it there," I add, but Eli

isn't interested. "She'd be upset to see us touching her books, moving them." I observe. "She didn't want them to leave her trailer."

"Really, Kate? We have no choice. These are extraordinary times, and we are now the caretakers."

Carefully, the boys fill cardboard boxes and baskets, and Tattler says, "Seventy-eight books, Miz Kate." The boxes are piled on the sled that had carried her casket. The boys leave and it's only Eli and me in the yard. He says, "Did you see the wooden chest?"

"No. Where?" I had stayed outside her trailer while the books were boxed.

"Near her cot, covered in a scrap of quilt."

We enter and shuffle toward the empty cot and pull aside the quilt. "What in the world?" I whisper.

It's a glorious chest, etched with exotic markings. An intricate inlay of a crow is on the lid. It belongs here as much as fine bone China or the queen's jewels. I try to lift the lid, but it's locked.

"I saw a brass key on her table," Eli says and walks the length of the trailer, his head six inches lower than the ceiling. "Got it," he calls out, then returns. Half teasing, he says, "Maybe it's a treasure."

"And what would Birdie be doing with a treasure?" I argue. "She didn't care about earthly possessions. She didn't even own a cup that wasn't chipped."

He hands the key to me and I slip it into the keyhole. It turns effortlessly as if it's used often. Together, we lift the heavy lid unprepared for what we'll find. Eli reaches out a trembling hand and whispers. "*Sweet Jesus.* Is that silver and gold?"

# Chapter 16

## DOUBLE NEWS

### Lydia Brown

My telephone rings twice on Saturday, and the calls change everything.

The first is from Kate Shaw with tragic news, and I slide to the floor holding the receiver. "Dead?"

"It happened a week back."

"Oh." After my awkward introduction. After she banished me. After I was busy doing things that didn't include Birdie. I missed my chance to know her, and I am heartsick. Death waits for no one, but the sad truth is that Birdie died and I had no warning, no whiff of her pipe tobacco, no portal opening to announce the news. Baines Creek lost its healer, and I lost my link to answers.

There is bittersweet news. Kate inherited Birdie's stacks of books, and she has spent the past week wandering through the pages lost. She needs help. Tuesday we'll meet at the schoolhouse.

Later that same day the phone rings again. It's my sister Lucy calling about her thirteen-year-old daughter, who is wreaking hell on the family's ordered life. Miss Augustina Rose Flannery, Lucy's youngest child—named after her triple-great-grandmother and with the little-girl nickname Teeny—now wants to be called Gus. That insistence has stretched Lucy's patience in unbecoming ways. Lucy wants to send Gus here for the summer, and I say yes.

We'll meet at Little Switzerland Inn two miles from my place but thirty miles from Lucy's home on the other side of Burnsville. Lucy teaches at Mountain Heritage High School, and her youngest will start there in the fall. I haven't seen them since Christmas. *We're busy* is the excuse to stay apart, but our ties to each other have grown thin. And there was Jack's death two years back. Only now grief is releasing me.

I wait at a table on the flagstone patio, face the Catawba River valley and sip a glass of chilled chardonnay. Little Switzerland was the vision of North Carolina Supreme Court Justice Heriot Clarkson. The original inn built in 1910 was demolished in 1961 and rebuilt as a seventy-room chalet. It was my task to review historic records for this place, and they now reside in Special Collections at Ramsey in Asheville.

This summer day, gentlemen play horseshoes and teenagers play badminton. In the heated swimming pool, children wear water wings while mamas sip spiked lemonade, and I glance over to see a frazzled Lucy cross the terrace.

She turned fifty last January and looks matronly and pinch-mouthed. My sister with a penchant for ten-dollar words and Nancy Drew mysteries is gone. The girl with a dream to write the Great American Novel is gone too. Or is lost. That unfinished manuscript gathers dust on a closet shelf. She teaches English at the local high school, but I imagine the stimulation is limited. My sister weaves around tables ahead of her daughter who lugs a duffel bag large enough to hold a body. At least I think that's Gus. The change is shocking. Fair hair has been replaced by purple tips spiked with gel. Metal piercings pinch her ears, eyebrows, and lips. A black tank top sits atop budding breasts.

Cargo pants hang low, and heavy combat boots carry my niece forward.

"Hello, Lucy," I say and rise to give her a hug. "Can you stay for a visit?"

"No thank you. I've got to get back."

"Date night with Ryan?"

"Really, Lydia? No. A business dinner I'll endure for Ryan's sake." She adds, "Teeny isn't feeling well," and my niece rolls her eyes. "She has an upset stomach but wanted to come anyway. Sorry to dump a sick child on you…"

I look at my niece and her pale face and wonder if it's partially the makeup. "We'll take it easy the next few days," I say. "It's supposed to rain tomorrow, so that's a reason to relax. Gus can stay as long as she'd like."

Lucy smirks at her daughter's preferred nickname, then delivers a weak kiss on her forehead and slips away trailing disapproval. I turn back to this tiny Gothic stranger. "I'm sorry you're not well, Gus, but I'm glad you're here."

She cuts dark-rimmed eyes at me. "For real? You haven't asked me to come since Uncle Jack died."

"And that's too long. I've missed you, and when you're better, I could use your help."

"For real? Doing what?"

"Two things: to find a lost graveyard and go see the secrets left by a witch who died."

"For real?" Gus scoots up straighter.

"Let me feed you first, and then I'll tell you what I know."

We order fries and burgers from my favorite waitress, Sandy. When she asks my niece how many piercings she has, Gus recognizes a kindred soul. "Eight," is the prideful answer.

Sandy points to the eyebrow hoop. "I bet that one hurt."

"Not really."

"I been thinking bout getting a second hole *right here*," the woman says, pointing next to a simple gold hoop.

"You should do it," Gus says and grins for the first time and looks more like herself.

Sandy winks. "I'll put your orders in lickety-split."

Gus sits forward and puts her elbows on the table. "Tell me bout the witch first."

"Her name was Birdie Rocas," I begin and recount my traipse up the mountain to her trailer, her dresses that dragged the ground, her corncob pipe and how she shunned me as she sat beside a girl half Gus's age being taught lessons by a master healer. I even confess my brazen behavior.

"She went inside and closed the door but you stayed? How come?"

"I hoped she'd take pity on me and talk."

"But she ran you off instead."

"But not before she came out to say that she could read my thoughts and that I couldn't have her secrets yet."

"What kinda secrets?"

"The good kind, I hope. I did see stacks of homemade books inside her trailer."

"Books about what?"

"We'll find out Tuesday, but I'd guess they're like diaries where she wrote happenings. Since she was a healer, there's likely plant cures and living history about her part of the world. Three years ago, I saw Birdie's name on a piece of handmade paper covered with her words. Someone had sent them to Uncle Jack's department. I've been looking for her ever since. At least I had that brief encounter before she died."

Our food arrives and Gus dips one fry in a puddle of ketchup. "What about the girl? Who's gonna teach her now?"

"I don't know. You want to hear a strange thing?"

She nods.

"When I was leaving that night, I thought I saw her in

the clearing. My headlights flashed across a child, but when I got close, no one was there. My eyes were playing tricks on me."

"Maybe it was her spirit but not her."

"The two can separate when we're alive?"

"Maybe," she says and shrugs delicate shoulders.

I finish half my burger before I think to ask Gus, "Are you afraid of witches?"

"Not the good kind."

"How can you tell the difference?"

My niece looks at me like I'm too old to be that dumb.

"Good witches celebrate the full moon. They protect Mother Nature and become healers and midwives. They're part of the circle of life, Aunt Liddy. I thought you knew those things."

I'm glad to see her sassy spirit surface. "Where'd you learn that?"

"Might've dreamed it." Gus looks down at her fingernail and picks at the black chipped polish. She hesitates before her tone turns more furtive. "I tried talking to Mama bout my dreams back when I was little. She called me a foolish girl having foolish thoughts."

*My palm itches. Trula Freed told me I came from a line of psychics, but I never thought about the gift being current.*

"Do you hear whispers in the night? Messages from the other side?"

My niece's eyes widen.

I explain, "The first voice I heard from beyond was Oma. She had died months before and I was starting to forget her when here she came, whispering in my ear while I slept. I smelled her Dentyne chewing gum; that's how I knew who it was. Lucy didn't believe me."

"What was her message?"

"To be on the lookout for Wade Sully, Aunt Helen's first

husband. He was already dead in the war, but we didn't find out till later."

"But Mama found out what you said was true, didn't she?"

"She did, but she never acknowledged my dream about it."

"She doesn't believe me either."

"But I do." I squeeze Gus's hand.

Of all my siblings, Lucy was the most critical of me when our parents were killed. She thought I had been trying to get attention all along. I'm not surprised Lucy doesn't support Gus.

"You are not foolish, Gus Flannery. That you are not."

Gus has barely touched her food so we have Sandy box it up for later. We leave the inn and drive to the cottage. On the way Gus says, "I haven't seen it since it's done."

"The cottage? Well, shame on me. That's about to change." I don't explain that I've been slow to heal and isolation in this place was a necessary part of the process. Only now can I share it with her.

Storm clouds thicken as I pull off Crabtree Road onto my dirt road that winds up the steep hill and stops at the tree line. We follow the path through the forest that leads to the cottage on the cliff. Gus struggles to carry her canvas satchel, so I grab one handle, and we cross a carpet of lush moss and braided roots and the suspension bridge. We climb two steps to the porch then fat raindrops pummel the tin roof. I open the door—

"You have a cat," she shouts above the downpour.

"No, I don't."

She points. "Then who's that?"

A white feline sits on the swing cleaning its paws like it's at home. It vaguely looks like the apparitions I sometimes see at a distance. It jumps down and rubs against Gus's leg and the three of us enter the unlocked door. I close it to muffle the rain while the cat jumps on the counter looking for food.

I find a can of tuna in the pantry. It's a mannered creature but forthright.

Gus looks beyond the vintage hooked rugs, tall custom-built bookcases, rocking chairs, and goose-down sofa to Jack's framed photographs lining the walls. "I remember this one," she points to remnants of a cabin smothered in kudzu with vibrant rays of sunshine filling the center. "I was with him that day. He waited and waited for the right moment to take the picture. I never saw how it came out."

She touches the protective glass and speaks softly. "Uncle Jack loves it here and he loved you at first sight, Aunt Liddy. Am I on the right or the left?"

"What?" I mumble, disoriented by her spooky declaration that is tied to a logistics question.

"Is my bedroom on the left or right?"

"Oh. You're on the right, honey. My room's on the left."

I am stunned at the girl's easy reference to Jack's ghost being happy here and his loving me at first sight. I feel a stab of abandonment and envy and joy all in one swoop. Such a sweet memory when we met on a blind date arranged by friends and Jack's first words when he shook my hand were, *I think I love you, Lydia Brown.* He was shocked he had said those words aloud, and it made us laugh. I love a man who makes me laugh, but did I ever tell Gus that story? I don't think so. With the duffle stored in her room, she heads to mine to see the wolpertinger with the white cat on her heels. Rattled, I put on the kettle for tea.

Gus will find the curious creature on top of Oma's Bavarian armoire that crossed the sea from Germany. The stuffed creature that sits on top was fabricated a hundred years ago, made on a lark by my great-grandfather. It has tiny antlers and falcon wings sewn to a rabbit's body and stands seventeen and a quarter inches tall. It was made to lure tourists into the Black Forest on the trail of the Brothers

Grimm. In my childhood home in Riverton on story night, whenever fairy tales were told, the wolpertinger held center stage as proof such fantastical things were real.

But the Bavarian armoire it sits on is more than it appears to be. It holds a secret that no one knows but me. One day I'll show Gus the hidden latch that releases a felt-lined compartment. A catch that is invisible in plain sight, such is the clever craftsmanship. After Oma died, only Mama knew about the hiding place till she showed me. A place where I have hidden stolen pieces of my family history: forty-two glass marbles and a paperweight with purple forget-me-nots. Mama cherished those things that linked her family to *good* German people, not evil Nazis. My German people created lasting things of beauty that I now possess because, in my grief on their dying day, I went to Mama's bottom dresser drawer and took them. Before my sisters came home for the funeral. Before their sorrow dissipated. Before they began coveting Mama's things. Before they remembered the marbles and the paperweight. At seventeen, I became a thief. My unique pain gave me that right.

Great-grandfather's glass marbles should have gone to my brother Grady, who is ten years older than me. You wouldn't know looking at the reticent man he's become, but when he was a boy of sixteen, he was a marble-playing marvel who made us proud. He never lost a local game. When the German prisoner-of-war camp was built in our hometown, masterful competitors emerged, and the first international marble championship was held inside the fence topped with concertina wire. I was too young to stand among the Nazi prisoners back then, so Mama banished Cora and me to the care of Aunt Fanniebelle, but good family stories take on a life of their own. This one grew to epic proportions. We learned every move in the retelling.

Grady was twenty-seven when Daddy died, but he was

already becoming a shadow of a man in the presence of Daddy and our older brother Everett. After, Grady never found his true place, and with Daddy gone, he let Everett make every decision. There was a time when I thought he was smitten with Bert Tucker, the daring girl who lived her teenage years under our family's roof. She was magnetic and irresistible and had her eye on *more*. That *more* never included Grady Brown. Her heart was never his to have. That loss changed him.

Next time I speak to Grady, I'll ask if he'd like to have the handmade German marbles. I hope he does and that he'll cherish them and remember what it felt like to be an international champion.

And the coveted paperweight. Maybe it's time for it to come out of hiding. My siblings have stopped asking if I know where it is, as though it sank into the muck of the Roanoke River with our parents on the day they drowned. It should sit on my window ledge in the light.

I open the front windows to let in washed air coming across the valley and, with my mug of tea in hand, head to the front porch to sit in the swing. Gus joins me carrying the cat. "Does he have a name?"

"No, honey. I told you I've never seen it before."

"I'm gonna call him Uncle for Uncle Jack." The cat's underbelly is exposed.

"Well," I point. "It's a girl cat."

"I'm still gonna call her Uncle."

When she speaks the name, the cat looks up in recognition. "You don't mind being called Uncle, do you, pretty thing?" Gus kisses the top of her head.

"How are you feeling, honey?"

"Not so good."

"Let me feel your forehead." She leans forward. "You're warm to the touch. Let me take your temperature and get you some aspirin. This damp night air might not be the best thing for you."

Gus sits on the kitchen stool with the thermometer under her tongue and watches me pull a tray of ice from the freezer, wrap the cubes in a dish towel, and use my hammer to crack them into tiny pieces. I fill a glass with chipped ice and add ginger ale. Gus's fever is nearly 101, and without complaint she takes an aspirin and lets me tuck her into bed with pillows propped at her back and Uncle by her side as if the cat belongs. I feed her teaspoons of ice nuggets and ginger ale like Mama used to do for me when I had a fever. I spoon-feed Gus till she's had enough.

"I'll stay right here, honey," I say and settle in the easy chair by the window where I can watch over her. She looks vulnerable in the bed wearing dreadful makeup and spikey hair, and she drops off to sleep and so does the cat while I think about her mother, my sister Lucy.

She surprised us when she married a safe, quiet, good man after junior college. There were no stars in her eyes and nothing brilliant in his. Ryan Flannery became a life insurance salesman, and I was disappointed for Lucy. I had pictured her penning a bestselling novel in a charming hut built for writing. When I was little, she was a thoroughbred living on our working man's farm. When I was little, I thought that once she could, she'd break free from the mundane and rise to her potential.

After high school, she went to college in the western part of the state alongside Bert Tucker. Lucy said that the first time she came to this high country when she was fifteen, it stole her heart away. That oddly she knew she belonged here and would return. To stay rooted to family, she named their first two children after our parents, David and Minnie. The boy and girl were always mannerly and never spoke back or missed a curfew or broke a rule.

They now live safe lives. Then a decade later along came Augustina Rose. Teeny. Gus. A spitfire of a girl who dreams about the other side and fights her battles like a warrior.

# Chapter 17
## OVER

**Kate Shaw**

I bribe the children to come through the last day because I fear no one will if I don't. I promise cake and ice cream and a present if they come. Preacher and I started making plans after the *good news* was delivered.

"I want to give them something they can hold on to after I'm gone."

"Like a lucky rabbit's foot?"

"No. Something that reminds them of their success."

We settled on framed copies of a *Creekrise* story that features each child's contribution. Something they can hang on the wall. Something that has one foot in tradition and the other in their future.

The day before that final day, Eli goes to town and prints copies of *Creekrise*, buys black frames, and finds small plastic trophies that read *1st Prize*. He also buys chocolate cupcakes with white icing and ice cream. He hides the treats at the Rusty Nickel. That night we frame the students' stories and place them on their desks. Now it's Friday, June 13.

All ten children come this morning intrigued, and find their gifts, and then Eli comes bearing cupcakes and ice cream in little cardboard cups with wooden spoons stuck on top. The children clap with excitement and eat treats and take turns reading their framed newsletter stories aloud, and I hand out diplomas with their names typed on the blank line and Eli gives each one a trophy. We have made a bona fide party for them, and it is a proud, fleeting moment.

By midday it's over. The children have gone and Eli and I stand alone in the empty quiet left behind and our shoulders slump. These last weeks have been exhausting since the *good news* was delivered, then Birdie died, and now school has ended.

"There's only a few hundred left, you know," Eli says.

"A few hundred what?" I say while I collect cupcake wrappers and cardboard cups in the trash can.

"One-room schoolhouses. Once upon a time, every county had one when people were born and stayed close to home their whole lives. Before roads and cars and opportunities multiplied and scattered them."

"Where are the ones that are left?"

"Mostly out west in wide open spaces or deep in Appalachia. This was the last one in North Carolina. There may be one in Kentucky. You were part of history, Kate."

I wipe crumbs from the desktops and slide them against the wall. Eli and I set up sawhorses and sheets of plywood he collected, lay out Birdie's books as best we can, and stand before them overwhelmed. "Now what?" he says, exhausted.

I was waiting for that question, the one that would easily segue into my next sentence. "I have an idea." I hold out a business card. The one with Lydia Brown's name and telephone number. "I believe we have two choices, Eli. We can wander for days and weeks and make a mess of Birdie's things or we can call for help."

"You'd bring in a stranger?"

"This woman does this sort of thing for the library at the

college in Asheville. And she's not a stranger. She met Birdie two weeks back," I say, but leave out the part where she had been dismissed by the witch. He doesn't need to hear that.

Eli studies the card and I think he's going to cry the way his nose reddens. He digs out his handkerchief to wipe his perspiring face. Maybe I've handled this idea all wrong. Spoken too quickly.

"Can we at least start on our own? Spend a few days by ourselves?"

"Yes. We can do that if it makes you feel better," I say, knowing we'll eventually invite Lydia Brown to bring order to this sea of confusion and hope she's willing.

But before we do, something comes and takes us to our knees.

# Chapter 18

## MESSAGE

**Lydia Brown**

My niece feels better after napping through a rainy Sunday, sipping ginger ale, eating chicken noodle soup, then sleeping twelve hours straight. On Monday her energy is still lackluster, and a mild fever persists. She stays inside and reads aloud to Uncle curled on the sofa beside her. The cat is mysteriously domesticated and tamed and content, and they nap curled in a little ball. I worry Gus will have a sleepless night and the light will stay on and she will roam the cottage restless, but again, her sleep is deep and restorative, and the house is quiet.

This early Tuesday morning, Gus is awake at first light and comes out of her room stretching and yawning, wearing Saturday's clothes and the ghastly makeup. I haven't pushed her to move faster than she can. With a sleepy *mornin'*, she heads to the bathroom, and I hear the water running in the tub for a bubble bath, then faint humming from a distance. An hour later she emerges wearing faded jeans and a pink T-shirt with M E in big letters. *Mother Earth* is scripted beneath. Mostly gone are the purple tint and spiked gel in her pixie hair that were meant to shock. Gone is the ghostly makeup and the harsh liner around hazel eyes. Only chipped black polish remains as a reminder of the Goth girl from before.

Like all young girls on the cusp of womanhood who don't know their allure, Gus is achingly beautiful. The skin as smooth as mercury, the blush that can't be manufactured, the arched brow that isn't critical, and the pouty lips that hold no disdain. Every woman who gazes upon this bloom of freshness at thirteen wonders if she ever held such fleeting power. A backbone effortlessly straight. Hips loose and limber. Though Lucy may have tried to remold and change her daughter, Augustina Rose Flannery is a wild and perfect marvel.

I don't do the foolish thing and ask why she put on her armor in the first place. I don't ask why she is now shedding it. This cottage in my haunted wood is a healing place where Gus feels safe and loved. She pours a cup of coffee, adds heavy cream and two heaping spoons of sugar. With mug in both hands, she faces me.

"I had a dream last night," she begins.

I look up quickly from my blueberry muffin. To rein in my sparking nerves, I tease, "For real?"

She nods. "It was about you."

*Oh my stars.*

Suddenly I am intimidated by this girl standing barefoot in my space. Is this how it felt to be on the receiving end when I was the young messenger that delivered dream truths or clues difficult to decipher? I never thought about how unnerving it had been to have a girl bear news that hadn't happened. But this girl is braver than I was. Her voice is confident when mine was hesitant.

"Tell me," I say and feel a flutter of fear but more excitement. I top off my cup of coffee and settle on a stool at the counter. When my hands tremble, I put the cup on the counter and clasp my fingers together to still them.

"Something is coming," she says without preamble. She looks me in the eyes, and I am pierced. "It's important in ways you won't understand at first, but the something spans centuries, and it won't be long now."

I am unsettled the rest of the morning, trying not to dissect and overthink the cryptic message. I find busy work to do before we leave for Baines Creek at noon. I make my bed, water plants, sweep the porch, fluff the pillows. We'll meet Kate at one o'clock at the schoolhouse and I'll get to lay eyes on the mysterious Books of Truth bequeathed to Kate Shaw. I believe those findings might hold evidence about my birthmark and an understanding of the word *Keeper*. The books might become a star in Special Collections. Might be findings so rich and rare that Appalachian history will expand. Jack would have been in his element today, and I regret he'll miss this discovery. The lingering question is whether my message from beyond is connected to Birdie's books. But her books have been written in one lifetime. They don't span centuries.

I'm rinsing the coffeepot when the phone rings. It's Kate. She has shocking news once more: Loretty Dillard has gone missing.

She was last seen yesterday.

Everyone is desperate to find her.

Nothing else matters.

I can't come today.

Abruptly Kate hangs up, and I stand stunned, thinking back to that final Saturday in May when I was in Birdie's yard. What was it that she said to Kate and me about the child? Did she ask us to watch over her? Keep her safe? No, it was something specific. *Y'all watch over this marked girl.* That was her cryptic request. Coming on the heels of Birdie's death ten days back, this news must have Baines Creek reeling.

Against my wishes, Gus and I have a free day.

# Chapter 19

## GONE GIRL

**Kate Shaw**

Buck faces the crowd in his front yard with Sadie snug against his side. She holds two-year old Baby Blue in her arms with Mary Harris clinging to her mama's dress. Buck's voice is pained as he confides, "We be shameful parents cause we ain't laid eyes on her since bedtime last night. And this morning, everybody thought she was somewheres else. Mary Harris say her side'a the bed was empty when she woke, but she thought her sister was doing chores."

A sob escapes the big man, and Sadie pats his chest and picks up the telling. "It won't till breakfast that we turn worried. We thought she be with Aunt Marris cause she checks on her every day." The old woman sits in their midst in a yard chair. Her face is serene and empty. "But Loretty won't there."

Sadie's jaw is set hard and her voice tight. "Y'all know our girl be different and sit with dying folk to ease their way over. Some days she head to the laurel hell near Peavine, so Buck hightailed it up that'a way thinking she might'a got hurt. But he couldn't find hide nor hair of her. No fresh dug holes. On a normal day she don't stay gone. Today ain't normal."

Sheriff Sykes from Burnsville twelve miles away pulls up in his squad car without sounding the siren. His lone deputy Clayton Booker is with him, and that signals serious business. The crowd parts so the officers can reach the Dillards. They shake Buck's hand and tip their hats to Sadie, whose eyes are now glazed over. Sheriff takes out his notebook and pencil and turns to us.

"We need to take these folks' statements then I'll come talk to y'all. We gonna need your help to bring Loretty home." They follow this hurting family through the yellow front door, which looks too bright against today's sorrow. The news continues to spread, and here comes Fleta Wright and her Crusaders for Moral Fortitude, a group of judgmental women formed to run me off when I came. The women are a social group now and have become more friends than foes to me. Today they hug me.

Mr. Turner, the mailman, stops his car and offers to ask at every house on his route if they've seen a traveling girl. Ellis Dodd, who makes fiddles, and Roosevelt Lowe, with his wooden leg and aging Plott hounds, have come to help. So have Tattler, Jerome Biddle, and his nephew Harlan. These men possess tracking skills that are renowned in these parts. We stand around the yard and wait for officials to organize the search. This June Tuesday our hearts have turned stone heavy.

The lawmen come back into the yard and the sheriff spreads a map of the county on the hood of his car. "We're here," he says, pointing to a dot on the map with *Baines Creek* written on the meandering stream but not a village. "We don't know which direction Loretty went, but we're going to start with a two-mile circle around here." His pointer finger loops the map. "We hope to find her or clues about her whereabouts. We aim to search the woods, barns, chicken coops, gullies, abandoned wells, and question every neighbor who ain't here helping."

Sheriff takes off his hat, scratches his buzz cut, and settles his hat back on his head.

"You walkers spread out and travel slow. Look for a child's footprints, broken twigs, and disturbed leaves." He looks at his wristwatch. "It's nearing ten, but we don't know when she left, so we don't know how far she got."

Roosevelt Lowe shouts, "Time's a wastin, Sheriff. Let Beanie and Weenie get on the hunt. Give 'em somethin that smell like Loretty." His buckskin Plott hounds are as weathered as he is.

"I hear you, Roosevelt. If anybody finds her, fire two shots in the air. Two shots," he repeats. "Let's get going, friends."

I join the wide search line that leads to the north where there are more boulders and thick underbrush and trucks can't go. We carry walking sticks to gently poke in the bushes and rock overhangs. I walk near Eli and Tattler and his hunting dog Skunk. Eddie and his older sister Weeza are with us, along with Jerome Biddle, the little lopsided man who has been a good neighbor to me. He keeps me in firewood and venison and squirrel.

We don't rush this beginning as we call out her name. We don't want to miss the leaving clues if she came this way. We walk slowly with eyes downcast, walking and calling till our necks are stiff. For hours we walk at a slow, thorough pace till we are surely past the two-mile mark. I roll my shoulders, crane my head backwards and breathe deeply—

That's when I see it. A child's sweater caught in a high branch.

"Is that Loretty's?" I point and everybody stops. They cluster beneath the tree, craning their chins up. "What do you think, Weeza? Does that look like it belongs to Loretty? But if it does, what's it doing stuck up in a tree?"

"Ain't never seed it. Don't think it be hers."

With his walking stick, Eddie snags the little sweater which has holes in it. He hands it to me and I put it in my backpack. It's hard to stop looking, but by early afternoon with no other signs, our search party returns to the Dillard home. We haven't heard two shots fired that would signal the girl was found. The only thing we bring back is the sweater hung up in a tree branch that Sadie confirms isn't Loretty's. A pan of biscuits sits on the table, potato soup simmers on the stove, and three coffeepots perk to give sustenance to the search party. We stand and eat and drink in silence, and trucks begin returning. The men drag frustrated hunting dogs. No news is not good news.

Sadie stands at the front window with her forehead against thin glass, eyes closed, her pain palpable. Before tender Buck and their children became her family, she fought a mighty war against a cruel husband and lost her baby. Surely the universe won't be as demanding of another innocent sacrifice, but all the same, I was wrong to think Sadie's love and determination could keep her child safe.

Mr. Turner's truck pulls in the yard and Sadie and Buck hurry toward him, hopeful. He gets out with a long face and is heartbroken to say no one saw Loretty today.

How can that be?

Then I think about Birdie, who's only been dead ten days. Could Loretty have gone there to grieve? I say, "Did anyone check Birdie's grave? The girl might be there missing her friend."

I don't say that Birdie asked Lydia Brown and me to watch over the girl. It made no sense that day and it still doesn't, but guilt burrows in my mind. Was I supposed to do something to protect her?

Tattler, Eddie, and Harlan take off running over the ridge toward Birdie's with their hunting dogs in tow. Sheriff yells after them, "Two shots if you find her, one shot if you don't."

Sadie Blue's face lights up with hope. "She and Miz Birdie was awful close. Loretty was learning the healing ways from her. Her dying cut a hole in my little girl's heart. I bet she be sitting by Miz Birdie's grave, don't you, Buck?"

Hope is a revitalizing thing, and we feel it ripple through the crowd. The most direct way to Birdie's place takes you through overgrown woods and massive boulders over a high ridge. I can't travel that way, but with youth on their side the boys should get there in fifteen minutes. I glance at my watch. It's twenty after three. There's abnormal quiet in the yard. Even the birds are silent. Everyone looks in the direction the boys went. Sadie and Marris sit side by side and Buck brings out an extra chair for me.

The old lady reaches over and pats Sadie's hand and says, "You a good girl, Carly."

Hearing that name shocks us.

Carly is Carly Hicks Blue, Sadie's floozy mama who abandoned her at birth into the care of a tender-hearted drunk named Otis Blue. He thought he'd won the prize when pretty Carly married him, but all she wanted was a daddy for her baby. When that baby was born, she didn't stay. She left for something *more*. When Otis died, Sadie had to move in with her granny Gladys. The name Carly isn't welcome at the Dillard place.

"I'm Sadie, Aunt Marris. I ain't Carly," my friend says firmly. "Carly run off with a fancy man and leave me behind. Don't go calling me Carly."

Marris says again, "It be all right, sweet Carly," and the smile on her old face is proof that what mind she has left has come unhinged. It's why young Loretty spends her days tending to her.

I've never heard anyone up here speak about Carly Hicks except to say almost exactly what Sadie said: At sixteen Carly birthed Sadie and ran off with a fancy man. That well-worn statement is a sad testimony to her character. Makes me wonder why Marris is focused on that wayward woman now after twenty-seven years.

Better than most, I understand the complex tie between mothers and daughters and the way an unkind mother can work misery in the heart. I had a lifetime of disappointments and judgments. Sadie only has a ghost to hate. A ghost we thought was long gone.

Minutes tick by.

My watch nears three-thirty-five. Time enough for the boys to get there. The lot of us hardly breathe, hoping.

Then a shot reverberates through the forest.

Only one.

# Chapter 20

## LOST AND FOUND

**Lydia Brown**

"We'll have to wait another day to see the witch's books."

"How come?" Gus wears her combat boots and is ready to go somewhere. Anywhere.

"A child is missing. It's the girl I met in Birdie's yard. Everybody's looking for her."

"That ghost girl you saw?"

"Yes."

"That was a forewarning, Aunt Liddy. She knew what was coming." I wondered the same thing.

"So, what do we do now?" Gus asks, clearly feeling stronger.

"We can still go on an adventure."

"Doing what?"

"Finding a lost graveyard."

"How did you lose a graveyard?"

"Truth was I forgot to look for it again."

After Jack and I bought the property and discovered the graveyard on our first ramble, we spent every weekend working at the cottage and guesthouse and didn't take time to explore. When he died, I was set adrift and never thought about that ancient burial ground. But it's time to find the headstones and learn about the family that time has forgotten. My niece could do with a project.

I make peanut butter sandwiches and fill a thermos with hot tea and add them to my backpack with charcoal and a roll of parchment. Gus loops her camera around her neck.

"That first time your Uncle Jack and I came upon the graveyard was the day we bought the place. Memory says we walked southwest from the bluff. Here's my compass. If you keep us walking southwest, logic says we'll find it."

But the white cat Uncle has different plans. He marches in the lead without need of the compass, as though on a mission; Gus blithely follows. We pass a boulder with a second white cat perched regal and serene. "Would you look at that?" I whisper, but the cat has scampered away.

"How long did y'all walk?"

"Twenty or thirty minutes maybe."

"Did you pass any landmarks or odd-shaped boulders?"

"None that I can recall."

"What does *sylvan* mean?"

"Sylvan? It means a wooded setting or an inhabitant of the woods. It's a lovely old word from the sixteenth century. Why'd you ask?"

"Uncle Jack likes that word. He uses it in some of his poems. *A sylvan chorus* and another time he wrote about *the sylvan-clad French Broad*. I wondered. That's all."

"Were you reading his book of poems?"

"I've got it in my room. It makes me feel close to him."

I follow Uncle and Gus walking in this *sylvan setting* and only mildly regret I'm not with Birdie's books turning wondrous pages and finding answers. But instead, the citizens of Baines Creek are on the hunt for their missing girl. A girl Birdie was mentoring and worried about. I'm lost in thoughts when my niece stops and I almost plow into her.

"I asked you three times if you like it."

"Like what?"

"My name. Do you like *Gus*?"

"Sorry. Yes, I like your new name. It suits you."

"I wish Mama did."

"Give her time. She's used to your old one."

"I didn't pick that terrible old-lady name. What were Mama and Daddy thinking?"

"Did you ask them?"

"Once. They said it was my triple-great-granny's name like it was special, but it's not. Nobody remembers her. Nobody talks about her. I think they went plumb crazy when I was born."

"I don't know, honey. Your mama didn't tell me."

She leads on and I add more conflict to the task of naming babies. "Did you know that some countries have strict rules for naming a child?"

"For real?"

"Yes. Germany, Sweden, Denmark—Iceland, too. They believe a baby requires a name that is distinctly a boy or a girl's name. While it cannot cause offense, above all, the first name must be gender specific."

"Who decides that?" Gus turns and wrinkles her nose in distaste.

"A Naming Committee," I say to her back as she walks on. "They create an approved list of male and female names. If you want a name not on the list, you pay a fee to have it considered. The committee accepts or rejects it, but if they reject it, the requested name can't be entered on legal documents."

"That's plain terrible specially for girls who want to sound strong, boys who want to sound sweet, or anybody who wants to sound different," Gus argues. "Why is it anybody's business? Do they get paid to do that job?"

"I don't know." I offer as a small kindness, "I do know your given name Augustina means 'great and magnificent.'"

"I still hate it. You'll never find anybody called that in the whole wide world. It's child cruelty is what it is. And 'Teeny' for a teenager is torture."

"When you're eighteen you can change your name. That's little more than four years from now. If you could pick a new name, what would it be?"

"Lydia."

"For real?" I say and she turns around so I can hug her, and she hugs me back. The sentiment is precious.

Only minutes later she says, "Is that it?" and I look up to see the walled graveyard. The cat was the perfect guide. It's even more forsaken than I remember. The porous surface of the stones is pitted. The wall is beginning to tilt. We enter the square plot through an arched entryway, and I kneel in front of the tallest headstone, unroll parchment paper, and use masking tape to affix it while Gus takes photos of the wall and headstones from all sides. Her 35mm Pentax camera is loaded with a twenty-four-print roll that she'll shoot today and put in tomorrow to be developed.

We kneel beside the middle stone. "Press the paper flat," I instruct, and I rub the charcoal block downward on the parchment beginning at the top, then across. The obscured carvings begin to emerge. The family name is Morrigan, and the dying date is October 31, 1768. Gus glances at the other two markers.

"Aunt Liddy, they all died on the same day. It'd be like David, Minnie, and me dying together and leaving Mama alone."

It's the first time Gus has mentioned her family, and it's poignant. "And on Halloween, too," she adds.

"It is odd. Our Scottish forefathers originally called that night *Samhain*. They believed it was the one night in the year when the veil between the Otherworld and ours thinned so the dead could pass through. Do you know where the name *Halloween* came from?"

"Where?"

"It was the Scottish poet Robert Burns who used the word Halloween in a long poem that had over two hundred lines. He wrote it in the late 1700s, and though he used *Halloween* only once, it struck the public's fancy. That was about the time these tombstones were carved."

"What do you think happened to the Morrigans?"

"Could have been a feud or sickness." I sit back on my heels. "Speaking of sickness, I don't feel well."

"Me either," Gus says, and I look at her gray face with lips turning blue from a peculiar chill in the air. "But it feels different than the fever."

"Let's have some tea to warm our bones," I suggest, and we step outside the square and are shocked to feel the balmy June warmth.

"What happened in there?" Gus looks through the arch. "Did we disturb the spirits?"

"I don't know," I say truthfully, for our bodies are proof that inside that wall we felt sick. "But let's go home. I don't want you to relapse. We have one rubbing. We'll come back another day."

# Chapter 21

## CONUNDRUM

**Kate Shaw**

Loretty Dillard stays missing, and the tragedy is a wet wool blanket that weighs us down. For all our united efforts on Tuesday, Wednesday, Thursday, and Friday, the sun rises and sets without finding that child. Not a clue, not a hint, not a scrap of hope. We grieve with every ragged breath we take, and the pall in the community is worse than when Birdie died.

Saturday starts with a desperate plan. Eli and the Dillards have made a list of all the people Loretty helped by collecting their sins and burying them at the laurel hell. We cross off names of folks who are part of the search teams, then volunteers visit the ones who didn't come forth. They ask questions and look for signs that the child is there to help somebody else. Everyone is on high alert, and the woods that surround Baines Creek feel perilous.

Sunday, I'm told church attendance swells to an all-time high to show support for Buck and Sadie, who shuffle in and sit crumpled over, pitiful in their sorrow. Today we're at the one-week mark, and I sit in the schoolhouse by the telephone, hoping for a good-news call that she's found. I sit in a neglected sea of Birdie's books where I worry for Sadie's sanity.

She was the first person to welcome me ten years ago, me scared of my shadow, her hungry for more. She offered to help me that first day in exchange for learning to read. I saw a pregnant, barefoot girl in a thin cotton dress carrying a dog-eared magazine with a big-haired woman on the cover. But I discovered that Sadie was a warrior who had battled dangers I couldn't fathom till she stood firm in my cabin on a day the rain wouldn't stop. Her drunk husband wailed outside like a spoiled little boy, and Sadie fought hard to keep her unborn child safe.

She lost that precious baby, then was widowed and life gave her new choices. She married kindly Buck Dillard, and on her wedding day she carried a red rose from Aunt Marris's miracle bush that shouldn't grow this high. I thought Buck's love would protect her from ever being hurt again. I thought Sadie had suffered enough for one lifetime. Now I realize that loving someone gives the Fates fresh ammunition.

Today, determined women file into Eli's church and join Fleta, Alice, Laura June, and Ima Jolly, who pray with greater zeal. They make a noisy spectacle that makes me ponder Eli's god. Why don't they see that their god has turned a deaf ear to their plight?

But they don't doubt. They pray harder, and begging for help is part of the process. Some of them are kneeling on the rough wood floor with arms raised and eyes closed while their arthritic knees throb and swell. Enduring pain calls god's eyes toward them. At least that's what they believe.

I'm angry. Angry that the world would be so cruel to my friend who has already known unfathomable loss. Loretty is Sadie's oldest living child, who was named for her big-haired hero. Loretta Lynn hailed from Butcher Holler, Kentucky, and that famous Loretta inspired young Sadie and gave her a reason to rise up and better herself. But now the talons of despair have Sadie in their grip again. It's harder to hold on to hope as we pass the one-week mark.

The next day, through the open door of the schoolhouse, I watch Lydia's yellow Jeep pull into the clearing. She has come by invitation, and steps out wearing a denim pantsuit and oversize sunglasses. She glances toward the church and the determined voices inside spouting Scripture. A young girl with hair cropped short as mine gets out of the passenger side. She wears faded jeans, a T-shirt, and leather combat boots. Her ears, lips, and eyebrows are pierced with tiny steel rings like a stapler holding her life together.

"Thanks for coming," I call from the doorway.

"Happy to help, but truly sorry for the tragic circumstances. This is my niece Gus," Lydia says then looks back at the church. "What's going on in there?"

"They pray for Loretty. Every day. It's something to do."

"Has there been any news at all?"

"Not a snippet. Now folks are venturing out further and praying louder for her return, but nothing has turned up. The not-knowing is pure hell. Those believers are doing what they can, but we're running out of ideas that make sense. It's like Loretty up and vanished."

The niece clutches her heart in sympathy, and Lydia says, "I wish we could help."

"Having you here looking at Birdie's books that I've neglected is helping, and it'll pass the time. I can't think of a single thing I can do now but wait. The preacher will stop by later with an update."

"Kate, I can't believe this tiny settlement has been dealt another blow."

I nod. "If I were superstitious and believed in curses, this is something big." I head inside the schoolhouse with Lydia following. The girl goes to the Rusty Nickel, probably for a soda and a snack, and I close the door as the lamenting prayers in the church turn to wails.

And there they sit. The lot of them lined up as best I could figure. I had randomly thumbed through looking for order. Lydia pulls white cotton gloves from her pocket—the kind I used to wear to tea and church when I was a girl living under my mother's formal scrutiny, and I cringe at sour memories. Those gloves were always too small for my oversize hands. They pinched my fingers and cut off circulation. When I tried to loosen their grip, Mother's glare scorched my cheek with shame. I let my fingers go numb. I like that Lydia is showing respect for Birdie's works, but I never thought to wear gloves. Birdie never asked me to. I don't think I even washed my hands.

Lydia walks across the room to the book that started it all and scratches her right palm through her glove. Out of all of them she knew which one came first, and she looks at it with wonder, and that makes me wonder, too. For the first time I see Birdie not as the wrinkled prune of a witch but as a girl with a lithe frame and clear eyes. Then it strikes me that the pages I read held little about her beginning. It was as though she was dropped from the stars to fend for herself. It is only the mention of the Cherokee Gray Wolf when she was young, the crows that saved her in the blizzard, and the arrival of Samuel that are personal. If there is more, it's hidden in other pages or written in gibberish I can't understand.

Lydia carefully opens the first book and sees something I don't. She whispers, "I need to sit," and I slide a metal folding chair toward her. The frame is bent and it sits cattywampus.

"You all right?"

"A drink of water, please," she murmurs.

I fill a jelly jar from the water bucket and bring it to her.

Lydia looks both stunned and flushed. She looks toward the closet. "What's that buzzing sound? You hear that? It sounds like a hive of bees."

"I hear the prayer group but that's all."

"How did all this end up here?"

I pull a second chair close to the plywood table. "You know where her trailer was, so after she was buried nearby in a family plot, Eli and I and some of the boys packed her books in cardboard boxes and brought them here. They stayed locked in that closet during the last week of school, then we spread them out on plywood. I did the best I could to organize them. It's a good thing we moved them because her trailer burned down the next day."

Lydia's eyes grow wide, horrified. "What? All this could've been lost?"

"Without Birdie to protect her things, all it would take would be lamp oil and the strike of a match. The sheriff didn't try hard to find the culprit. He said what was done was done. I'm sure you've noticed the burned ruins next door. That used to be the teacher's place before I came. Those ruins and Birdie's serve as reminders that folks up here take matters in their own hands. This place is above the law, literally, and there are few consequences."

"What did Birdie tell you about all her books?"

"Sometimes she'd have me sit and read a page or two, wanting me to learn something in particular. One of her rules was that a book could never leave her place."

Lydia chuckles. "Sounds like my daddy and his rules about our family library."

"After Birdie died, taking her books from the trailer felt wrong. Like we'd violated them or at the least disobeyed her."

"But lucky you did," Lydia drags a finger on the leather. "You ever see her make one of these? The paper and ink? You think she made all these on her own?"

"Eli and I talked about that. We think she made them but we didn't see her do it. In the ten years I knew her, she added new books without much fanfare. But this is a close-knit community, so word would've gotten out if anybody helped or supplies came through the mail. I don't think anybody else was involved. We did find a stack of her special writing paper and stuff."

"Where's that?"

"In the closet with the chest."

Lydia looks at the locked door. "There's a chest in the closet?" and she sounds idiotic repeating words as though her hearing is off. "May I see it?"

"Sure, but I need help getting it out." I unlock the door, remove the quilt, and slide to the inside. Lydia is on the outside, and we carefully carry the chest into the light.

"*Oh my stars*," she exclaims when she sees the workmanship. "This is amazing. What in the world was this doing in Birdie's trailer?"

"Don't have a clue."

At that moment, Lydia's niece and Eddie come in with sodas and Moon Pies. Gus says, "What's that buzzing sound? Y'all got bees in here?"

# Chapter 22

## MEDIEVAL

**Lydia Brown**

I could kiss Gus for hearing bees buzz. It means I am not the only one plugged into this dead witch's world. Birdie read my thoughts and Gus delivered a dream message, so something is coming together. Here, surrounded by Birdie's words, my path to the other side seems possible.

"What does it hold?" I ask.

"Something unbelievable," Kate says, and she smiles for the first time and pulls an ornate brass key from her pocket. "Want to do the honors?"

The key has heft, and the shank and bow are a Celtic design. Even the barrel sports fine etchings. The key matches the box in its quality—but the quality does not match Birdie Rocas. I slip it in the lock and turn, and when I lift the lid, the buzzing stops. Gus hears the change, too. And what's inside *is* mind-boggling. The object shimmers with gold and silver and spectacular semiprecious stones.

"What is it?" Gus whispers, and Eddie leans closer and whistles.

"An illuminated manuscript," I whisper. "And a smaller book. They were made long ago."

"Ever seen anything like it?" Kate speaks reverently.

"In Appalachia? No. But medieval manuscripts, yes. In London, behind a protective wall of glass. At J. P. Morgan's library, in New York, there are over eleven hundred manuscripts spanning ten centuries. And at the Rare Book School in Charlottesville. It makes sense for illuminated manuscripts to reside in these places, where they can be properly appreciated and cared for. A witch's trailer in the middle of the forest is not one of those places. And from what I know, the content is usually religious. Based on the cover, this one is an apothecary book."

"How old do you guess?" Kate asks.

"Hundreds of years. Maybe four hundred or five hundred. We'll know more after they've been examined."

Kate says, "That's twice as old as the United States. There were barely white settlers here when this was written—assuming it was written here." She adds, "Eli and I didn't touch anything when we looked inside and saw it held precious things. We didn't want to risk doing damage."

"A wise move. The smaller book could be a journal."

"But why would Birdie have these things?" Kate wants to know.

I grin. "That's the million-dollar question, isn't it?"

Still wearing gloves, I reach inside to lift the ornate cover of the larger book, which is roughly sixteen by twenty inches, and six inches thick. I lift the cover and reveal a marvelous first page. The colors are brilliant on the drop cap and intricate border. Lapis lazuli for the light blues and indigo for the dark. Red lead for orange and lead tin for yellow. Artists who knew how to unlock nature's colors that could last for centuries. I gently close the book cover and the chest. It doesn't hum.

"This part of history isn't my specialty in Special Collections, but I know where to find someone who can help. Do you agree that the first order of business is to secure these treasures? We need to move all of this"—my eyes scan the room—"to a place that is safe and better protected against the elements and the curious. Your lock isn't enough."

"Where would that be?"

With that question, I'm encouraged Kate will support my proposal. "I'd like to take them to my workroom in Little Switzerland. It's where I review collections being donated to Ramsey Library in Asheville. It's only an hour from here. It's a private and secure space."

Kate is tied to deep emotions, and I'm the interloper, the thief wanting to steal away these riches in broad daylight. I go on. "You've done a wonderful job with Birdie's endeavors, moving her books and protecting the chest—but this is a big job. Too big to stay here in a public place." Then I remind her, "You reached out to me for help, and that's what I suggest."

Kate nods but won't meet my eyes. She runs her fingers over the nearest book. "It's all happening so fast, isn't it? It's only been a few weeks since Birdie died and we dismantled her world and the rest burned to ashes. I can't guard them around the clock, I know that, but when they leave the mountain there will be nothing tangible left of Birdie except her grave."

I soften the blow and say, "I could use your help, Kate."

"Doing what?"

"Being my research assistant—if you have time."

She pauses, so I sweeten the pot. "There's a guesthouse beside my cottage where you could stay. We'd only be a few miles from Birdie's things."

Then I deliver the hardest part. "But I'd like to start today. Take everything in my car and yours. If you come with me, you could oversee the transition."

"But we need to find Loretty. I can't walk away. Wouldn't that be heartless?"

I say tenderly, "What can you do about the missing child that isn't being done?"

"I'd be turning my back on this place," Kate says and looks to Eddie for a response but he shrugs.

"No, you'd be caring for Birdie's legacy, which means a lot to this community. Left here, this is all at risk."

"She's right, Miz Kate," Eddie says.

The teacher confesses. "I haven't slept well a single night since they've been here, but if I'm going with you, I need some things from my cabin."

"May I come with you? I'd like to see what's left of Birdie's trailer and where she was buried."

My niece quickly says, "I'll stay with Eddie. We can watch over the books while y'all are gone."

Kate explains, "Eddie is uncle to the missing girl. I think they'll be fine here, and Eddie will like the company. He'll listen for the phone if there's news. When we get back, I'll wait for Eli to tell him this decision. I don't want him to find the books and me gone."

"You'll be freeing him so he can focus on the girl," I add as encouragement.

"Everybody will be helping except me."

"You can come back often to give Eli a report on what we discover and see what's happening here. It's only an hour away. And there's the telephone."

Kate closes the flimsy door with the books and treasure inside and two children as protectors. As before, we follow the creek up into the hills while a bird follows overhead.

"Is that a crow with white feathers?" I say.

She glances up. "That's Samuel. He was Birdie's crow for over twenty years. His feathers have been turning white."

"Birdie had her own crow?"

"She writes about him in her books. He used to ride on top of her head. It was strange to see at first, but then I got used to them being together. Without her he's lost. Spends his days on a branch outside the schoolhouse or up at her grave site."

Our walk turns quiet and the acrid smell of ashes grows stronger, a reminder that as long as Birdie's books are on the mountain, they're in danger. The sooty remains of her trailer come into view, and we pause beside the shell, which is pitiful and small. It doesn't hint at the powerful soul who lived here.

"Tell me again when this happened?"

"Eli found her dead on Saturday the week after the big news about school closing and you came. She was buried Sunday and we put her books in the school closet that day. Then her place caught fire after her burying day. It's been a rough two weeks."

"You said they didn't look hard for the culprit, but do you have a guess?"

Kate starts walking again, and I keep up this time. "No. How this place felt about Birdie Rocas was complicated. She was a necessary, indispensable character. Wise, impatient, judgmental. Strict yet generous. Over and over her witchy ways mystified me. You'll learn more when you read her books. It's a half mile more to my place. When we come back, I'll show you her grave."

Birdie's crow stays at the ruins. Corvids inhabit my haunted wood, and I know they are smart and faithful and even vindictive, but nowhere have I read of such a love bond with a human. It speaks to the transcendental qualities of the crone and the crow.

We reach Kate's clearing, and a mongrel dog steps from the shadows wagging his tail. She says, "His name is Rachel. He needs to come with me. He's no good on his own," and she goes inside and leaves the door open. Wind chimes jingle without a breeze. I enter the single room with a sleeping loft while Kate stuffs shirts, trousers, shoe polish, and toiletries in a canvas backpack. She adds books, tucks the half bag of dog food under her arm, and leaves the scrap of bread on the counter. "—For the mice," she says.

"What happened?" I point to a dead bonsai tree.

"It was old, a gift from a student in a former life. I was careless and the killing snow got it."

A card is tacked to the front of a pie safe: EXPECT A MIRACLE. I point and ask, "Did it work?"

"It did." She puts the card in her pocket. "Again, it was in the killing snow. I'll tell you on the walk back." She eases me out the door, and her dog leads the way to the burned trailer and an overgrown footpath draped with kudzu.

"This vine came from Japan." Kate uses her walking stick to lift the climber so we can stoop under. "Came to America a hundred years back. Thought it would solve erosion problems. You familiar with it?"

"Yes, I live in the south."

"It has some merits. Birdie wove baskets, cooked the young leaves, and made medicine."

"I didn't know that."

We pass an abandoned cabin being consumed by the woods, then round the final bend in the trail, and I am stopped cold: *Birdie's graveyard looks like my graveyard. Three ancient headstones in a row inside a stone wall.*

Kate sees my shocked expression, and when I explain, she says, "It must be a coincidence."

"I don't think so." I point to the fresh grave. "And Birdie's buried outside the wall."

"It's what she wanted."

"And you didn't think that was strange?"

Kate repeats, "It's what Birdie wanted."

I stare in the distance southeast, across a meadow, into thick trees, toward Little Switzerland. "You know, as the crow flies, only a dozen miles separate my graveyard from here."

"And that makes you think what? That this graveyard is somehow connected to yours? But why? What would they have in common besides three old headstones?"

"I don't know yet," I answer honestly. And truthfully maybe I'm overthinking and overreaching because I grieve for what I lost by a hair's breadth: the chance to know Birdie.

I clear my throat and rush to know more before Kate wants to leave. "Do you know anything about this meadow?"

"I told you," Kate's voice is tight. "I only saw it the day Birdie was buried. I'd never been here before and I haven't been back since."

"It's shaped like a bowl."

"So?"

"I wonder if it played a part in Birdie's life. Maybe in ceremonies or rituals. If you squint your eyes you can see magic forming. See women swirling around a bonfire while the tall stones watch." I blink twice and the scene fades.

Kate shakes her head in disbelief. She's unhappy with me. She repeats, "Like I said, I never saw this place till Birdie was buried. Never heard of anybody coming here either. To my way of thinking, the overgrown trail from Birdie's place was a warning to keep out. This is a forgotten place, Lydia. It's not special at all."

Kate walks away and I hurry to keep up, but I'll watch for mention of the meadow in Birdie's books. I'll find out who comes to this hidden place. I'll unearth the old customs that mattered to Birdie.

My trigon pulses.

# Chapter 23

## MYSTIC

**Kate Shaw**

Lydia is talking plain foolishness. Even when I squint my eyes, all I see are weeds and rocks. She sees something that belonged in Birdie's world. How can we see differently what's right in front of us?

But then I'm reminded of those nights in midsummer when the moon was full. I'd hear drums pulsing through the woods. That primal beating kept me awake, stirred my core, and pulled me to rise from my bed and gaze out the window. Those nights there was a glow through the trees, and embers rose high in the sky from a giant bonfire, and I could hear faint yips of joy and chants. But I never went to explore. The drums came only in the dark. Once I asked Birdie if she heard the beating drums, and she ignored me. Now I wonder if it was this very meadow that was alive with her rituals.

For all of Lydia's enthusiasm and enlightenment, standing in the presence of Birdie's grave I feel the crone's disapproval. It's oily and clings to my skin and smells mildly rancid. Is it because I brought Lydia here? Is it because we've decided to carry Birdie's books off the mountain? Did she really think that on my own I could unravel the purpose of her compulsive journals and understand a fancy chest that doesn't belong? And why did she give me the burden of protecting something so priceless and perplexing? Why not give it to someone who belongs here? Someone who cares. Birdie's death alone would have taken me to my knees, but the *all* of this place is too much.

We head down the trail and Lydia reminds me to tell her the story of the miracle card and the killing snow. I was hoping she'd forget. I say, "It feels trite talking about that ordeal, especially since Loretty isn't home," is how I begin the story from four months back when the woods became a frozen hell and I faced my demons.

"The *Old Farmer's Almanac* had predicted 'the snowstorm of the century' was coming," I start and feel my heartbeat quicken at the memory. "Seasoned souls had been preparing and so had I. Chopping firewood became the daily task as walls of split wood got stacked in sitting rooms, on porches, and encircled houses like a wall of defense. My neighbor Jerome Biddle had cut enough seasoned wood to last me two winters. A line of five-gallon buckets were filled with spring water for cooking and drinking. At the Rusty Nickel, shelves of canning jars, candles, kerosene, batteries, and lamp oil were stripped the day they were stocked. Folks prepared for something big coming. Something that would be slow to leave."

I pause and turn. "Where were you when it came?"

"At the Rare Book School in Charlottesville. The storm didn't reach that far north, but it was all the news."

"You're lucky," I say, and we walk on.

"When it started, Rachel and I went to the top of the ridge and watched the world turn into a pretty snow globe. On the second day, my wall of firewood was covered with ten inches of snow, so I brought the wood furthest away inside to dry. Rachel and I took another walk before we'd be snowbound, this time past Birdie's empty trailer. She asked me to join her in the mushroom cave. Said temperatures would stay steady there, even if the snow piled high. I declined her invitation. I felt claustrophobic in the cave. To my way of thinking, I had enough food to feed an army, a fresh stack of books to read, and my dog for company. I thought I was prepared.

"On day three, snow reached twenty inches, so, again I used my broom to keep the top of the woodpile clear and brought in more logs to dry and thought I was staying ahead of the game. I read and listened to my transistor radio. I had extra batteries. But on day four, the wind howled and the snow came down as though it was only now becoming serious. That's when I thought about that card you saw: EXPECT A MIRACLE.

"I got it at the October Festival at the elementary school in Burnsville when Eli and I took the children to wear paper masks and get free candy. We watched town people bob for apples, eat cotton candy, and carve pumpkins into scary faces. The bluegrass band played tunes and a man on stilts defied gravity, but it was the fortune teller's tent that captivated Loretty and young Crystal Mayhew, who thought it would be fun to have my palm read."

I stop when I say Loretty's name and turn again to face Lydia. "What if we don't find her? How can we stop looking? Who would harm a girl born special?"

"Special how?"

I hesitate. Should I trust Lydia with the secret of Loretty? Do I dare say what is common knowledge up here? I decide to speak bluntly. "They call her a sin-eater."

"I've heard of them," she says without a whiff of disapproval. "But they're usually older people who are willing to carry a burden. I've never heard of a child taking on that task."

I turn away from her acceptance of such preposterous

folklore. I'd hoped she would challenge Loretty's gift. I'd hoped that Lydia's beliefs were based in the logical world, but I stroke the miracle card in my pocket like a worry-stone. That card has changed me, and my feet now straddle the divide between common sense and the mysterious.

I continue. "The girls were fascinated with the crystal ball in the middle of the gypsy's round table, and she played her part to the hilt. She spoke words about my fate line, my Girdle of Venus, and my love line intersecting my lifeline—not once but twice. When I left she gave me the card EXPECT A MIRACLE. And when my cabin sat under four feet of snow with drifts above the roof, I made a list of miracles I would appreciate. At first I was cavalier about the exercise. I did it to pass the time. It was a game. Then something changed when I reached for the kettle to warm my tea and heard a terrifying sound. *Sleet.* It clattered dangerously through the forest like spilled BBs.

"In an instant, I realized I wasn't prepared for a felled tree crushing my roof or a branch crashing through a window. I had been careless. I'd seen abandoned cabins swallowed by kudzu like the one beside Birdie's graveyard. They were somebody's shelter until they didn't shelter."

I stop talking because the retelling is upsetting, and Lydia doesn't pressure me. I don't say out loud the part where the door latch rattled and I could barely breathe, certain that something starving was on the other side. I stared at that flimsy door and wondered what animal smelled me through the wood. Then, on its own, the door opened a crack and ice chips swirled inside like bizarre confetti, and I nearly fainted. I pried the door open on the alert for the swipe of a claw, the whiff of rancid breath, but all I saw was a wall of ice pressed against a latch that could no longer catch. The eerie blue wall of ice filled the doorframe. I was in a frozen tomb.

I finish the story in a hurry, about Birdie sending two

boys to rescue me. How they dug through the ice, broke a window to get inside and pulled Rachel and me out, us barely conscious. We huddled under Birdie's bearskin on their sled, which took us to the Rusty Nickel.

I end by saying, "It was a miracle we survived."

Lydia asks, "Did anybody die?"

"One man. Billy Barnhill. He froze to death under a stack of deer hides in his trailer. He'd become a recluse since killing his buddy in a hunting accident. Billy was never the same after. He kept to himself, drunk and addlebrained. Only one woman was faithful to the man everyone else forgot: Loretty's mama, Sadie Blue. She brought him food every week: a quart jar of stewed tomatoes or green beans or cabbage soup. She would knock and leave the food outside his door. Next time she came, the empty jar was waiting. What she did was enough to sustain the hermit locked in a narrow hell of his own making. But the killing snow did him in."

# Chapter 24

## LEAVING

### LYDIA BROWN

Kate and I make the rounds to her cabin, to Birdie's burial site and the mystic meadow, then back to the clearing. Gus and the boy have loaded Birdie's precious cargo and divided the boxes between my car and Kate's.

"We were real careful moving them," she says. "And guess what? Eddie's going to Mountain Heritage next year and is gonna be in the same grade as me."

They sit on the front steps with empty soda bottles between them and the glow of youth lying easy on their skin. It's good they can't see but so far down the road to life. It's littered with deceitful promises.

The prayer group at the church has dispersed and the settlement is quiet, and Kate whispers, "Here comes Eli." He carries a weariness that says the news isn't good. Introductions are made and he says, "Nobody's seen hide nor hair of her."

Kate says, "It's been eight days. Do you think we need outside help? Could Sheriff Sykes ask for more officers to broaden the search?"

The stoop of the little man's shoulders and set of his jaw are pitiful. "Nobody knows these hills better than us, Kate. If we expand the search, that means we think an outsider took her, and that's terrifying."

Kate doesn't argue but says, "There's something I haven't told you. Birdie's last words and Loretty's—they were confusing, but they might be a clue."

"What did they say?" He perks up.

"Birdie wrote on her last page about sin and misery and a grave. Loretty talked about a kinship sin, but I can't remember what she said exactly."

Eli says, "The child collected more sin than most could tolerate, and kinship sins are common up here, but it doesn't sound like clues."

"So, you don't think they were warning us about a special sin? Something different?" Kate wonders. "That's what I keep worrying about. That I'm forgetting something important I'm supposed to tell you."

Gus and I watch this struggle to manufacture hope.

"There's something else you need to know," Kate says.

"What now?"

"We've loaded Birdie's books in our cars. We're taking them to a safe place where we can study them, Lydia and me."

Eli looks over at the schoolhouse, which is now empty. "Where's that?"

Kate looks to me to explain.

"An hour from here, in Little Switzerland. I have a workshop above the bookstore. Birdie's things will be safe while Kate and I review them."

"You taking the chest, too?"

"We can't leave it behind," Kate says. "We need to understand why it's here. That answer might be in Birdie's books."

I say, "I know experts who will help us understand what you have. There are people in the academic world who specifically study Appalachia." I'm quick to add, "You'll be kept informed every step of the way and can read a final transcript when we're through, but it's going to take forever to sort through so much stuff."

"She didn't leave the books to me, Kate, and I'm relieved they'll be safe. And we got enough to worry about with Loretty missing."

Kate hugs him awkwardly then steps back. "Lydia, can you give Eli a phone number where he can reach me?"

I write the guesthouse phone number on the back of my business card, the same card I left with Kate only two and a half weeks ago, hoping to meet Birdie Rocas at a more cordial time. "That number on the back is where Kate will be staying. You can call her there or reach us at the office."

Kate says, "So that's it. We were waiting for you and hoping for good news, but that's not coming today, and I don't know what more I can do."

Gus shocks us when she steps forward and takes Eddie's and Eli's hands in hers and speaks words we never expected.

"Tell Loretty's mama and daddy that the girl left of her own free will. She's doing good work. She'll come home when it's time."

# Chapter 25

## SIGHTING

**Kate Shaw**

Eli and Eddie don't know what to say. The strange girl with the piercings speaks riddles as cryptic as Birdie's. At least they're hopeful words that may comfort the Dillards—if Eli or Eddie tells them. I hope she speaks the truth, but if she does then I am yet again confounded. It is as though I'm living in a different dimension and the ground beneath my feet is shifting sand.

I crank the old Edsel and it starts on the first try, though it's been months since I've driven it. This behemoth could swallow Lydia's Jeep and still feel hungry. It's almost as big as my cabin and now carries Birdie's precious books off the mountain.

Rachel's head sticks out the open passenger window with his ears pinned back by the breeze, his tongue lolled to the side of his grin. In my rearview mirror I see Eli and Eddie watch me abandon them and I almost hit the brakes and stay—but why? I can't fix the hardships this place faces. Baines Creek is more desolate now than when I arrived, and I wonder what's been the point of it all?

When they are out of sight, I breathe easier and follow

Lydia's Jeep as it cautiously fords the creek and weaves around blind curves. Where we are going, what I will find, and what I will do are unknowns that are more appealing than staying. When I told Lydia the story of the killing snow it brought other memories to mind. Memories about Mother and my love, Rachel, both long dead. Women who still flavor my days when I let them. Mother would call today's spontaneous decision reckless, foolish, dangerous, desperate. Rachel would be tickled I'm going on an adventure.

We enter Burnsville and its center square, then head east on an unfamiliar road with the setting sun behind us. The further I'm away from Baines Creek, the more right it feels to go somewhere else. Why have I not left the mountain more often except for summers? Maybe I needed a reason and now have one.

Five more miles at a cluster of buildings called Micaville, my eyes play tricks on me. *Outside a country store I see Loretty!* She wears a familiar faded dress and walks beside a small woman with bent shoulders and pale hair. They hold hands, and each carries a basket. I pass by so quickly that I only have a glimpse and think I'm surely mistaken. Loretty would never leave her parents in such a miserable state if she could help it. The child I passed wasn't conflicted or in danger. Wasn't being held against her will. I need to talk to that girl, but I don't stop for fear I'll lose sight of Lydia's car. The further I drive, the more I doubt myself.

Twelve more miles and we drive through the town of Spruce Pine, then Grassy Creek, and enter the shaded Blue Ridge Parkway, which I've read about but never had leisure time to drive. Politics rerouted this scenic road around Asheville to end in Cherokee—not in Tennessee as originally planned. The political stakes were high and the battle long and likely the rewards substantial. We dart through a blackened tunnel then exit into Little Switzerland. I follow Lydia's Jeep into the gravel lot at the inn, which is modeled after a Swiss chalet with heavy timbers, exposed beams, and decorative brackets. They park, and I pull beside them.

"Thought we'd eat supper now," she explains. "My treat. Have you been to Little Switzerland before?"

"No. Only the real one."

"Switzerland? When?"

"Thirty years ago."

"Did you go by yourself?"

"No. Went with my sister, Rachel," I lie.

My dog stays in the car with the windows cracked, and a promise I'll bring him a doggie bag. Lydia opens the heavy entry door, walks through the expansive lobby and out to the patio. A waitress recognizes Lydia and her niece, shows us to a choice table, and gives us menus.

Gus says to the waitress, "You got a second one!" and her hand flies to her ear as she grins.

"You turned me brave. Got it three days back."

"Looks good," the girl says about a fresh piercing, and I wonder why lovely Gus with skin as smooth as a pearl would sully it with piercings. Is it to declare that her body belongs to her? That she'll do with it what she pleases? And, if so, isn't that a good thing?

They give me the seat facing the valley and I admit, "Haven't been in this kind of luxury for a long while."

Lydia explains, "The original inn was torn down twenty years back, and this was built in its place."

"It feels perfect in this setting, doesn't it?"

Our drinks arrive and we order dinner, then I ask what I should have asked an hour ago, "I followed you over hill and dale without asking what should have been my first question: What *will* I be doing here?"

She chuckles. "Rewarding work. We'll study Birdie's books with fresh eyes, and for the parts we can't decipher, we'll find somebody who can. We'll be careful to preserve each book as Birdie left it. The books she handled most will be evident and have greater wear and tear and possibly be more important to her. We'll have plenty of secrets to unravel and organize. But the trunk and manuscript will require a curator's help." Lydia adds sugar to her iced tea, stirs, and asks, "I'm curious about you as well. What's your educational background?"

I list my pedigrees. "Vanderbilt for an English degree and a year abroad at Oxford in my third year. Then a master's degree in anthropology." I add as a footnote, "Vanderbilt was my mother's alma mater." This is true but not the whole truth.

Lydia plops back in her seat. "Kate Shaw, if an alien sat down at our table, I could not be more surprised. And you've spent the last decade teaching in a one-room schoolhouse? Did Eli know?"

"I'm not sure Eli saw my résumé. I was the only one who answered his plea tacked on a church bulletin board. He was relieved."

"But today's timing is all strangely perfect. Your education, the closing of the schoolhouse, and possibly the most intriguing discovery ever found in Appalachia laid at our feet. I'm grateful you invited me to help with this project." She raises her glass of tea and salutes me. "To conundrums and curious minds."

I add somberly, "And to finding a lost child."

A day that started with bland oatmeal, weak tea, and worry is ending in promises I don't deserve. Dinner is a perfect pork chop, creamed potatoes pooled with butter, tender asparagus, and decadent peach cobbler for dessert. I save half my chop for Rachel and he smells it when I get in the car. I don't wait on formalities but open the foil and let him enjoy a rare treat, and then we follow the Jeep across the road and around the corner to a line of connected shops: the Diamondback Café, a general store that doubles as a post office, and Books and Beans. We park near the bookstore that is closed for the day, but Lydia has the key. We three carry boxes up steep stairs to the workroom. She unlocks the door and turns on overhead light to reveal a white, spacious room with windows on three sides. This is where Lydia processes donations to Special Collections. It's where Birdie's books will be safe. Our last task is to deliver the wooden chest to its new space and cover it with the old quilt. When finished, Gus, Lydia and I give a sigh of relief. Suddenly I feel very tired and very old.

Lydia declares, "It's time to go home and start fresh tomorrow."

On the drive, I reflect on my sin of omission. I was honest with Lydia about my Vanderbilt degrees, but the truth is more complex. Mother went to Vanderbilt, so I went to Vanderbilt. Her greatest achievement was being named president of the local chapter of Alpha Delta Pi. I was rushed by that sorority on her merits, but it was an abysmal fit. I offered none of the aesthetics focusing on gentility and privilege. I was never the Southern belle hoping to catch the eye of a future politician or doctor. I was too smart for men, too studious for my sorority sisters, and too antisocial to be of any use for Mother's mahjong conversation. I had a small world filled mostly with books until Rachel Harrison chose to love me.

# Chapter 26

## PARADIGM

**Lydia Brown**

It's two miles to home, up Bear Wallow Road, through the opening beneath the parkway and onto Crabtree Road. Once past the white church, I pull into a steep field of wild grass and follow the narrow dirt road that zigzags to the top with Kate following. We park and walk the path into the wood, me with the dog food and my flashlight, Kate with her backpack, and Gus the box of incidentals. We walk single file.

"How did you find this place, Lydia?"

"Part luck and part destiny. A few years ago, my husband and I lived in Asheville but wanted a retreat with a view. One of our weekend hunts brought us to this back road. We found a faded *For Sale* sign that had fallen in the weeds and took this trail to two abandoned buildings. The view at the bluff was what captivated us."

"Does he live here, too?"

"No. Jack died two years ago." I say impossible words that always lead to an awkward silence.

Beneath regal pines we pass mossy boulders and blooming rhododendrons with fat pink blossoms aglow in the dusk.

Then the outline of the structures comes into view, backlit by traces of the sunset. Gus and I lead Kate to the stone guesthouse perched on the edge of the cliff a hundred yards from the main cottage. Inside, I click on soft lights, drop the bag of dog food at the door, and take the box of things Gus carries so she can leave. The dog curls up under the oak table on the hooked rug while Kate turns full circle to see a persimmon-colored sofa facing a stone fireplace, a large matted photo of a mysterious glen hanging above the mantel, and narrow bookcases framing each side of the fireplace. An oversize rocker sits beside a brass reading lamp, and the side table is large enough for a book and a mug of tea or coffee. The kitchen has a small electric stove and refrigerator. A coffeepot, two mugs, and bowl of apples sit on the butcher-block countertop. And tucked in a nook is a comfortable bed covered in a vintage quilt and stacks of down pillows. I say, "The bathroom is through that door. It too has stunning views."

"It's perfect, Lydia," she whispers. "Absolutely perfect. Was it like this when you bought it?"

"Heavens no," I chuckle. "Both the cottage and this structure were sound but in need of a lot of work. Jack and I spent every weekend for a year doing repairs. When the hard work was done, he had a heart attack sitting at his desk at the university. It was so unfair."

Kate sympathizes. "Do you find it hard to be here or a comfort?"

"A comfort really. His work here was a labor of love. I see his talent everywhere. Now this stone house…we were told it was built last century. We were also told that locals believed this wood was haunted. Buyers were scared away. It was the reason the property came at a bargain price."

Kate's eyes widen. "Haunted?"

"That was the story, and when we started spending weekends here we heard moans and whispers and creaks that sounded spooky until we realized it was only the wind crossing the canyon. It hummed through the rocks and cracks in the chimney and the poorly fitted windows. The more we repaired, the fewer ghosts we heard, until now they're gone."

"I don't like haunted places." Kate's voice is tight.

"But this place isn't haunted. It's all imagined. In truth, I had hoped to find ghosts here. Would welcome seeing ghosts."

"Why, for heaven's sake?"

"I'll save my personal story for another day but trust me. Your stay here will hold nothing supernatural or frightening. If you hear a moan, it's only the wind. But I do want to warn you. Be prepared to be awed when the sun comes up. The view is stunning. Will this do for your new home, Kate?"

She shakes her head and grins. "You know where I've been living. I collect drinking water from a spring, use an outhouse that has spiderwebs, and cook simple meals on a woodstove. By those standards, these accommodations are pure luxury. Thank you. And thank you for caring about Birdie's books. I honestly don't know why she left them to me."

"I can hazard a guess."

"Then enlighten me, please."

"I don't think Birdie wanted her books to stay out of the public eye forever. I believe they hold universal knowledge that will benefit a larger audience. The illuminated manuscript is proof that her legacy spans centuries and goes far beyond the boundaries of Baines Creek. Somehow, it's all one big mystery, and you and I are being tasked to find the pieces of this puzzle and put it together. It's a privilege to be part of something so important. May you and your dog be happy here, Kate. Come for breakfast around eight. I'll have the coffee on."

# Chapter 27

## ASTONISHING

**KATE SHAW**

When I am alone on the day that changed things, I turn off the light and stand at the wide window and watch stars appear. I stand in luxury while Baines Creek's grieving heart beats and its citizens carry on with their hardscrabble lives. Birdie has grown cold and Loretty stays missing.

Who did I see in Micaville walking with that older woman. Was it Loretty? Maybe—but why was she so far from home? After days of looking, no one wanted to reach beyond the village, beyond walking distance, beyond the familiar. Only my serendipitous drive with Lydia through a crossroads I've never seen may have shed new light. Tomorrow, I'll call Eli and tell him to go to Micaville. He needs to ask at the store if a new girl has come. But if she has, then the bizarre questions are *why*, and *who assisted our girl to travel so far from home*?

Rachel snores under the table, and I head to the bathroom and flick on the light to see a claw-foot tub long enough for my six-foot frame. A bottle of pearly bubble bath sits on the window ledge, and I pour in decadence and fill the tub with steaming water that didn't need heating on a woodstove.

I step out of my trousers, unbutton my shirt, and cast aside dingy underwear. I turn and catch sight of my nakedness in a full-length mirror and stare. I've not gazed upon my body in ten years because there are no mirrors in my cabin. The only reflection of my form is what I've seen in a still pool of water.

Full-on, I face the mirror, which is kind with the golden cast from wall sconces. It reflects toned legs that have carried me thousands of hard miles. My muscles are as defined as in an anatomy book. Above lean hips and flat belly, my small breasts sag. A silver bush of hair springs from my armpits and between my legs. My calves are a sheen of silk.

But it is the span of my shoulders that pleases me most. The sculpt of my collarbone has carried burdens that could have broken me but didn't. What I see is an Amazon with straight posture and wide feet, planted strong. I've become something *more* without trying, and what comes to mind is a poem Rachel often quoted to me. It's by Hafiz, a Persian poet, written in the fourteenth century. *I wish I could show you / When you are lonely or in darkness / the astonishing light / Of your own Being.*

And this is what my Being has become. It is pleasing.

I step into fragrant bubbles, sit, breathe deeply, and lie back to float. I close my eyes and think about Rachel. Physically, we were lucky to look alike. Tall and angular, we were prone to wear trousers and polished boots and tailored shirts, like the movie stars Lauren Bacall and Katharine Hepburn, who were famous when we met. We kept our hair cut short and had the same quirky cowlick at the crown. When mistaken for sisters at the start, we never corrected anyone. We were *Kate and Rachel,* and we perpetuated the lie. Sisters could go behind closed doors. Travel together. Share the same hotel room. Sisters could gain entry to a hospital room where only family was allowed to comfort the dying.

When I see my body tonight, I see Rachel's body the way it would have aged naturally had she not been mutilated by breast cancer in the summer of '73. Three years after I got fired for helping a student get an abortion. Three years after I came to Baines Creek for my punishment that included leaving Rachel in the legitimate academic world where she belonged. Ironically, the year she died, constitutional law legalized abortion and changed the rules. A fair resolution at last.

I allow myself to be at peace tonight and float and let go. When I open my eyes, I see a symbol on the painted ceiling. An eight-pointed star in shades of lapis. Birdie had an eight-pointed star that hung beside her humble door. Her Cherokee friend gave it to her when she was a girl. It kept her balanced. Hers was rudimentary and made of sticks. She touched it when she entered her trailer. It reminded me of a child's craft project, crudely made but deeply loved. Maybe this blue star on the ceiling will help me find balance.

# Chapter 28

## RED HAIR

**Lydia Brown**

The table on the porch is set with blue pottery and gingham napkins. When we see Kate and her dog come down the path, Gus pours coffee and I bring out a platter of pancakes. Crispy bacon, a bowl of berries, and a pitcher of maple syrup are already on the table. Oma's cuckoo clock strikes eight.

"Morning, Gus. Morning, Lydia," she calls out. "You warned me that I would be awed with the view, but I wasn't prepared," is how she starts. "I've been up since sunrise watching the awakening. Every minute it changes. It's hard to look away."

"I agree. When we found this place, I promised myself not to take for granted living on the edge of the world, and every day I'm still enchanted."

The languid white cat watches Kate's dog approach. They touch noses. Gus says, "Her name is Uncle. She likes your dog."

Kate steps on the porch. "We blur the gender lines without guilt, don't we? I'm guessing your name Gus wasn't your birth name."

Still holding the coffeepot, my niece wrinkles her nose.

"Augustina. Who names a girl *Augustina*? It's a death sentence is what it is."

Kate says, "I like Gus. It suits you," and wins a friend for life.

I pull out the chair with the best view for our guest and sit beside her. "Did you sleep well?"

"Like a rock. It was only the glittering stars out the window that kept me awake. I've lived beneath the tree canopy for years, so seeing the open night sky is a gift." She shakes out her napkin. "This looks wonderful."

"I want to fortify you for our first day of work. It will be spent organizing and walking through the process. If you'd like, before we head to the office, I can give you a ten-cent tour of the cottage."

"I'd like that. What did it look like when you bought it?"

"Rough. Neglected. Unloved. It had been abandoned for decades except for the occasional drifter or teenagers looking for shelter. They left trash and graffiti, but the ghostly sounds likely chased them away. The stories of our wood have become legendary."

"Like what?"

"You sure you want to know?" I tease.

"You said they weren't true."

"They're not, but they're clever. My favorite is the one about a witch's coven that lived underground. And then there's a widow woman who roams these hills looking for her dead husband's head. So far, I've found nothing to support these tales."

"Do you know who lived here before you?" Kate pours syrup on pancakes drenched in butter and takes her first delicious bite.

"The Johnsons we were told, but that's one of the most common names in the area. They lived here sixty years ago then were gone. The realtor thought they may have died from the Spanish flu of 1918, an epidemic that killed fifty million people. It wiped out whole communities up here. My daddy's people in the east were killed by the sickness. He was the only survivor."

I pour cream in my coffee and add blueberries to my pancakes. "We inherited his family's library. Some of the classics are here and in your guesthouse. Daddy's children are all bibliophiles who love to read. Every night of my childhood we read stories aloud to each other. Every weekend, neighbors could come and sit in the yard and listen to classics like *The Velveteen Rabbit* by Margery Williams or *Twenty Thousand Leagues Under the Sea* by Jules Verne. My family was a literate lot. It's no wonder that Gus's mother Lucy wanted to be a writer when she was a girl. I believe she still has a bestseller in that excellent head of hers."

Gus says, "I forgot about that."

Kate says, "Does she live close by?"

"They live on the other side of Burnsville. We came within ten minutes of their home yesterday. Gus is spending the summer with me as a junior intern."

She grins at the honorary title.

"It sounds like a wonderful childhood. You were lucky, Lydia."

We fall quiet and eat till the platters are empty. This isn't the time to tell my dark truth about how a lucky life can be cut short and taint what comes after.

Gus clears the table while Kate gets the tour of the great room with its line of windows and waxed pine floors scattered with loomed rugs. Above the mantel on the stone fireplace is a close-up of the exotic jack-in-the-pulpit, a bewitching beauty that is poisonous and perfect for a haunted wood. Spider plants, a trio of jewel-tone African violets, and trailing philodendron line the baker's rack. The sofa and chairs are placed for easy conversation and reading and comfort.

Kate whispers. “Another perfect place.” She smiles at the needlepoint pillow, *Too Much of a Good Thing Is Wonderful*, then touches the cornflower blue shawl over the arm of the sofa, ready to ward off a chill. More pottery lines the mantel.

“There are two bedrooms. I’m on the left.” The morning light turns my robin’s-egg blue room into an impressionist painting. “We installed floor-to-ceiling corner windows to see the wood in two directions. Do you recognize the rocker?”

“There’s one in the guesthouse.”

“Yes. They’re made by local craftsmen at the Woody Chair Company. It’s said that President Kennedy had this rocker in the White House to help his back problem. They don’t use nails in construction. It’s exceptional Appalachian craftsmanship.”

“But this armoire isn’t local.” She runs her hand over its painted surface.

“No, it’s from the Black Forest in Germany, home of the Brothers Grimm and my ancestors on my mother’s side.” I point to the creature on top. “That creature was made from three animals by my great-grandfather. As you can see, folklore and ghost stories run in my family, so we are at home in a place the locals still call haunted.” I grin.

Kate loves to touch things. She runs her fingers over the diamond patchwork quilt and the woven throw at the foot of my bed and skims the stack of books on my bedside table. She looks up. “I see what’s been missing from my cabin. I treated it as temporary, and it was.”

“It certainly holds none of your talents and promise.”

Kate bristles at the compliment. “Talents and promise? You confuse me with someone else. I’ve failed miserably.”

I ache for dear Kate, who is riddled with guilt about God knows what. She stares out the window and bites her lower lip to hold back emotions. This marvelous, educated, responsible woman is filled to the brim with self-doubt. Who did this to her? Why did she allow it to happen? But then I stop judging Kate because the same could be said about me.

I deflect. "Do you know the saying *You can't see the forest for the trees*?"

She nods.

"I believe you've been on your path for important reasons but haven't been granted clarity yet. You're too close to see the details, but the closing of the schoolhouse has freed you. Your unexpected partnership with me is a gift to us both. We are in the right place at the right time. Let's be patient."

We climb the stairs to the second-floor workshop and find Birdie's treasures where we left them. We'll start with the medieval chest because it's more manageable than the mass of books. Kate removes the worn quilt and pulls the brass key from her pocket and unlocks it.

"Gus, photograph our process, please." Kate and I put on white gloves, and she lifts the inlaid lid to reveal the manuscript and the smaller worn leather book and a worn pouch. We gently remove the items from the box.

Gus peers in the bottom. "What's that?"

Hidden beneath the books is a painting on velum. A drawing of stately figures in black robes surrounding a girl with red hair. Using tweezers, I lift a corner to see if it's stuck to the bottom by mildew or wood rot, but it comes up easily. I place it on the examination table and we lean in; our three heads almost touch.

Kate shocks us when she says, "I've seen these people. The red-haired girl and the robed figures."

"Where?"

"At Birdie's funeral. They were in the distance, across the meadow."

"You'd never seen them before?"

"No. I wasn't even sure they were real. They looked *ethereal* and when the congregation lifted their heads after Eli prayed, they vanished. And now this." She looks back at the figure in a drawing that may be centuries old. "It doesn't make sense, does it? What could it mean?"

"That, my friend, is a delicious conundrum." I suggest, "This drawing might have been done by a young artist. Maybe the girl with red hair. Maybe she's related to the scribe or illustrator of the manuscript." I grin. "So many marvelous loose ends fluttering in the wind to collect and tie together."

"But how could these robed figures and the red-haired girl be at the funeral?" Kate shakes her head in disbelief, doubting what she saw.

I offer a possibility. "This was protected in Birdie's trailer. Hidden under a simple quilt. She knew what and who they are, though they're long gone. Now she wants us to know."

Kate adds, "Are they nuns?"

"Nuns or witches," I say. "In the Middle Ages, people who practiced medicinal and chemical arts—usually women—were first depicted dressed in white. But later they were associated with black magic. Nuns wore black and some were healers, and the lines between them blurred yet their purpose for good never changed. Only the public's perception—one often influenced by male physicians. Historians have always marginalized the work done by women healers. They've simply been written out of history.

"And let's consider the source of these treasures: a witch in Appalachia who understood nature's gifts and recorded truth. From the little I know, it makes sense that she's part of a powerful lineage that goes back deep in history. The contents of this chest are part of Birdie's legacy."

Gus bends closer to the drawing. "I think they're leaving. Being cast out of their home. There are satchels and trunks." She points to a box loaded on a cart. "Is that *this* box?"

"Could be." We straighten up and step back.

Gus points to the pouch. "What's that?"

I carefully unroll the fine leather and expose tools, likely the ones used to make the illuminated manuscript. First are quills, but not from swan or goose feathers. "These are magnificent crow feathers," I explain. "They've been slit and prepared to hold the ink. But it is this"—I hold up medieval reading glasses framed in dried, cracked leather—"that dates the tools and works. This tool was invented in the thirteenth century and helped the scribes do detail work when their eyes got older and the light was dim. Before these were created, scribes used a large glass bowl filled with water and suspended it over the page. Candlelight lit the work, and the water enlarged the details being painted."

"How do you know so much, Lydia?"

"Jack and I earned degrees in library science. He got a master's. One small facet of that study was illuminated manuscripts, but I never expected to find one in Appalachia, and sadly, I don't read Gaelic."

"But you know someone?"

"A curator at the Rare Book School might be willing."

"What do they do there?"

"Study the history of printing, for one thing. After the invention of Gutenberg's printing press five hundred years ago, scholars had to decide common fonts and formats. Had to declare a uniform alphabet. The school houses those trials and errors. But nowhere in the modern world are bookmakers doing what Birdie has done."

Kate turns appreciative eyes to me. "This is extraordinary care being given to her work. It's far beyond what Eli and I could have ever done."

"It's my pleasure."

We carefully turn pages of detailed plants, herbs and flowers, but none of us are privy to the lessons in Gaelic. We close the book midway and save it for the expert.

In the small book we find beautiful penmanship but again, written in Gaelic. Dates appear to separate the entries, so we think it's a journal—but written by whom and when? We have been intent for hours and our shoulders are tight and eyes blurry. Gus has taken pictures of each step.

"Coffee break?" I say, and we go downstairs into the warm energy of a bustling bookstore selling baked goods alongside mystery and travel and knowledge. The three of us carry our mugs to the table beside the fireplace and are quietly sipping coffee when Kate confides, "I didn't mention this at supper last night because I felt foolish…"

"About what?" I ask.

"On yesterday's drive from Baines Creek, I thought I saw Loretty."

"Where?"

"In Micaville. We passed a girl walking beside the road holding an old woman's hand. They each carried baskets. The girl even wore a cotton dress like Loretty's."

"Why didn't you stop?" I ask.

"I was following you."

"We would have come back for you."

"But there's nothing much to say. I saw them then they were gone. It was literally two seconds, and it didn't make sense. The girl didn't look frightened or in danger."

"Are you going back to look?"

"I was hoping Eli would check it out. I tried calling him last night and again this morning, but I didn't get an answer. I'm probably imagining this out of guilt."

"Possibly, but maybe it's a new piece of the puzzle.

Call him from upstairs if you'd like, and keep calling till he answers."

"Miz Kate," Gus interrupts, looking shy. "Can I ask you a question?"

"Of course."

"What can you tell me about Eddie Dillard?" She blushes and her freckles glow.

"He's Loretty's uncle, as you know. He's smart and comes from a good family. It's going to be a big transition for our students going to county in September. He could use a friend at Mountain Heritage."

"Want me to help him get ready?"

"He'd like that, Gus. He'd like it very much."

Professor Covey comes by our table, and I introduce Kate, then lower my voice. "When you have time, come upstairs and see what we have."

He lowers his voice in playful conspiracy. "Do tell."

"It's a witch's ancient legacy that spans the sea."

# Chapter 29
## HUNCH

**KATE SHAW**

My voice is strained talking to Eli on the phone. There's no privacy in the workroom, and I'm embarrassed for Lydia to hear me beg.

"I know what I saw doesn't make sense, but it *might* be her." I grip the telephone receiver tighter and listen to his breathing. "It was last evening on my way here. Near the country store on Route 19. The sign said Micaville. Do you know anybody who lives there?"

Lydia scratches her right palm. It looks painful.

"Can't say that I do," Eli says without enthusiasm.

"Does Sadie or Buck know anybody there?"

"Don't know that either."

"Would it hurt to go to Micaville and ask? Somebody would have noticed, wouldn't they?"

Eli is silent and annoyingly resistant, but I plow forward.

"If you can't go, maybe the sheriff can stop by. It's only a few miles from Burnsville. It should be an easy question to ask: *Have you seen a new girl?* You don't have to tell Sadie and Buck what you're doing unless you think they can help."

He's quick to speak, "I'm not delivering false hope, Kate. Sadie's taken to the bed and stopped eating. No amount of coaxing will get her to swallow food. What I need to bring her is Loretty, not a story or a wish." He is tired and dejected from ten days of dead ends, but so is everybody who cares about the girl. "Lord, I wish Birdie was here," he mumbles, "She'd know what to do. She'd conjure up a vision in that red bowl like she did when Sadie lost her first baby. Birdie saw three more coming. You remember?"

"Eli, you're talking about witchcraft while I'm talking about asking a simple question."

He sighs. "I'll try to go this afternoon. What time did you see her?"

"A little after five. We were driving east with the sun behind us, and they were walking west."

"Anything else?"

"They each carried a basket, and as usual, Loretty was barefoot."

"Okay," he sighs. "I'll call when I get back."

"You have the card with my phone numbers?"

"Yes, I have the card."

"Thank you, Eli. Truly. Thank you."

I return to the worktable. "He's going to check. He'll call when he gets back. I don't think he believed me," I say, then point to Lydia's inflamed palm. "Did you get into poison ivy?"

"It's been bothering me since I saw Birdie."

"Would ointment help?"

"Maybe. I'll get some when we break for lunch and then wear a glove to protect the books."

Lydia is taking notes on the first book and I the last while Gus is downstairs exploring in the bookstore. My hope is still to find a clue as to how Birdie knew death was coming. Her last book starts in late fall with a list of nature's signs predicting the brutal winter, and I skim over them because it's tedious and I won't remember. Then I'm surprised to find my name mentioned along with a small group that Birdie asked to join her in the cave. I was the only one who declined. She even noted sending Tattler and Harlan to save me from my own demise.

Loretty's name is entered often along with the lessons she was being taught, and Birdie noted the school closing and then there's the entry *Lydia Brown come to my door—*

I call out. "Lydia, you'll want to see this."

She comes and looks over my shoulder, and when she sees her name in Birdie's handwriting she gasps and reads, "*Lydia Brown come to my door but it ain't time.*"

One sentence, but what a weird sentence.

"What does she mean?" I ask. I thought that week before Birdie died was the first time the two had met, but if the witch knew Lydia from before, why did she turn her away? One week later and the witch was gone, so when was the right time to talk if not that night?

Lydia clears her throat and explains. "That's the only time I saw her, but three years back I found her name in a stack of papers at the library. It was on an index card attached to a piece of homemade paper and I made a copy." She pulls a file folder from a drawer and shows me copies of the index card and the sheet attributed to Birdie. It's the illustration that is easier to understand: a palm with a trigon and the word *Keeper* beneath it.

I say, "Birdie had that triangle mark. And so does Loretty."

Lydia holds out her hand with the inflamed palm. "As do I. I was born with this birthmark. Until now, I knew of only one other person who had it. Trula Freed. What does this discovery mean, Kate?"

I grin. "You're asking the wrong person. I don't understand mystical things, but it appears that you are tied in mysterious ways to Birdie and Baines Creek."

In a daze, Lydia returns to the first book and, confounded, I flip ahead to Birdie's final pages, the ones written closest to her death. The first time I looked I was numb with grief and could barely make out the words through my tears. In this place distanced from the pall of Baines Creek, I see more clearly—and what I see is chilling. *A kinship violation… Loretty the innocent… To right a terrible wrong.*

For the first time, I think the missing child may be on a mission. May be doing work only she can do. I'll tell Eli when he calls. After he goes to Micaville. After he asks about a girl. After he sees if my eyes deceived me.

We walk to the Diamondback Café for lunch, and Lydia knows I'm nervous to be away from the phone. She says, "If he calls while we're eating, he'll call again. Especially if he has good news," and we order fried green tomato sandwiches on homemade bread and glasses of sweet tea.

"How's your palm?"

She holds it up and the redness and swelling are nearly gone.

"Did you put ointment on it?"

"No, I forgot."

"Then how did it heal so quickly?"

"Maybe it was trying to tell me something and now it has."

But Lydia's healed palm is the last miracle of the day. Eli doesn't call that afternoon, and we lock up the workroom, find Gus among the stacks, and go to the cottage. Lydia fixes a light supper of lemon pasta and salad. It's now been eight hours since I spoke with Eli. Time enough to drive to and from Micaville over and over.

"What's keeping him?" I ask as if an inquiry will make him call.

"I don't know," Lydia says and mixes dressing for a salad of dandelion greens, heirloom tomatoes and goat cheese. "While you wait, why don't you tell me about your preacher. You obviously respect him and his hopes for Baines Creek."

"I do—most of the time," I start, then feel guilty for criticizing the dedicated man. "Every Sunday he makes stone soup. Makes it in a big pot over an open fire. He wants his congregation to go home filled with more than the good word. Have you ever heard of it?"

"I have. It's a clever folktale of fair trade: the traveling storyteller enticing his audience to add a little of this and that to the stones and water, until something edible cooks while he regales them with his tales."

I remark, "I'd never heard of it before Eli. His starts with potatoes and onions then folks add a handful of whatever: mustard greens, ramps, scallion, wild mushrooms. That first time we met, his shirt sleeves were rolled up, and he was washing out the soup pot.

"One of the first stories he told me was about an exorcism. His daddy and granddaddy performed it on a man believed to be possessed by the devil. Eli witnessed it as a boy and said it was the pivotal moment that determined his future as a preacher." I reach for a glass of Lambrusco wine Lydia has poured and take a welcome sip.

"And you thought…" she asks.

"It was useful and quaint. It supported his beliefs."

"But not yours."

"No. Not mine. Not at first. Not back then."

"But something changed?" Lydia is genuinely curious and kind.

"Nearly dying but being saved changed things. Seeing mysterious lights. Hearing Birdie foretell. Baines Creek has been slowly wearing me down.

"A more recent faith story Eli tells is about Gladys Hicks.

That's Loretty's great-granny. She passed away in April. I'm told that the last time she went to church was when I came and spoke before the congregation. She'd heard I was tall and wore trousers and my hair was cut short as a man's, and her curiosity got the better of her. She thought I'd be gone before I even got started.

"Anyway, Eli couldn't get her back to church after that, but when she lay dying in her front parlor, he'd come by every day to pray for her. She wouldn't let him inside, so he stood on her porch and prayed loud enough for her to hear. It wasn't till she'd fallen into a coma and the family stood around her deathbed that Eli came in with his Bible.

"Now here comes the funny part," I say, settling back in the chair. "After days of being unconscious, her eyes started fluttering and she started grinning her toothless grin because her false teeth were in a glass beside the bed, and when she opened her eyes and saw everybody hovering over her, she declared in a raspy voice, *Oh shit, I'm still here.*"

Lydia giggles because it's funny, and I get tickled too, and we're having a laugh at the expense of an old woman who thought she'd passed through the tunnel of light, when I ask, "What do you think happens after we die?"

"We go home."

"You don't mean our childhood home."

"No. Further back to where it all starts at Finally There."

# Chapter 30

## DISCREPANCIES

**Lydia Brown**

Saturday after breakfast, Kate heads to Micaville. It turns out Eli never did go. Not on Wednesday or Thursday or Friday while we were in the workroom bringing order to Birdie's books and Kate was desperate for the phone to ring. When she finally reached him, he spouted a litany of vapid excuses: a flat tire, then a funeral to preach and his sister Prudence getting stung by yellow jackets. And there's no news about Loretty either, so today, Kate follows her own hunch and goes to talk to strangers.

Gus and I ride to the general store in Little Switzerland to pick up the photos she took last week at the Morrigan graveyard. Then we walk to the bookstore to show Professor Covey the rubbing we took of the headstone. We follow him to a long counter in back with space to unroll it.

"Thank you for including me in this exploration. Let's see what we have here..."

He places bean pouches on the corners of the page to keep it flat. I say, "I sprayed it with fixative so the charcoal won't smudge."

"Good, very good..." he mumbles then gasps. "Had you

told me the family name was Morrigan?" He looks up and slips off his readers.

"No, I misremembered it as Morrison. Does Morrigan jog your memory?"

"Not for a family from these parts, but from Celtic mythology. The Morrigan was an ancient Irish warrior queen. A shapeshifter who loved to stir trouble on battlefields. She was fearless."

There it is again. That odd link between the shapeshifter Romi and potentially my graveyard. I say, "I found that reference in my Celtic dictionary as well. But what would my graveyard have to do with a Celtic warrior goddess?"

"The ties between Appalachia and Celtic lore are tight beginning in the 1700s. But your headstone is chiseled Morrigan, and therein lies a distinction. The warrior goddess was referred to as *The* Morrigan."

He slips on his readers again and his eyes travel across the charcoal image to the dates. "May I jot down notes?"

"Certainly, but you'll see some odd things."

He remarks, "The obvious dying date is clear, but the birth date of February 29, 1702, is wrong."

"I know. It's not divisible by four, so it wasn't a leap year. I didn't bring rubbings of the smaller tombstones, but their birth dates are wrong as well. The birth months don't have thirty-one days."

"Fascinating, isn't it? Do you think the stone carver chiseled three wrong dates by accident?"

"Of course not. One could have been off, but not all three."

"I agree. He's playing with us, but why?" He picks up his magnifying glass to study the charcoal border. "This daisy wheel at the top is a symbol to protect from witchcraft. That has me think your Morrigans believed in witches but weren't witches. And their dying date: October 31, 1761, is earlier than most recorded history in these parts. We didn't become a state till 1789."

Professor Covey sits back and grins. "It appears finding the lost graveyard has brought more questions than answers. You have unearthed a wonderful enigma, and I'd enjoy being part of the quest."

"Gus took photos of the graveyard. We had them enlarged and picked them up a few minutes ago. Would you like to see them?"

"With pleasure."

I reroll the rubbing, and Gus lines up the prints on the counter. Magnifying glass in hand, Professor Covey shuffles along muttering *excellent, interesting, well done.* I follow behind and marvel at the clarity of the photographs. My niece has an artist's eye like her Uncle Jack. The lichen looks three-dimensional, and the carving on the stones is more pronounced. While at the site, Gus had me hold my flashlight from the side, and the angle of light revealed the writing better than the rubbing. Professor Covey jots down more notes.

"The puzzlement is the errors in the dates, isn't it?" he says. "Why would there be such obvious mistakes? All three women have birth dates that don't exist. And the symbols that frame the stones are a combination of religious or pagan and Wiccan, and that's an unlikely marriage. But the borders are all identical. Something fishy is going on." Professor Covey takes off his glasses and out of habit polishes the lens with his handkerchief. "Your mystery is holding tight to secrets, ladies, and it grows more complex."

"There's something we haven't told you." I nod toward Gus to explain.

She says, "We got sick. Sick to our stomachs. When we were inside the wall making the rubbing, it was getting really cold. But when we walked outside the wall, the air was fresh and warm."

Professor Covey studies our somber faces, then shocks us. "Ladies, we need to go back to that graveyard, and I need to accompany you. Are you free this afternoon?"

# Chapter 31

## ANOMALY

**Kate Shaw**

The clerk in the general store is standoffish to a stranger with questions.

"An old lady and a girl? What's so special bout that?" she says while stacking the *Yancey Journal* on the counter. She doesn't look me in the eye.

"It was only five days back, last Tuesday before five. They were walking west, each carrying a basket. I think they were coming from your store." I stretch the truth.

She scrunches up her nose and stares into space like she's thinking but doesn't speak.

Then I take a chance. "Is there a woman named Carly in these parts? Does that name sound familiar?"

She rings up an order for tenpenny nails and a ball of twine, then calls out to the man stocking honey jars on a shelf. "George, what be the name of Granny C what comes down from the hills now and agin. You know what that *C* stands for?"

"Don't recollect."

"Could it be Carly?" I add.

George says, "Might could be, but I won't swear to it."

"Did you see her with a girl a few days back?" I push.

"Maybe," he offers weakly.

Disappointed, I thank them for their time, and drive to Baines Creek with Rachel to catch up on Loretty news. The peculiar thing was hearing Marris speak Carly's name when the search for the child was only hours old. What prompted a forgotten name to come to light? Was there an incident that sparked her fading memory? And was her speaking that name tied somehow to Loretty's disappearance? I'm not the best detective, but these questions now carry possibility, and hope spurs me on the winding drive, across the creek and into the clearing.

But no one is there. The Rusty Nickel is closed. Irma Jolly's boardinghouse is empty. The schoolhouse and church stand hollow. I don't go to Eli's home where Prudence and her bitterness live. I ride over to the Dillards, but their yard is empty except for the iron plow where Gladys's husband Walter was struck and killed by lightning long ago.

I knock on the yellow door and step back. Buck's mama Jolene opens it, wiping her hands on a dish towel. She leaves the door open, and that's an invitation for Rachel and me to follow her inside through the parlor to the kitchen, to the smell of a molasses pie baking in the woodstove. She sits at the table and nods toward the coffeepot then gazes out the window. I pour myself a cup and Rachel settles at my feet.

"Where is everybody?"

"Babies wid they daddy." She drags her hooded eyes from the kitchen window toward the stairs. "Sadie be upstairs near broke in two."

"What's happening with the search?"

"Nobody sayin'."

"They've given up?"

"Nobody been by."

I shake my head over the travesty but resist sharing a

theory I can't confirm. "I need to talk to Eli. Do you know where he is?"

She shakes her head.

"How bout Marris? Is she home?"

"I reckon. Ain't seed her fer two days."

"I'm gonna walk down to her place then come back. If Eli comes by, ask him to wait for me or send him to Marris's. Can you do that?"

Jolene doesn't answer or show me to the door. Everything about her is sluggish like the blood in her veins is tired of trying. She's back to staring out the kitchen window and stirs her coffee over and over. I say, "Watch your pie. Smells like it's starting to burn."

It's a three-minute walk down the dirt road and round the bend to Marris sitting in a yard chair by her dented mailbox. I call out as I grow near, "Afternoon, Marris."

She pivots her chicken neck in my direction. "That you, Miz Kate?" she asks, though I'm only a dozen feet away. Her eyes are milky. Her sight is gone.

"It is. You doing alright? Waiting on the mailman?"

"Naw. Waitin on Carly. She be by directly."

I gulp and work to keep my voice normal. "What makes you think she's coming today?"

"She bring Loretty home," she says easy as pie and startles me even more.

"How do you know that?"

"Cause she say so." Her voice is calm and sounds rational, but I'm not sure how far Marris's mind has wandered. I believe her enough to wait with her.

"I'm gonna step inside and get a chair if that's okay." Rachel lies down beside Marris.

"Suit yourself."

The inside of Marris's home is dark and neat. There's only one window to let in daylight. The packed dirt floor is swept clean, the faded quilt on the featherbed is pulled smooth, the water bucket is half full, the table is wiped clear, and a basket holds a half dozen brown eggs. I carry out her other ladder-back chair and sit beside her. "Which way will she be coming?"

"From that'a way." She points to the right with her arthritic finger, away from Sadie's house.

"Does she come often?"

"Now that Gladys be dead, she come now and agin."

"What does Gladys dying have to do with Carly coming?"

"Cain't say."

"You mean you don't know or you can't tell me?"

She repeats, "Cain't say."

"What *can* you say?"

"She be coming along today...or maybe tomorry."

"Oh." I thought we were talking about an imminent arrival, but Marris is good at waiting. She can no longer tell time. Her world has grown small, and waiting is what she does best. But she may be speaking part-truths, and the truth that I hope is real is that Loretty is with Granny C, and the *C* stands for Carly, and that they'll be coming to Baines Creek soon.

I take a gamble and say, "I thought I saw Loretty with Carly last Tuesday." I watch her face but there's no change in her expression. "I was driving through Micaville and saw a girl who looked like Loretty. I went by the store this morning to ask questions. That's when I heard the name Granny C. I wonder if that's what Carly calls herself these days."

Marris looks to the right and kneads her turkey neck with one hand and chews on her gums like a cow its cud, but she doesn't speak. I never knew her when she had teeth or a spring in her step. The soft skin of her thin lips folds inside her mouth. I know so little about this woman except that she is the first to come to the aid of anyone in need. The second is how she got her name. Sadie told me her rightful birth name is Mary Harris Jones, named after the warrior hero Mother Jones who was the famous female labor activist of the nineteenth century. Marris's mama and daddy witnessed the hero standing in the rain on the back of a caboose talking about fair pay and rights. With hope for bravery, they bestowed that powerful name on their baby. Sadie bestowed it on her second born "because it is the name of a great woman," she said. I think she was talking about her Aunt Marris.

The only anomaly in her humble place is a glorious rose bush blooming red in a spot of sunshine. It defies logic in this high country. From ten feet away I can smell its sweetness as the minutes tick by and I wait on a back roads with the oldest woman in these parts.

She reaches over and pats the back of my hand. "It be all right, Carly. Yor kinship sin be coming out the dark. It be here directly, sweet thang. It be wrote down in Birdie's books."

# Chapter 32

## STILL LIFE

**LYDIA BROWN**

Professor Covey rides in the front seat and Gus in back, and we park on the ridge and follow the path. My cottage is the best starting point to the graveyard so we don't get lost. We pause long enough for our visitor to gawk at the view that overwhelms new eyes, and I promise tea and a tour when we return.

He's quiet on the walk and holds on to a clue that puts pep in his step. Gus has loaded film in her camera for this second excursion, and as before, the white cat leads the way. It's as though Uncle's natural compass is on point and the graveyard is her true north. We walk on a mission of the professor's making, and I don't think about our destination. I think about the cat that has captured Gus Flannery's heart.

My heart has never been owned by an animal, and that's a shortcoming. The closest was my affection for a mule on my family's tobacco farm. He was as hardworking as any field hand, and he never complained. When I was a child, Daddy could put me on the mule's wide back and know I was safe. Someone had misnamed him Assassin long before I was born. It was years after his tail had been set on fire by a hateful boy trying to get Lucy's attention, and later when the mule was poisoned, that I understood the cleverness of his name gone wrong. Donkeys are asses. Not mules. Our mule was called an *ass* twice in his name, but he didn't care. When he was murdered, I gave him as good a funeral as a girl of six could muster. Despite barn cats and stray dogs that showed up, Assassin was as close to a beloved pet as I've had. He was my friend.

Professor Covey keeps a good pace and only needed two breaks. The thrill of an adventure has recharged him like a man twenty years younger. Each time we stop, I spy another white cat in the distance. If they were lined up beside Uncle, I wouldn't be able to tell them apart. No one else seems to notice but me. We arrive at the graveyard in forty-five minutes.

The professor points to a bubbling spring I'd missed. He instructs us to circle the outer wall and note the misalignment of the middle headstone, then asks, "What do you see?"

We don't answer his rhetorical question because we must not see what he sees. He steps inside and walks around the three stones. Using his walking stick, he brushes aside leaves, plucks moss, and tosses twigs. He drags the stick along the top of two parallel roots. He examines the large stone and rubs his palm against the markings then pauses over the daisy wheel at the top. He traces the outline with his knotty finger, pulls a penknife from his pocket and clears the outer groove. Then he presses against the marking.

Nothing happens.

"Ladies," he says, and we join him and press on the stone till we hear an odd squeal. Like freight train brakes on tracks. *The headstone moves.*

We step back and breathe heavily, shocked at what happened. He says, "I opened the lever, but we need to push harder near the top. Ready?"

We dig in our heels and use our upper bodies to force open a crack in the ground the width of the main headstone; a cloud of chilled, fetid air escapes. "Don't stop," he urges, and we push harder, and the gap broadens. Are we opening the crypt of a witch's tomb centuries old?

When we have a six-inch gap, Professor Covey is winded and holds up his hand. "I need to catch my breath." We step back and rub our hands to release the grit and dirt. Our palms are dimpled and sore. Professor Covey rests on the rock wall and leans his head against the walking stick. His face is flushed but proud. He chuckles and hands his flashlight to me. Gus pulls hers from her back pocket.

"Go on. Take a look."

My niece looks first, confident there is nothing to harm her. "It's a ladder."

"As I thought," he says. "Now, Gus, you need to go on the back side of this headstone. You'll find parallel tracks." She hurries around the stones. "You see them?"

"I do." She drops to her knees and uses a stick to clear the dirt and roots.

"Now let's press on the large stone again," he says, and it moves more easily along the freed rails. Soon the opening is wide enough to descend. He warns, "Use care, Gus. Test each rung before you put your weight. The ladder may be rotten."

At the bottom, Gus says, "It's solid. Come on down. You guys gotta see this."

I turn to the professor. "This is your amazing discovery, can you make it down?"

"Wouldn't miss it."

And I follow till we stand in a cavernous room dimly lit by the opening, braced by timbers, lit by our flashlights. Rusty lanterns hang from iron hooks at all four corners. There are dented copper pots connected by tubing to wooden barrels.

Empty gallon jugs and rows of smaller bottles with cork stoppers sit in rows. Professor Covey grins like it's Christmas.

"How did you know?" I ask.

He chuckles. "I've heard every moonshine story ever told. The clever ways moonshiners disguised their stills to trick revenuers. There's an entire bookcase in the store dedicated to the craft. Your headstones contained too many errors to be accidental. The stonemason was poking fun, especially putting a single death date on Halloween. He might have offered his skill in exchange for hooch. Add the facts that the border combined pagan and Christian symbols and that there were no homestead remains close by, I had a good idea we were looking at a moonshine cover-up. Not a haunted wood but rumors designed to keep the curious away. When I saw the natural spring, I knew before we even opened the chamber. Water's essential for moonshine but not for a graveyard. They would run a pipe when needed and dismantle it when not. The smokestacks are contained in the headstones. Very clever engineering."

The space is roughly thirty feet square. Chunks of upended logs serve as stools, probably where the shiners sat while the moonshine cooked. A dusty miner's coat hangs on a wooden peg.

"How old is all this," Gus asks, "and where do the tunnels go?" She shines her light toward the black holes framed with roughhewn planking. The puny light is swallowed by inky black.

Professor Covey guesses. "It could connect mica or gem mines. It might lead to a cave on a neighboring mountain. And while this room goes back decades, it's not centuries old as the dates imply. Those dates were made up. Why it was shut down is the big question. It wasn't revenuers because they would have destroyed the still."

Gus snaps pictures and I look for something that would

give us a clue to the time frame. A newspaper or calendar. Empty burlap sacks are neatly stacked, and I take one off the top and shake off the dust. I also take the old miner's coat. My headache ratchets up, but now I know why: a sealed underground room where 110-proof liquor was made.

I feel a pinch of sadness that this mystery is based on something as common as illicit liquor. But there are still things to understand. Who devised this clever ruse? And if we ever followed those dark tunnels, will we find the bones of men whose dreams came to a tragic end?

We're back at my cottage late afternoon, and I put on the kettle for tea while Gus and Uncle sit on the porch with the professor. The door and windows are open, and I put earthenware mugs on a tray and a plate of oatmeal-raisin cookies Gus made yesterday. I hear her ask, "You said moonshiners are sneaky. What other things do they do?"

"A common one was wearing clip-on deer or cow shoes on the bottom of their own shoes, much like adding roller skates to saddle oxfords. The imprint in the dirt hid their man-made footprints leading to the still. It can be a cunning game."

"What was the clue that told you about ours?"

"There was too much *off* in that graveyard, but when you and Lydia felt sick and chilled kneeling by the headstones, that was the kicker."

I bring out the tea tray. "Professor, is there a map of the tunnels?" I pour Earl Gray in our mugs and pass the cookies.

"You're asking a complex question, Lydia. There are hundreds of independent mining companies in these counties, especially mica, and there's iron and copper mines too, but there's no reason to share tunnel information. They'd have a stake in their own enterprise on their own land, but not their competitors'. And then there is a labyrinth of ancient mines discovered in this county that goes back thousands of years. You're easily talking about a thousand tunnels. Personally, I believe there are more miles of underground tunnels than there are county roads, but I'd be surprised if anyone has compiled an overall map."

"Does anybody live there?" Gus dips her cookie in her tea.

"Sometimes strangers come to town with grime etched in their pasty skin. They blink beady eyes against the light like a mole. Folks speculate where they come from. In desperate times, finding any place out of rough weather would be a prize."

The burlap bag sits on the old man's thin legs. He fingers the material and stitching and notes the printing on the sack: Lester Pfister. It held a bushel of corn and weighed fifty-six pounds when full. Mr. Pfister printed proof of his product's quality on every bag. *Grown and processed under my personal supervision from inbreds developed by me.*

"What are inbreds? I know what the word usually means, but clearly it's different here if Mr. Pfister is boasting about it."

"Inbreeding involves the transfer of pollen from an individual plant to the silks of the same plant. It's tedious work done for several generations of corn before it stabilizes. Plant breeders create varieties with specific traits. They might be fast-growing or able to tolerate drought, or they're particularly resistant to a pest like the European corn borer. That extra work would be reflected in the price. Your moonshiners had a first-class operation."

He sets the feed sack aside and holds out his hand for the denim coat I took off a peg. It's a worker's coat caked with dried mud and smelling of the dank. The familiar name *Levi Strauss* is legible at the neck. The coat has lived a hard life. Professor Covey fingers the seams.

"What are you looking for?"

"Secret places to hide gems or gold," he grins, "or notes from a ghost."

"Really?" Gus stops petting Uncle and leans forward.

He finds an inside slit in a seam and pulls out a thin notebook smaller than an index card. He hands it to me, and I squint at the tiny print. Gus leans over to see. It's a ledger of clients. Dated 1918. Sixty years back. She says, "Looks like moonshine was going for six dollars a gallon and a dollar a pint. There are pages of names in tiny print—first initial, last name. I wonder if they knew their names were being recorded?"

Professor Covey returns to the denim jacket when something crinkles in the upturned cuff. Paper? Money? It's a folded note. He pulls out a small magnifying glass from his shirt pocket and catches the light. What he reads aloud turns our world upside down.

# Chapter 33

## KINSHIP

**KATE SHAW**

I need to find books Birdie wrote before Sadie was born. I've got a sick suspicion about that kinship sin that involves Gladys Hicks and Loretty. To my way of thinking, Marris confirmed that Carly is involved in the girl's disappearance. I'll tell Eli and he can tell the sheriff. Maybe they'll want to track down Granny C, but I no longer fear that the girl is in danger. She's on some kind of quest. Relieving some of Sadie's numbing grief is my goal today.

I leave Marris sitting on the side of the road and return to the Dillards. I climb the stairs, knock on Sadie's bedroom door, and open it a crack. An army blanket is tacked over the window, so the room is dark except for the light from the open door. Sadie's body in the featherbed is so slight that at first I think it's empty. But then I see her small head on the flat pillow and her open eyes staring at the water-stained ceiling, her chest barely rising.

"Sadie?" I speak her name tenderly so as not to startle her. "It's Kate."

She doesn't move.

There's a washbasin and I wet a rag in cool water, ring it

out and gently wash her moon-pale face. She leans into my hand and sighs. I want desperately to tell her I know where Loretty might be, but I bite my tongue to keep from spilling an unconfirmed truth. What I whisper is, "Hold on a little longer, dear friend. Hold on, please."

I can't find Eli to share Marris's news of possibility, so I drive back to Little Switzerland. It's near closing time but Nancy lets me in the workroom at the top of the stairs. I count back twenty-seven books to find a starting point near Sadie's birth year. I find 1947. Before Sadie Blue was conceived. When Carly was young.

I'm tender with the pages as I glide through the story of a traveling family that stayed in the mushroom cave while Birdie tended their ailing child. And there's the notions man whose wagon came once a year with buttons and colored thread and ready-made fabric. And then I find what I'm looking for: the name Carly Hicks.

She's described as a bright girl with the patient soul of a healer. Her backbone is strong. There's no hint that she was the kind to run off with a fancy man. I take rudimentary notes about every Carly entry in that book, then move up to the next and watch the girl grow and stay loyal to mountain ways. She becomes such a vital part of Birdie's days that her name isn't spelled out. Birdie simply writes *C*, and I know it's Carly, a girl who is thorough and doesn't complain. There are no references to her seeking something more, so what happened in '53 to change things?

I've filled three pages with notes in Birdie's words before dread seeps in. The girl doesn't want to go home. She finds excuses to stay with Birdie. When she stays away too long, her daddy Walter comes for her, but he doesn't enter the witch's yard. He stands at a distance, afraid of the power

Birdie is teaching his girl. He always found a way to pull Carly to him.

Then the girl got in the family way. A euphemism that could not be misconstrued. No boy or man was mentioned in Birdie's books—only Walter Hicks. Now in a pickle, Carly married a tender drunk named Otis Blue and birthed her baby girl—then did the only thing she could to get away from Walter. She left. Birdie wrote, *Them Hicks need a great reckoning but Carly say no, and I do what she say.*

The scene is set to right a nasty lie that spans twenty-seven years.

# Chapter 34

## TABOOS

**Lydia Brown**

The hidden note holds an incredulous find: *Romi say see Birdie. Go leff at fork 5 X then rite.*

My Morrigan graveyard connects powerful Wiccans, and I can't wait to tell Kate. We'll revisit Birdie's graveyard and see if it hides an entrance to the tunnels. Why else would a witch be buried outside the rock wall rather than within? Why else would there be a note written decades before with directions from Romi to go see Birdie? The similarity between the Morrigan graveyard and Birdie's can no longer be denied.

Professor Covey enjoys two cups of tea and a tour of the cottage but is fatigued from our unplanned adventure. I take him back to his car at the bookshop eager to share our news with Kate when I see her car parked outside and find her upstairs surrounded by a half dozen books.

"Hello, Kate."

"Oh, hi," she says, distracted. "Nancy unlocked the door and left the key with me. I hope you don't mind."

"Of course not. I need to give you your own key. Was today's search in Micaville successful?"

"Sort of—maybe—but what I found out from Loretty's Aunt Marris is most disturbing. And now Birdie confirms it in her books." She holds up a fistful of notes.

"Tell me." I sit. My news about the note can wait.

Kate begins. "First off, no one is searching for Loretty anymore. No one was at the Dillard home except Buck's mama. Buck was off with the children but Jolene didn't know where. Sadie was upstairs in bed weak as water. I couldn't find Eli, and Marris was chattering about Carly coming since Gladys died in April. And now I'm ninety percent convinced that the girl I saw in Micaville is Loretty, and she's with her grandmother Carly."

"That's wonderful! You found proof?"

"Not exactly. Oddly, no one in Micaville remembered seeing a woman and a girl last Tuesday walking by the road. One man thought it might be a local healer called Granny C. When prompted, he said the C *might* mean Carly."

"And that led you to believe what?"

"That the healer might be Loretty's grandma."

I nod toward the stack of papers. "Does Birdie write that Carly became a healer and settled in Micaville?"

"No. Nothing so explicit. At least I haven't found it yet." Kate responds with her usual edge, always on guard against criticism. "In the years leading up to Sadie's birth, Birdie referred to young Carly by her initial *C*. The girl was close to Birdie until she got pregnant, married Otis Blue, birthed Sadie, and then left."

"So you now think Birdie's reference to Carly with the letter *C* is tied to Granny C?"

"Lydia," Kate rubs her temples. "I'm trying to help, and I might have found something that makes sense and you're not helping."

"I'm trying to understand, that's all. I know the temptation to make things fit that don't. You began with a girl the age and size of Loretty. It's logical that you wish they were one and the same, and that you were at the end of the search, not lost in the middle."

My friend lifts doleful eyes to me and declares, "You might be right, but I did discover there was a double crime committed against Carly. Of that, I'm certain."

"What crime?"

"The first was incest. Carly's despicable daddy raped and impregnated her." Kate sorts through her notes and finds the entry. "Birdie wrote, *Carly be in the family way and it ain't from a boy. It be Walter Hicks. I show C a tea what turn his pecker limp and another tea what end his seed, but she don't make neither.* Is that blunt enough?" Kate's on the verge of tears. "What gives a daddy the right to molest his child? Where does that disgusting disconnect come from?"

"Sadly, it happens," I admit. "In a lot of places, not only Appalachia."

She goes on. "And I know this to be true: The horrendous second crime was when Carly's parents created the lie that their daughter was promiscuous. That the seed that she carried was from a fancy man. That she abandoned the newborn and Otis Blue to be with that fancy man." Kate spits vile words. "Both Walter and Gladys sacrificed their daughter's reputation and future for Walter's wicked ways. That's the terrible, horrible kinship sin I found out today."

Our hearts are heavy, as they would be for any good soul who knows the difference between right and wrong. Gladys and Walter Hicks did not.

I ask tenderly, "And how does this all tie to Loretty?"

"She knows the truth. About the *wicked sin dipped in misery*. The *kinship violation*. That's what she called it," Kate explains. "It was when she heard the vile confession. She may not have understood it all, but she knows the truth about Walter and Gladys. So, I don't believe Loretty ran away or was kidnapped or is lost. I think she's on a mission to mend her broken family. You don't have to believe me, Lydia, but the folks in Baines Creek defy logic. They do things and know things that aren't normal. This is far from the only thing."

"You can't shock me, Kate." I lean forward and when she doesn't respond, I say, "I believe in magic and psychics and the spirit world. I believe in all the creatures our planet holds from the Little People to tommy-knockers. I believe in reading tea leaves and palms."

"Well, I don't," she says and clenches her hands in prayer. "But I'll start with the latest weird thing that happened. Three boys were sent to interview a taxidermist for the school newspaper, and they found him dead, sitting in a rocking chair, surrounded by stuffed animals. Then they said the chair started rocking on its own and phantom animals and red-eyed ghosts chased them. How can that be?"

"I can't explain it," I speak tenderly. "It's a lot like faith. A miracle happens, a gift appears, a voice is heard, and you just *know*."

Then Kate says, "And then there were the dancing lights."

"Near Birdie's place." I say.

"Yes."

"When you ran through the dark."

"Yes."

"I saw them, too," I say.

"When?"

"The day I met Birdie but she wouldn't talk to me..."

"...and yet you stayed," she finishes my sentence.

"Yes. I sat in her yard quietly thinking and hoping she'd open her door—when she did."

"She came back out? She talked to you? What did she say?"

"She scolded me. Said my thinking was too noisy. Called

my thoughts *yammerins*. Said she couldn't sleep and that it wasn't time for me to know her secrets. You know that now from that entry in her book with my name and our birthmarks."

"Why didn't you tell me, Lydia? Didn't you think I'd want to know?"

"What was there to tell, really? I never spoke to her again. I left as she instructed, and when I got back to my car, that's when I saw the lights. I guessed they were floating over Birdie's place."

"Were you scared?"

"Why would I be? They were mysterious and beautiful."

"And therein lies the difference between us," Kate says with a look of resignation. "I like science and proof for my truths, not myths and fairy tales."

"But myths aren't false or fabricated stories. They're based on truth. That's what C. S. Lewis believes."

"The writer of the children's series?"

"It isn't simply a children's series. Those books represent Mr. Lewis's spiritual quest. That intention has been documented. He called those books *a study of the connection between the physical world and beyond*. He believed myths are that bridge to the other side."

Kate says, "What other side?"

"The spirit world. Some call it heaven. That other side is why I wanted to speak to Birdie. To understand more."

"Understand what?"

"The failure I've carried since I was seventeen."

I glance out the window at the dark and then down at my watch. "It's suppertime. Let's go home and I'll warm a bowl of soup, and tell you my story."

# Chapter 35

## UNDERGROUND

**Kate Shaw**

Lydia and I share a common pain: We failed our parents. We spend our days trying to justify our existence. Lydia's spirit gift didn't allow her to forewarn her parents and defy death, and I was never good enough to be my mother's child. Those failures are heavy burdens for young girls to carry. They warp the paths we follow and weaken our spines. Lydia seeks the mystical while I seek validation, and we both fall short.

"Tunnels…" Lydia is saying, and I blink a few times to catch up. She stirs the pot of vegetable soup while I slice a loaf of honey wheat bread and spread creamery butter. Outside, Gus lights lanterns and sets the porch table.

"Like the tunnel near Little Switzerland?" I ask.

"No. Underground tunnels. From mica and gemstone mines. Literally a highway of tunnels that link mountains and valleys but all out of sight. Today, while you went to Micaville, we found an entrance on my property."

"Today?"

"Yes. We showed Professor Covey the photos Gus took of my graveyard. That excursion we took when we didn't get to see Birdie's books. When the professor saw the prints, he suspected the graveyard held a secret, so we went back this afternoon and confirmed his suspicions: The tombstones are fake."

"Fake? Who would go to that kind of trouble. And why?"

"In this case it was clever moonshiners. The center headstone hid an entrance to an underground room with remnants of a copper still. Remember how I said my graveyard and Birdie's looked similar? Three headstones in a row? Now I wonder if Birdie's hides access to the tunnels."

"But why?" I ask again. "Who would use them? Where would they go?" I shudder.

"Private spaces for private reasons. The one on my property has three intersecting tunnels branching off from that chamber. And look what we found hidden in the cuff of a jacket."

I wipe my hands on a dish towel and take the photocopy of the message. Lydia watches my astonishment grow when I read, *Romi say go see Birdie. Go leff at fork 5 X then rite.*

"But you live an hour's drive from Baines Creek."

"But much shorter if you go by tunnels that don't cross valleys or zigzag around mountains and through towns. The path goes beneath the obstacles."

"How long would it take to walk?"

"Don't know. But the fact that one *can* travel from my graveyard to Birdie's place all underground is intriguing. Professor Covey says there could be a thousand passageways."

"Do you think tunnels could run from Baines Creek to Micaville?"

"Maybe," Lydia says, smiling. "Why not? It would make sense as to why no one saw the child."

I cringe. "You'd never find me wandering in the dark like that."

Once was enough when Birdie took me to the mushroom cave and I almost got separated from her because my steps were unsure and I lagged behind. It's why I didn't want to go there when the killing snow came; the dark terrifies me.

Lydia continues, "It's clever or cunning or convenient depending on your purpose, isn't it? Whatever the reason, knowledge of the tunnels has exposed a mysterious world. No telling what we'll find. With this revelation, Kate, Birdie's world, and mine are connected."

Soup and buttered bread along with sliced apples and cheddar cheese are served on the porch by lantern light. After more conjecture about hidden tunnels, Gus asks if I like the Narnia books.

"I read them years ago. Even taught them in middle school. The children loved them."

"And you didn't?"

"They're good but simplistic."

Lydia interjects. "They're more than simple stories. Mr. Lewis created a fantasy world full of talking animals and kingdoms that revealed truths and the meaning of life."

"Which is—?"

"Love, sacrifice, and redemption. That there's something greater than ourselves."

"But all I see are fairy tales."

"And that's a good start. Lewis believed fairy tales were important, both in their structure and message. Every time I read one of the Narnia books, my faith is reaffirmed in something bigger than mankind. The universe gets righted. There's a set in the guesthouse."

I use my standard refute against Lydia's argument. "I think myths and folklore are man's fabrications. They're meant to elicit control or fear or power. Blind faith has always eluded me. I've never seen the need for mythology and organized religions." I hate my righteous tone.

But Lydia isn't put off by it. Her voice isn't condescending. It's kind when she says, "The timing has to be right, Kate, and maybe your time hasn't come."

She speaks as though I don't know what I'm missing. That whatever it is, it will wait for me. What does that even imply? That I need to grow up or grow young or merely grow?

To lighten the mood, I say, "And the Bavarian armoire in your bedroom. That's the portal to Narnia, isn't it?"

Gus says, "I thought so. Hoped so. In the dark insides I could squint my eyes and almost see Aslan and the Witch and Mr. Beaver."

"The armoire *could* be the door to Narnia, couldn't it?" Lydia chuckles. "I was mostly grown when Narnia was published, but even as an adult, I was frustrated when my wardrobe didn't open at the back and let me step into a snowy world more purposeful than my own. Narnia would have been a great escape when I needed to go somewhere, anywhere else. I do know this: Fairy tales are indispensable to our lives, Kate. They connect us to our imagination. They shape our values and beliefs. Fairy tales are the vehicle to truth."

# Chapter 36

## OUIJA

**Lydia Brown**

"What's this?"

On Sunday, Kate stays at the guesthouse and Gus and I are having a lay-low rainy day. I'm on the sofa reading a compilation of Gloria Steinem's latest essays called *Outrageous Acts and Everyday Rebellions*. She is my hero for embracing the vision of equality for everyone. My favorite quote is *We are the women our parents warned us against, and we are proud*. Gloria is the voice of my generation—both the vocal and quiet ones. While I read, Gus and Uncle explore. I hear them rummaging in the bottom of closets and through the cavities of the armoire, except the one only I know how to access. I didn't think I had anything to hide.

But I forgot about Ouija.

Gus found the dust-covered box under my bed. The box that always lives in dark chambers, hidden, waiting for an inquisitive girl. The box from Aunt Fanniebell that I last touched two years back when the cottage was finished and we brought our possessions here—then Jack died.

Aunt Fanniebelle was a tiny, complex, funny woman who always treated me like a grown-up. When I was still single-digits old and the last of the Brown children, she let me sip brandy, then moonshine, me sitting on her portico in a wicker chair detesting the vile tastes but relishing the privilege. Once she showed me a worn deck of cards with naked ladies on them that she'd found in Uncle Nigel's liquor cabinet. We took our time marveling at each pose and making fun of old men who liked to look. I didn't tell her that I tried some of those poses at home and nearly hurt myself. It was harder than it looked. For a Southern Baptist, Aunt Fanniebelle was different in good ways, but Ouija was serious business.

"Lydia, it may look like a game," my aunt began, "but it isn't. And with you being a bridge to the other side and all—well, you gotta be *extra* careful." As protection, Aunt Fanniebelle taught me two prayers. To begin, I pray: *In the name of God and the Sisterhood of Light, let us only communicate with the Powers of the Light.* And before the box is closed, I speak with reverence, *Thank you for answering our questions through the Angels of Light.*

I was thirteen when she gave me that black wooden board painted with golden moths, mushrooms, and coiled snakes ready to strike. Thirteen is a dangerous age to get dangerous games. When Ouija was moved for the last time from the bottom shelf of Aunt Fanniebelle's secretary and became mine, no one would join me in the ritual. Lucy and Bert had outgrown such nonsense. Cora wouldn't touch that planchette for any amount of bribery, and I trusted no one in my circle of friends because they already knew I was different. At college, I used the power of Ouija three times with my timid roommates before they grew too cautious to play. How many times have I used Ouija in thirty years? Eight times? Nine? Does it grow tired of neglect and need to move on to someone else who is more curious?

"It's my Ouija board."

"How does it work?"

I set aside Gloria's book and hold out my hand.

# Chapter 37

## NARNIA

**Kate Shaw**

Sunday has been declared a day of rest, and this morning the world outside my window is a pale watercolor of a primordial land. I have nowhere to be and nothing to do as I sip coffee and ponder a miracle I witnessed last night.

After dinner, Gus and Lydia had invited me to walk by flashlight along the rim of the canyon away from the cottage, into the pines and down a ravine to smooth boulders that surrounded a circular glen. Once seated, we turned off our flashlights and the dark became a fairyland. *Blue ghost fireflies.*

Gus said they are one of two thousand species of fireflies and the most rare. Tiny quarter-inch beetles skilled at the mating game. Their pale blue lights glowed for a long minute as they floated two feet off the ground on the hunt for a mate. This kind of firefly doesn't live in Baines Creek. I would have noticed.

In a reverent voice, Lydia said, "These are the only fireflies who guard their offspring. The tiny female carries as many as thirty eggs attached to her belly. Their bioluminescence is unique. We're near the end of their dance of love."

Rachel and Uncle were with us, and they were respectful.

The magical moment felt like silk and organza and sensual nights, things I have no knowledge of in recent years yet recognized from my past. What has led me to this time of awakening, sitting in an enchanted woods in the midst of a miracle? Who grants wishes that haven't been dreamed?

The Sunday's gentle rousing continues with thick fog gathering and pressing against the window. For today I let go of worries about Loretty and Birdie and let myself *be* in this peaceful place. Tomorrow we will dig deeper into the witch's mysteries. Tomorrow I will call Eli and tell him about Loretty. But today I reach for a book in the Narnia series: *The Lion, the Witch and the Wardrobe.*

I lied to Lydia when I belittled these books. I read them because Rachel insisted. "Keep an open mind and engage your imagination," she had said, knowing that wasn't my usual practice. "You may enjoy this alternate universe."

And I did. Even in my thirties, I yearned for a portal to magical Narnia. To escape a world ruled by a witch called Mother. A world that made me hide my sexuality. I wanted to be brave like Aslan. Wanted good to triumph over evil.

On this Sunday in a stone house on the edge of a cliff wrapped in fog, I climb into the familiar covers of Narnia, and the story is even better after my years as Birdie's student. I read while wearing thick socks against the chill, sip more coffee, heat a bowl of chili, then doze stretched out on the sofa with Rachel snoring beneath the oak table.

In my dreams I roam through snowy woods on a mission, trying to unravel a puzzle, but I become distracted by the ringing of a bell from far away that no one hears but me. A bell that doesn't belong in this dream, and I wake to find it's the telephone. I stand and rub sleep from my eyes.

"Hello?"

"Oh, thank goodness you're there." Eli's voice is breathless.

"I'm here, Eli," I say and yawn.

"And, indeed you are," he chuckles and draws out news he deems important enough to call about but not enough to tell me right away.

"Wish you'd been at church this morning."

"Why's that?" I play along and stretch.

"We had a visitor."

"Oh…" I whisper and come to full attention. "She came home."

"She did. Walked through the door of our little church when I was preaching, and our congregation rose up and shouted hallelujah, and hugged and cried with each other. She didn't look any worse for wear though her bare feet were coal black with dirt. Buck and Sadie bout squashed her with their loving and right away Sadie got color in her pale face. It was a blessed resurrection of sorts, and I wish you'd been there."

"Me too. What time is it?" I glance around for a clock.

"Near bout five."

*Five o'clock?* Church was hours ago. Eli didn't reach out to me right away. I was an afterthought.

"We've been in a joyful frenzy since she got back, celebrating and spreading the good news. We ended up in the Dillard yard and food kept coming and we had a homecoming dinner nobody planned on. And when I thought the day couldn't hold any more surprises, it did."

He makes me ask. "What happened?"

"You were right, Kate. All along you were right. Loretty's been with her Granny Carly. I'd gone on home to give the Dillards some privacy, trying to think of anybody who might have been left out of the news, when I found myself walking the trail up to Birdie's place. Something pulled me that'a way though I knew Birdie was gone, and that's when I saw her: Carly Hicks. She was coming from behind Birdie's place with her arms full of Birdie's things."

"What things?"

"That red bowl, candles, crystals and such."

"Where did she get them? The trailer burned down."

"Don't rightly know, but here's the thing: She says she's gonna stay. And she's gonna live in your cabin so she can be close to Birdie's place."

"*My* cabin? But where will I live?"

There's an awkward pause. "Kate, you've moved on."

"Eli, I left last Tuesday. You act like I've been gone for months."

"But school is over and so is your job." He adds as an afterthought, "But a job done well."

"And the cabin was contingent on my teaching job," I say and realize that's the truth. Still, I thought I was more than a hired teacher. I thought I belonged. That before I left for good I'd have time to say goodbye.

"You did your job admirably—"

"But it's over." My voice is flat. "I understand." Now my voice is blunt.

"Please don't be upset, Kate. This is good news for Baines Creek. Granny C—that's what she wants to be called now—will be our new healer. Sadie Blue has her mama back. And Loretty is safe and sound. And you have a new life somewhere else."

The seconds tick tick tick. Then he says, "You can always visit."

I am crushed more deeply than I thought possible. I strike out.

"Yes. Some of it is good news, but the coming of Carly isn't all good news. Those nasty wounds for Sadie and Carly are gonna be slow to heal," I say, sticking my nose into something that is none of my business.

Eli and I haven't talked about the real reason Carly Hicks left her newborn behind. Loretty knows about that kinship violation. Will she tell anyone? It will have to come to light now, won't it? Now that Carly's name is on everyone's lips, won't people keep picking at that old scab? At least that's how I see it. But I could be wrong. The folks of Baines Creek might not ask questions at all. As quickly as they open their arms to Carly Hicks whose blood is their blood, they'll turn away from me.

# Chapter 38

## INQUIRIES

**Lydia Brown**

I build a fire to take away the chill while Gus takes the Ouija board out of the box. The cuckoo clock strikes three, and we kneel on opposite sides of the board with our fingertips barely touching the planchette. The air crackles. The glow on Gus's face tells me that the portal to Ouija's world has widened. She says the opening prayer—twice, and commands it to memory. Evil is not child's play.

I haven't touched the board since I was eighteen and looking to fight and bite, hoping for a confrontation after being shunned. At forty-two I feel more trepidation because time has beaten me down and been a stubborn enemy. My bridge to beyond may be closer, but it's still out of reach.

Gus asks Ouija standard teenage questions. This mindset must be etched on an age-old tablet: *Will I be happy, will I be rich, will I find love—que será*. Every new seeker asks the same questions because we humans are abysmally predictable. A small gasp escapes when *E-D-D-I-E* is spelled out as her true love. Then she asks harder questions. *Am I good enough? Does Mama hate me?* Mercifully, Ouija responds *YES* then *NO* to the tender ones. Ouija may help her sleep better.

"Your turn," she says, pleased with her answers. "Go on, you can do it," she urges, as though I am the hesitant child new to the game. Our fingertips still rest on the planchette, but there's only one question I want answered, and asking it has become tiresome. *Will my spirit gift return?* But I ask it again, and the disk begins to move like a lazy serpent, weaving, teasing, taking the long way to its destination before stopping in the middle of nowhere. Like it's out of gas.

Hasn't there been enough headway in the last weeks for me to feel progress? A dream message from Gus, the ghost girl Loretty in the clearing, a tunnel that leads to more, a birthmark I share with a witch—and unprecedented access to Birdie's truth.

I drop my arms and start to pack the board and planchette back in the box—and I almost forget to say the closing prayer and Gus dutifully repeats it twice. *Thank you for answering our questions through the Angels of the Light…*

My niece kisses me on the forehead like I'm the child. The cuckoo clock strikes four, and we curl up at each end of the long sofa and our bare feet touch. We stare at the flames while the rain on the tin roof is a muted kettledrum.

"Wanna talk about it?" Gus says.

I know what she's asking. "It's dark stuff, honey."

"I'm not afraid of dark stuff. It's part of life." The girl's voice is not naive. "Your dark stuff is my dark stuff, isn't it?"

"No. You do not carry my burdens."

"But what if I want to? Really want to? I may look like a child and sound like a child, but I'm not, Aunt Liddy. Do you understand what I'm saying?"

I nod and blow her a kiss. "I do understand, and I won't make that mistake again," I say mostly to pacify Gus.

"Thank you. So the dark stuff. I think it comes when your mama and daddy died. What happened after that? Mama never says what came next."

I choose my words carefully. "You know that our family's tragedy arrived in 1955 when I was seventeen. I was supposed to go to market with Mama, but I woke up with the start of a cold. Daddy went in my place, and that's where the day started going downhill."

I take a deep breath.

Gus says, "You think you should have had a premonition."

"Of course I do. I'd had dreams before that warned people. But it was more than that. It was Daddy doing my job at market. He went in my place. It should have been me in that truck. If somebody needed to die that day, it should have been me."

"It doesn't work like that. We can't pick and choose, and we can't volunteer."

"I know that, honey, but the guilt was too heavy from every angle. I was only seventeen."

"Only a little older than me."

I nod. "Everybody stopped what they were doing when they got the call. And you wanna hear an odd thing?"

She nods.

"I remember vividly your Uncle Everett's final riddle that he told the night before at supper. He used to tell one every day, but he stopped when our parents died. My sister Cora says he's never told another."

"What was it?"

"*What can you break, even if you never pick it up or touch it?*"

Gus says, "It's a promise, isn't it?"

"Yes. A *promise*. When I was little, I struggled to solve Everett's riddles. It was your mama who figured them out quickly. Like you did now. You have a deductive mind like hers."

I've tried to wander off course to softer memories, but Gus pulls me back to my telling. She won't let me stray. "Tell me about that dark day."

I look out the window and the fog is pressed against the glass, listening as I spill secrets like spilling blood. I end with the confession, "I left and never went back."

"Maybe you weren't running away, Aunt Liddy. Maybe you were going where you were supposed to go."

Anger spikes in my chest, and I think this child isn't following my story at all. She isn't feeling my pain. I say sarcastically, "Like following my destiny?"

"Yes. Your destiny is a very real thing that can't be denied. You are where you should be, but you don't know that yet."

I take a deep breath. Isn't that what I said to Kate? That she was where she needed to be? Did I think that comment would bring her comfort? What a hypocrite I am that I can't accept that I am on the right path too. I whisper my hard truth. "My home is gone, Gus, and I miss it with an ache that could sink me if I let it."

"Then don't let it." She gets up on one elbow to see me better.

"What?" I shake my head, confused.

"Don't let it sink you."

"Oh, honey, you make it sound simple—"

"—*when nothing is simple or easy*, right?"

I stare at the fire. The flames are hypnotic. "But there's more," I say. Now the flames crackle like static on an old-timey radio. "Trula Freed, my childhood friend, died four years later." My right palm itches. I hold it open so Gus can see. "Trula had this mark in the same place. And now I find that Birdie Rocas and the missing girl, Loretty, have one. Birdie called it the *mark of a Keeper*, but I haven't a clue what that means. I do know I don't commune with the spirit world anymore like you do or like Trula or Birdie did. But it is Jack's death that is the cruelest reminder of what I've lost." I bite my lip to keep from crying.

"I loved Uncle Jack," says Gus sweetly. "When he died I

was heartbroken because he always treated me like a grown-up. He taught me things and called me an excellent student. The last thing he told me three Christmases back was about an aspen grove in Utah called Pando. Did he tell you about it? He read in *National Geographic* that it's the oldest and largest living thing on earth. Over forty thousand quaking aspens cover a hundred acres with a single root system. He promised to take me there but he didn't say when. Maybe you and I could go, Aunt Liddy. To honor him."

"I'd love that, honey. You set the date. And like your Uncle Everett's last riddle, it's a promise."

# Chapter 39

## RETURN

**Kate Shaw**

"She walked in the church door while Eli was preaching," I blurt out in excitement now that I've gotten over Eli's insult. My pants and shoes are soaking wet because I ran through the rain with my slicker over my head.

Lydia exclaims, "Simple as that, she came back?" and hands me a dish towel to wipe drips from my arms and face.

"Yes, ma'am. On the fourteenth day, she came waltzing through the door and down the aisle. People wanted to reach out and touch her to see if she was real. That's what he said."

"Where has she been, Kate?"

"With her granny, she said, and that confused people. They knew she hadn't been with Buck's mama, Jolene. Then she said it was Granny C."

"*Oh, my stars.* You were right all along. Was her granny with her?"

"Eli said she brought the girl home but didn't come to Sunday service. He thought she didn't want to confuse people when Loretty's homecoming was the important thing. But that afternoon, Eli crossed paths with her on the trail to Birdie's place. She's living in my cabin."

"Your cabin? How do you feel about that?"

"I was upset for a quick minute, but it's the right thing. I don't teach there anymore. But, Lydia, don't think I'll overstay my visit. Your generosity is wonderful, but I'll find a place soon."

"That's not what I meant, Kate. There's no rush. You have a home here for as long as you want to stay. There's much work to do on Birdie's books. I only meant it sounded pushy of Eli. That the woman usurped your place and Eli acquiesced without asking permission. It was rude. That's what I meant."

I privately agree with Lydia, but my pride prevents me from looking pitiful. I try to sound confident. "Rachel and I were planning on leaving Baines Creek anyway. I'm thrilled at the turn of events for everyone's sake."

"Has Granny C spoken to Sadie?"

"Eli didn't say."

"So, we don't know how that reunion went."

"No, but it'll come out in due time. Loretty knows everything, and Marris in her addled brain knows everything, too. I do get sick thinking of the ugly weight the child has to carry."

"How did she find Granny C?"

"Eli thinks Birdie may have told her. Or Marris. He believes they knew the truth about Carly but were bound to her wishes, which were to ignore both the sin and sinners till they died. Carly understood that there would be no justice by the normal route as long as Walter and Gladys lived. Though Birdie offered the girl a cure, Carly took the high road."

"Kate, I am so relieved the girl has come home. It certainly lightens your heart. Starting tomorrow, we can now focus on Birdie's truth without this worry. I know you'll sleep better tonight."

I give Lydia the wet towel and am heading back into the rain when she hands me an umbrella. I fairly dance along the path back to the stone house that holds everything I need. Rachel is at the door curious as to why I left him. I ruffle his head and stand in front of the window blanketed in soggy clouds. I pray a timid prayer since I'm a novice to the practice. I lay my right hand over my heart, as though reciting the Pledge of Allegiance, but instead I say, *Thank you, Eli's God. You were listening all along. Thank you, thank you, thank you.*

The following Saturday, after a second week working beside Lydia, I return to Baines Creek. No work has begun on the bridge, but lumber is stacked on the shoulder. I park outside the schoolhouse where I did the first day. I walk the beaten path as I have ten thousand times. It became a walking meditation and it transformed me. But for all my effort, not much of me is left behind. A renegade breeze will erase my memory. It's already started. Rachel and I have been evicted. The cabin now belongs to the healer.

I have two goals today: to get my remaining things and to see where Birdie hid her witchy tools. When I enter the clearing, the woman I know is Carly Hicks stands on a stool washing windows. From the back she looks like Sadie Blue, small and wiry. Birdie's yard table has been moved and is at home here. Bundles of fresh herbs are ready to be tied and dried. The ground is swept clean. The door is painted blue. The place has been imbued with a soul.

"Hello, Carly," I call out, and the small woman steps down and wipes her hands on her apron.

Her stare is cold, and she looks up at me in defiance. But then I realize that it isn't defiance. It's strength. Carly is a woman to whom dastardly deeds were done. One who watched and waited for evil to die in human form, then stepped out of the shadows to claim what was hers. A legacy Birdie was saving for her.

Though we've never met, she knows who I am. "Hello, Kate Shaw. My name be Granny C. Carly died a long while back."

She doesn't apologize for taking my home. A home I never paid a nickel's rent for, but still… "You cleaned up the place. It looks nice," I say to be polite and to inch my way toward my intended conversation. I see a familiar eight-sided star nailed beside the blue door. It was Birdie's star. Now I know where it went.

I wasn't here when Sadie and her mother were reunited, but over the years I'd witnessed the scars the abandonment had inflicted on Sadie. When at seventeen and in this very cabin, she miscarried her first child. She begged god to take her life instead and let her child breathe. Even delivered dead, that infant was loved fiercely by Sadie. After, she asked a question in a raw voice. *Knowing love so pure, how could Mama leave me?* And what could I say to that? Sadie loved with unwavering innocence. Now I know Carly did, too.

I relied on Eli's description of the face-off, but what he gave me was puny. Both women are victims, and the words between them were cautious because Sadie doesn't know her mama's truth. Eli thinks Loretty will be peacemaker enough. What she can't do, time will.

Rachel heads to his favorite resting place, but a wide yard-broom leans against the trunk. I never thought to sweep the dirt or wash the windows. Inside has been transformed too, with the floor scrubbed and a drying rack hung from the ceiling. On the windowsill sit colorful quart jars of tomatoes, green beans, peaches, pickles, and apple butter. Gifts from neighbors happy to have a healer nearby is my guess. Or happy that one of their own has returned. A red-and-white quilt in a log cabin pattern is spread on the back of the sofa. It smells different from when I lived here, and that's because the place is cared for. Old cabins and worn-out souls need steady attention. I neglected mine.

In a small cardboard box are my remaining books, a few copies of *National Geographic*, three mismatched socks, and the eagle feather Birdie gave me. "What's all that?" I nod toward the bowls, candles, crystal pendulums, stones, bones, and tarot cards. Eli had mentioned Granny C carrying an armload of things up the trail. This is a staggering stash.

"Birdie's things."

"These weren't in her trailer or else they'd have burned. Where'd they come from?"

"Somewheres else."

"Nearby?"

"Near enough."

Though she is small-boned like Sadie Blue, she holds a powerful presence, and I think how fortunate Baines Creek is to have her confidence. She knew she'd return to this place when she was free to become who she was meant to be. She's already filled this cabin with purposeful things. She will do great good for those in need. Loretty will be by her side, learning the old ways.

"You know Lydia Brown and I are studying Birdie's books that were in her trailer, and there's information that could help you." I set the stage to drive a bargain for Birdie's hidden world. "The crone had a recipe for most everything. Would you like to look at 'em?"

She sees through my ploy. "I gots what I need."

I lay it out more clearly. "I'll help you if you help me. Giving you copies we've made would make your work easier. And I think sharing information would be what Birdie would want."

"How you figure that? Let me see your hand."

"What?"

"Right hand. Let me see."

And I hold it out, confused.

"You ain't a Keeper." Granny C pinches her lips around an imaginary corncob pipe, like Birdie smoked.

"Are you talking about the mark Birdie had on her palm?"

"That I am, and you don't got it."

"Of course I don't. I'm not like you or Birdie. But she left her Books of Truth to *me*. The night she died, she wrote *my* name on a scrap of paper saying so. You and I may not understand why, but Birdie had a reason. She trusted me to find that reason and you can trust me, too."

I'm exaggerating our friendship, but it's for a noble cause. If we don't have more strings, how can we tie together the universal mystery of Birdie Rocas? Thankfully, Granny C understands my logic.

"Sit," she says, and negotiations begin.

# Chapter 40

## UNRAVELING

**Lydia Brown**

Kate comes to my cottage as soon as she returns. She's got good news to share and it radiates off her skin. We settle on the sofa. "Tell me."

"I got evicted from my cabin," is how she starts and grins. "Like we thought, Granny C moved into my old place. When I went there for my things, I saw tools that Birdie used. The singing bowls and tarot cards and the red porcelain bowl Eli saw. And the reason they survived was that they weren't in her trailer at all. They were somewhere else," Kate looks impish. "But you already know the answer."

"An underground room," I state.

"Yep. We went inside the stone wall, and Granny C pushed a hidden lever on the center headstone and the ground opened up easy as pie. It looks similar to your moonshine room but older. Entering that room, I'd stepped back into the Middle Ages when scribes labored over writing desks. The modern day falls away when you're standing there. It's under Birdie's graveyard, completely hidden. It's why Birdie wanted to be buried outside the wall."

"So you went underground and saw what?"

"It's where she made her books and stored her witchy stuff. And there were more books on wooden shelves than I could count. Smaller rooms spun off from the main one that was at the intersection of three tunnels and held up with ancient timbers. The floor isn't packed dirt. It's covered in slate tiles laid as tight as a jigsaw puzzle. It was made to last."

"And nobody knew about this before?"

"I don't know. It's possible Granny C is the only living person who knew. Maybe she learned about it when she was a girl. Maybe when she came back she remembered. At least that's me filling in the blanks. She wasn't exactly forthcoming about those private things, but at least she let me see the room."

"This is a huge piece of the puzzle, isn't it? To discover that a connected world exists hidden and safe. I'm reminded of one of the tales we were told about our haunted woods. That a coven of witches lived below ground. Even I thought it was a made-up ghost story."

Kate sits back and looks proud. "What have we stumbled upon, Lydia? I feel like we've discovered a new planet in our solar system. An alternate world that's out of place. Can we hope to do justice to Birdie's mystery that keeps expanding?"

"We now know one thing: Birdie's on our side now. We only have to be patient and thorough and not miss a clue."

# Chapter 41

## CURATOR

**Kate Shaw**

Today comes a new contributor to Birdie's puzzle: Doctor Theresa Cotton, the expert in Gaelic and the curator from the Rare Book School.

"Why did she volunteer?" I ask again, worried.

"She wants to be part of this discovery."

"But she understands Birdie's things belong to Baines Creek."

"Of course. The joy of assessing rare books isn't to possess them. It's to bear witness to history and to understand it."

But I worry that this expert will exert pressure to steal Birdie's legacy. That she will manipulate me into a decision I'll regret. But she has to get here first, and on this first Monday in July, Mother Nature has thrown a wrench in Dr. Cotton's coming. It's not a good omen when an epic thunderstorm builds in protest and wind wails and trees lash like rag dolls. The air outside turns an eerie green, and Lydia and I are hypnotized by the fury. The bookstore closed early, but this is our meeting place with Theresa, so we can't leave. We worry she's had an accident or slid into a ditch blinded by the downpour. But a clap of thunder explodes overhead as an orange Volkswagen wheels into the parking place in front and the brakes squeal; Dr. Cotton is here.

Miraculously, the rain lets up as though a spigot has been tightened, and we open the front door as a flamboyant woman steps out. Her chartreuse trousers flutter in the wind like a pinned butterfly. An oversize turquoise tunic swings to her knees and billows on her five-foot frame. Her ginger hair is frizzy, and the frames of her round glasses are ruby red. She is a parrot, a circus clown, and when her silk scarf comes undone and flies into the churning clouds, she lets loose a belly laugh.

I whisper, "Not what I expected."

Lydia shouts from the open doorway, "Doctor Cotton," and the curator rushes inside seconds before a second round of rain lets loose and we close the door.

"I'm here, I'm here!" She's flushed with excitement. "Please call me Theresa."

We gawk at this pint-size character who smells of gingerbread and cinnamon. She vibrates with energy. Next to her, I am mud and moss.

Lydia introduces us and we shake hands; the curator's grip is firm.

"*Oh, my word.*" Theresa is mesmerized. "Mother Nature is having a tizzy fit, isn't she? It's deliciously dangerous, isn't it? How I love a riveting storm especially from this side of the window."

Clearly, Theresa is prone to excessive adjectives. She accompanies those adjectives with the wave of her arms and widening of her eyes. Outside the fury whips through the village, and lightning sparks garish-green. Ripped leaves swirl like riotous confetti. The light inside the bookstore darkens to an old varnish, and the wind forced through cracks around the window frames is a pained brass instrument. We are spellbound.

Theresa Cotton stands between Lydia and me and gawks. She isn't the stiff and imposing person I feared would want these treasures for personal gain, nor is she a mousy soul who spends her days in a library's dark inner sanctum. She is something more. But what exactly?

"Is that coffee I smell?"

Lydia says, "It usually is, but Nancy left thirty minutes ago, and I'm sure she turned off the pot but not sure she emptied and washed it. Let me check."

"Cold coffee will do. I need a pick-me-up quick." She checks the pastry shelves in the cooler. "And that lonely powdered doughnut looks good. I missed lunch and think I'm having a sugar drop." She holds out her hand for us to see it tremble.

"I can put on the kettle upstairs and make tea if you'd like. And I have shortbread," Lydia offers.

"No, coffee and a doughnut, but first, I've got to tinkle something fierce. Where's the loo?"

"Come with me," I say. "It's around the corner, up the steps, and in back," and we hurry and she locks the door and I come back to Lydia, who found cold coffee in the pot. She plugs in the microwave and heats a cup for Theresa. The seconds tick down on the timer, and I whisper, "Maybe she's having a sugar drop, but five whole days with this wild woman? That's a long time to be around such high energy."

Lydia whispers back, "We need her, Kate. We need her expertise. And she's helping us for free. We're not even paying for her hotel. Don't forget that." She holds up a finger. "Before she comes back, let me give Gus a quick call."

Her niece answers with a shriek I can hear through the receiver. "Wasn't that *awesome*?"

"You and the animals all right?" Lydia listens then nods and gives me the thumbs-up. "And the house? Everybody safe and everything intact?" The timer on the microwave dings and I put the lonely doughnut on a plate beside the steaming cup. Lydia concludes her call saying, "I'm at the bookstore then at the inn for dinner. Call if you need me. There's wild mushroom soup or leftover pizza in the fridge when you get hungry."

Theresa rounds the corner adjusting her layers of clothing. She spies the sugar fix and grins.

# Chapter 42

## HIGHLIGHTS

**Lydia Brown**

The curator surveys the line of Birdie's books, the manuscript, the chest, the journal, and the painting. Her hands are behind her back to resist touching them. There's powdered sugar on her cheek, but she's calmer after a caffeine and sugar boost.

"I need five months, not five days, but that's all the time I can spare right now."

"How would you like to set up shop?" I ask.

"That big closet would do for my workspace, away from natural light. Let's move the small desk inside. I've brought lights, extension cords, and book stands." Fifteen minutes later the workstation is set up to Theresa's liking, and I put on the kettle for a leisure cup of tea and we settle in three folding chairs facing each other. The rain has passed.

"We are so grateful you're here to help. Shall we tell you the highlights of what we know so far?"

She counters, "Every delicious morsel," and calmly sips her tea with milk, all traces of her hyper behavior calmed by a powdered doughnut.

The telling begins with a witch's legacy housed in a dilapidated trailer and bequeathed to a teacher, then a network of tunnels and chambers that interconnect, to an ancient masterpiece trundled across the ocean centuries ago, holding Gaelic enigmas.

I add, "At Birdie's burial place, Kate showed me a ceremonial meadow encircled with boulders. The place was choked with weeds, but there were clues of something more. The afternoon light cast a lavender tint to the air, and the smell of something sweet lives there. It isn't a forgotten place."

I conclude by saying, "Birdie Rocas lived too intentionally for her books to be a record of scattered thoughts. Too deliberately for the chest and its contents to be accidental. Too purposefully for the tunnel rooms and ceremonial meadow to be minor discoveries. No. All of it goes together in some complex web barely out of sight. Of that I'm certain."

Kate looks dubious at my notions while Theresa looks at her, bright-eyed and trusting, and says, "And to think it all started with a scrap of paper with your name on it."

The sun is shining when we lock our workroom and the front door of Books and Beans and walk out into a world of pick-up-sticks. Branches and leaves litter the road, and Theresa follows our car around the corner to Little Switzerland Inn, where she will stay the next five nights. She checks in, then meets Kate and me on the terrace for supper. We order tonight's special of pecan-crusted rainbow trout, butter braised leeks, chive and dill cream, and crispy capers. Wine arrives and I raise my glass: *To Birdie and Theresa and conundrums.*

"Speaking of mysteries, what led you to study rare books and learn Gaelic? Are your ancestors from Scotland?" I ask.

"Not that I know of. I was born in Charlotte, a few hours from here, and thought I'd become an archaeologist. I could see myself sifting through sand and stone to unearth buried history in the pyramids or riding a camel through the desert to a forgotten cave hiding ancient scrolls. But do you know what changed my mind?"

"Appalachia," I guess, and she nods.

"Yes. When you live a stone's throw from the oldest mountains on earth, why look anywhere else? And now this: a hybrid of epic proportions spanning the Middle Ages to today. Thank you for letting me be a part of this moment. It's a miracle this manuscript survived in good condition in such a primitive place. In rare books, we take many precautions to preserve treasures. The light and air humidity are regulated to the nth degree."

Kate says, "Yet Birdie threw an old quilt over the chest and called it security. Her trailer would have offered little protection from heat or cold or damp. And yet, at first glance, the manuscript and journal look to be in good condition when they shouldn't be."

Theresa is wistful. "How I wish I had met your Birdie Rocas. Very little is known about her at Rare Books."

"But you'd heard of her?" Kate is surprised.

"Yes, but only in whispers. Some people thought the rumors about the books were fabricated. A little like a snipe hunt for the educated bibliophile," she says with a grin. "But this I know from the start: These books are not here by accident. And neither are the three of us. There's a master plan at work, and Birdie Rocas is in charge."

# Chapter 43

## SPILLED SECRETS

**KATE SHAW**

The next morning before eight, Lydia and I leave for the bookstore. Gus stays home to work on a secret. When we arrive, Theresa's Volkswagen is there, and she sits at a small wrought iron table and chair outside the locked door. She's dressed even more electrified today in orange clothing down to orange sneakers. Where does she find such things? Did she make them or dye them or hire a tailor who worked for the circus? The woman doesn't have a reticent bone in her body.

Lydia says, "Sorry to keep you waiting. I'll get you keys today so your valuable time isn't wasted."

"No problem. I've been entertained by the motorcyclists on their touring machines. A few stopped to ask when the bookstore opened. They're headed down this stretch of road called the Diamondback. One rider told me there are a hundred and ninety steep curves in only twelve miles. It must be a thrill of a ride." She follows us up the stairs chatting about switchbacks and hairpin curves and the Harley-Davidson she almost bought when she was in graduate school. But when we enter the workroom she becomes all business.

"I want to start with the journal because it's manageable."

She turns on a soft, diffused light inside the closet and lines up her note-taking tools. She secures the journal in a bookstand with a page holder. The Gaelic writing on the opening page is artistic and remarkably legible.

We work independently until midmorning, when we hear familiar footsteps on the stairs and a light tap on the door. Lydia says, "Come in professor," and he enters shyly. "We've been hoping you'd come for a visit. This is our curator from Rare Books, Theresa Cotton."

She comes out of the closet with a pencil behind each ear, a smudge of lead above her lip, and red reading glasses perched on her head.

"Madam, my pleasure." Professor Covey bows.

"Likewise," she curtsies.

Lydia explains, "Professor Covey is the owner of this establishment and our landlord, but he was a history professor at UNC Asheville. He is also our primary resource for local knowledge and an excellent sounding board for research."

The old man grins bashfully. "You give me too much credit when it is your discoveries that are the rare ones. What has been unearthed this morning?" He looks over at Theresa's cubbyhole.

"You have timed your arrival perfectly, professor. I have news to report, so let me grab my notes and I'll read the opening translation. You will want to be seated."

We pull three chairs in a row like dutiful students.

"Your scribe's name is Florie Leslie." Theresa begins. "She was thirteen when she began this journal in the year 1592. She was a learned girl in a time that denied her gender those rights. I don't know yet if she is our sole author. Others may contribute later, but so far only her voice has appeared." She refers again to her notes, then raises her eyebrows. "The first sentence is a doozy."

We sit relaxed, ill-prepared.

Theresa reads, "*Mother says they will kill us.*"

*What?*

"Hold on, hold on." She uses her pudgy hand with orange painted nails to dampen our shock. "Let me read the full paragraph for context.

"*Mother says they will kill us. We must leave Elcho Priory under cover of night and travel to Schiehallion. Though I am afraid of the dark, we will travel all night. Once there, green witches will protect us. We will bring our tools to continue Mother's important work on the apothecary book. Mother believes the Wiccans will welcome us, but I am afraid our secrets are beginning to fray.*"

Theresa takes a deep breath and the three of us stare at her.

"Well, I never…" Kate says.

"Remarkable." I add.

"How marvelously frightening," the professor exclaims.

Theresa flips through more pages of notes. "I'm about eight pages in. Young Florie is quite the writer."

Lydia clears her throat. "Where were they going?"

"To a witch's cave, on a fairy mountain a few miles outside of Perth. That's an hour's drive north of Edinburgh. It's a strenuous climb for hikers, even today. Coincidentally, I visited there a decade ago and remember walking among the remains of Elcho, which the girl names. If my memory serves me, it was run by Cistercian nuns. It is thought that they dedicated themselves to the Virgin Mary and followed strict religious rules, but their written history is almost nonexistent. This is the first I've read that an illuminated manuscript was created there, and of the secular nature, not religious. History may be rewritten with this discovery. Or at least clarified. Let me continue translating and we'll know more by the close of day." She smiles sweetly to the gentleman. "And Professor, you're welcome to return for the next installment."

"Bless you," he says and reluctantly leaves. Lydia and I return to the twentieth century and the Books of Truth, which pale only slightly in comparison to Theresa's world. Birdie dedicates some sections to a specific topic. One is fungi. Mycelia edible mushrooms named chicken of the woods, chanterelles, black trumpets, hedgehogs, oysters, and morels. There's even an edible rare blue mushroom that I've never seen. She drew an illustration above its name. The medicinal mushrooms are a longer list with strange names like turkey tail, lion's mane, and reishi, which grows on dying hemlocks. But it is Birdie's map of the mountain noting where they likely grow that is extraordinary from a teaching standpoint.

The section that unsettles me most is called *Peculiar Forest Folk*. It reads like a science fiction story. I speak softly so as not to bother Theresa and say, "Are these made-up stories? Or do you think Birdie actually saw Moon-Eyed People who live underground and hunt at night, and Little People two feet tall with white hair and long arms? Do you believe these are real?"

Lydia whispers back, "There's proof."

"What proof?"

"About the Little People. In Special Collections at Appalachian State there's a child's skull that fits in the palm of your hand—but when you look closer, you see wisdom teeth in the mouth."

Lydia waits for me to understand. When I don't, she says, "Children don't have wisdom teeth, Kate. They don't come in till their late teens or twenties, but this skull was as small as a six-year-old's." She reiterates, "*But it had wisdom teeth.*"

"And I suppose you believe all those odd people named in Birdie's book? You think tommy-knockers are real and Bigfoot and Spearfinger the Cherokee shapeshifter?"

"Kate, I don't think Birdie was prone to lie or exaggerate, do you? Remember, her mission was truth."

"Maybe she wouldn't lie on purpose," I admit, "but she easily swallowed the preposterous. She never questioned anything."

"And you question everything," she counters. "Does that make her wrong and you right?"

I turn away from Lydia and look for a book based on more logic.

At noon, we break for lunch at the Diamondback Café and order spicy gazpacho and crusty bread. Theresa looks dazed.

"You're not going to believe this girl's story," she teases then dives into her soup. Between mouthfuls she speaks low. "The entries are insightful, but you already know the manuscript and journal survived against impossible odds. The women were threatened by locals who thought they were witches simply because their knowledge and gifts couldn't be explained. They were taken in by kindred spirits who helped them plan their escape to the New World. It took cunning for nuns to outfox the dangers of the time and arrange passage on a ship. But tell me what's going on in Birdie's books?"

I say, "The last story I read was about a Roma wedding held at the mushroom cave. It's about a fifteen-year-old bride and sixteen-year-old groom and how they violated strict traditions."

"In what way? Did they have sex?" Theresa refills her glass of sweet tea from the pitcher left on the table.

"How'd you know?"

"They're young. It's always sex that gets them in trouble."

"Well, they'd been promised to each other for three years as Roma tradition requires, and the wedding day grew close. But the boy and girl weren't meeting for the first time on their wedding day as they would normally. Their families had traveled together, and they had fallen in love and the girl found herself pregnant. That's where Birdie comes in.

"The girl sought a medicine woman because if it was known she was pregnant, she would be shunned by her family. The bride and groom might not survive on their own. At the end of the story, Birdie listed the herbs that would bring on menses."

Lydia says, "Did the girl abort the baby or not?"

"Birdie didn't say. Maybe she didn't know. Maybe the wanderers packed up their caravan and moved on before she found out. What I'm learning is that Birdie wrote facts, not her judgment. She didn't guess."

Theresa reaches for another piece of garlic bread and adds more butter. She says, "I bet one of the most common subjects in Birdie's books is ways to get menses flowing, right?"

I say, "You're right."

"And I'm guessing we'll find a similar topic in the apothecary book. It's the healer's knowledge of woodland plants that gave a woman a choice. An unwanted pregnancy is a dilemma as old as womankind, and it's never a simple situation."

Our waitress returns and we order blackberry cobbler and coffee. Conversation returns to the tender topic, and Lydia says, "I'd like to think that the young mother and her illegitimate child survived and were spared being ostracized. If she was, she would be in her eighties now with a passel of children and grandchildren tending to her. It's likely some of the girls she begot faced their own dilemmas. Time has done little to make a woman's road easier."

We return to the workroom and Lydia pulls out a stack of index cards and spreads them on the counter. "I started this exercise last night and forgot to show you. It's a list of major discoveries. Here's what I have so far."

*Birdie's 78 books*
*Mushroom cave (yet to be visited)*
*Medieval oak chest*
*Crow carving in oak chest*
*Birdie's crow Samuel*
*Illuminated manuscript*
*Tool pouch in chest*
*Florie's journal*
*Birdie's graveyard*
*Morrigan graveyard*
*Moonshiner's chamber*
*Note in miner's coat*
*Miner's Levi Strauss coat*
*Empty corn sack*
*Underground tunnels go where?*
*Birdie's writing chamber*

"What an impressive list," Theresa says. "I remember you mentioning the moonshiner's tunnel, but tell me again why it's pertinent to Birdie's quest?"

"It physically connects to Birdie's workroom. And though they are forty miles apart by county roads, traveling the tunnels is more direct. There may be other entry points. I'm probably overreaching here, but I'd like to include more in our discovery list than exclude anything."

I point to the card noting the mushroom cave and add, "There were paintings on the cave wall. Did I tell you that?"

"What kind?" Lydia says.

"Old and faded ones, and even some strange writing—and tall figures similar to the painting. It didn't make sense when I went with Birdie because I was frightened and only wanted to leave. I wasn't paying close attention."

Lydia prints *Cave paintings* on another card and counts. "Seventeen clues."

"We need to see that cave," Theresa says. "It may have been the first place the women settled."

# Chapter 44

## THE DARK

### Lydia Brown

On Thursday, we drive to Baines Creek and hike into the hills where Sadie, Granny C, and Eddie meet us at the mouth of the cave. Theresa, Kate, and I carry a flashlight and a sweater against the chill; Gus carries her camera. We breathe our last fresh air then head down the narrowing throat into the inky gloom. Kate's dog stays behind in the speckled sunshine. Granny C and Sadie take the lead, and then come Eddie, Gus, and me, with Theresa and Kate at the rear.

Today the curator wears black-and-white trousers and an oversize tunic in horizontal stripes, possibly modeled after prison garb from the fifties. To elevate the look, she has pinned a red plastic flower on her left shoulder. The effect would be ludicrous on anyone else, but the woman's self-assurance reigns. Our conversation bounces off the humid walls, and ten minutes in, Gus and Eddie run ahead like mountain goats on sure feet, their flashlights bobbing. Gus's tiny voice barks, "Found it!"

Once through the narrow side passage, the space opens and the ceiling vaults. A skinny waterfall from thirty feet high splashes into a stream, and emerald-green moss climbs the walls. Mushrooms glow in the damp shadows. Gus snaps photos of the painting and the message from different angles, then joins Eddie sorting colored stones in the shallow creek. Like children, they divide them into piles—but it is the painting on the wall that compels Kate, Theresa, and me. It *does* resemble the painting in the ancient box. Hooded figures wear black robes. They face right, and a triangle separates each figure, like the mark on my palm.

Kate and I are beside the curator, and the chamber amplifies Kate's voice. "It's Celtic, isn't it?"

"Gaelic, the ancient Celtic language." We follow as she points to foreign words painted long ago. "*Tha an luchd-gleidhidh ann mu dheireadh*," she reads, then whispers, "How very, very odd…"

"What?"

Her eyes widen. "The translation reads: *The Keepers are finally there*."

"Are you sure?" My palm pulses.

"Positive. Maybe being *finally there* refers to their ultimate destination. Or maybe the words refer to a universal understanding." Theresa steps closer to the wall to touch the figures. "They're moving toward the cauldron, aren't they, and a cauldron is a symbol for the divine feminine, for fertility and growth. It can also represent the element of the womb."

Rainbow blobs from fractured sunlight dance on the walls. With the talk of the cauldron, a red bead settles on the pot as though it's on fire.

Kate points to the triangles. "What's that symbol between each figure? Is that the mark Birdie had?"

Granny C speaks for the first time. "That be the sign of a Keeper. I got me one."

Kate flippantly exposes me. "Lydia has one on her palm, too. Show 'em."

Granny C and Sadie come to stand beside us with their

gathering bags full of mushrooms. Granny C orders, "Let me see," and shines a light on my palm and rubs her thumb over my calloused symbol. "It be the sign all right," she states calmly.

"Let me see yours," I say, and she holds out her palm. Everyone is huddled over our two upturned palms in the light.

"What did you call them?"

"Keepers. All Keepers got that sign."

Gus says, "So y'all are marked special, but how come? And Birdie was marked, too. But you two didn't lay eyes on each other till today, so how did you get tied together?"

Granny C and I step apart like sparring opponents in a boxing ring. She rubs her hand on her long skirt. I put mine in my pocket.

"I don't know, Gus. You have the gift of sight, but you don't have the mark. I lost my gift but still have the mark. It's all confusing."

"Did Birdie say who made these cave drawings?" Theresa asks.

Granny C shakes her head, but she has the air of leaving about her. I can see that the time in the cave is coming to an end.

"Naw. We come for shrooms when I be a girl back in '43. There be a fever killin' off folks, but we don't come the long way."

"If not the way we came, how did you come?" I ask.

Granny C squirms, caught in a confession of her own making. She doesn't answer, so I say what comes to mind. "It's the tunnels, isn't it?"

From the flash of her eyes, I can tell I'm right.

"You can come all this way—through the tunnels," I state with conviction, and she nods.

We're only now beginning to understand that the underground passages are a maze we can't fathom. A world hinted at by the note found in the cuff of the Levi Strauss coat. A world Professor Covey says has never been mapped on paper. Maybe it should be.

"Can we go back that way?" I ask.

Granny C hesitates but Kate quickly says, "I won't go in the tunnels. Rachel's waiting for me in the sunshine. Eddie, can you come with me, please?" More than a touch of panic is in her voice.

"Sure, Miz Kate. I'll come with you." He pockets some of the colored rocks and glances at Gus, eyebrows raised, a quiet invitation to join him, but she says, "I wanna see the other way."

I look at my watch. "It's eleven o'clock. Why don't we meet back at the trailer ruins. The time it takes each of us to get there will tell a lot about the distance."

I think we'll head back to the main vein of the cave, but Granny C doesn't go that way. She and Sadie loop around the waterfall and disappear. After a minute, Theresa, Gus, and I go too and find a slit in the wall. We squeeze through and step into an equally large chamber but with a low ceiling. Water drips and hits the nape of my neck and chills me. It smells like wet dog.

"What is this place?" My voice is amplified.

"'Twas the bookmaking room till de flood come."

"When was that?"

"Long while back."

Two tunnels lead from the chamber and Granny C takes the left one. When we round a curve, the trace of daylight from the waterfall is snuffed out and our flashlights struggle to penetrate the black. Granny is in the lead, then Sadie and my group. We walk an incline in a shaft a foot wider than my shoulders.

"Who made these tunnels?" I ask.

Sadie answers. "Miners or Cherokee could'a done it. But it ain't Little People, for sure."

"You believe in the Little People, don't you?"

"Gotta be dumb not to. Them and the tommy-knockers."

But this tunnel wasn't built for Little People or for tommy-knockers. Men made these tunnels possibly to unearth semiprecious stones and minerals. Treasure lies beneath every bucket of dirt in these counties—if you know where to dig.

My head pounds from breathing loamy air laced with decay. I hear skittering voices from inside the walls. They let out scraps of words and tapping sounds. A cool draft pushes against my back then lets go. Bones from small animals crunch beneath my feet. A rat the size of a cat scurries in a side channel.

"How do you know where to go?" I keep my voice neutral, but I'm beginning to be afraid. Granny C leads us down a path that has already forked three times.

"Blazes," she says, which doesn't make sense till we get to the next junction. She shines her light near the ceiling. "Yonder there."

A white bar is reflected in her light. Like the tree blazes on the Appalachian Trail to show hikers the way.

"That'a way," she says as she points and forks right to a path that looks the same—except for the blaze. After we shift left then right then right again, my sense of direction is dulled and I feel trepidation being led by a woman I only met today. If she had a mind to mislead us because we threaten her way of life, we'd never find our way out. Suddenly, this venture feels foolish. I wipe nervous sweat from my upper lip and focus on the bravery it must take to travel through the black heart of Appalachia. It's the perfect place to hide sins, treasures and bodies.

The dark is mind-numbing and, finally, after sluggish minutes, the air begins to grow lighter. Birdie speaks to me as we enter a large chamber. *You come for my secrets like I knowed you would.* The mark on my palm mimics my heartbeat.

Granny C climbs stone steps and slides the hatch open so fresh air and light flood the space, which is neat and orderly. It's different from the abandoned still at my graveyard. This place has not been neglected. It's been respected.

Gus turns and whispers, "All those sad voices."

"I know, honey. Go on in the sunshine and wait for Eddie. Sadie will show you the way to the meeting place. I'll be there shortly."

Theresa is starstruck and scans the chamber and the rooms adjoining it. Like Kate said, the walls are lined with substantial shelves holding books and neat rows of clay pots with flat lids. Colorful glass jars remind me of Trula Freed's apothecary. Here, the accumulated knowledge spans generations and centuries.

"This is extraordinary, Lydia," Theresa begins. "It's like an ancient monastery, with its wooden ceiling and stone steps. A place where monks and nuns lived their days hunched over, creating masterpieces to the glory of God and to honor nature. This chamber was likely created by Florie and her tribe."

But we can't explore the way we're inclined. Granny C yells down the hatch, "Y'all coming? Don't dally. We done finish the tunnel part."

# Chapter 45

## LONG AND SHORT

**Kate Shaw**

I hold Eddie's arm to steady myself on the slippery shale. My breathing is ragged. The flashlight wobbles at my feet. I say, "You knew about the tunnels?"

"Everybody does. They go a long ways, but there ain't many places to git out."

"Did you ever get lost?"

"When I was a kid it was kinda expected. But nobody died that I recollect," he teases.

"Have you found things?"

"Sure. Old tools and an ammo box, and that green stone folks call emeralds. Like what we found at Mister Sunday's place."

"Eddie, I'm sorry I doubted you that day." I start my apology. "It must have been terrifying what you saw, and there I was questioning you."

"It's okay. You ain't from round here."

My heart thuds at his bluntness. That easy dismissal that I've not earned my place no matter how much I invest. Makes me wonder if the last ten years counted for anything. But there's my inheritance from Birdie, so I did something right for her to trust me. She lived an intentional life and, like obedient children, Lydia, Theresa, and I are following the path to the heart of her story. I'm beginning to understand that our purpose is to expose Birdie's truth whether it's her apothecary knowledge or the wisdom of women who are the Keepers.

I ask Eddie, "What's the best thing you found?"

"A rifle musket from the Civil War back in the 1860s. Took it out of a skeleton's hands, him with his mouth wide open, likely screaming or crying for his mama, but he got caught all the same. Still got it."

"So, somebody did die."

"I guess, but he was a damn Yankee. Serves him right for sneaking round thinking these tunnels was meant to hide the enemy when they ain't. They belong to us."

We exit the cave, and Rachel's tail wags his whole body as he comes toward me and I love on him. Now our strides widen on open land and in blessed daylight, and Eddie and I make good time. This is my chance for closure with my star pupil.

"You ready for school?"

"I been there once. Preacher took me. Went inside and walked the halls. It's big."

"How'd you feel?"

"I could get lost, I guess, sorta like the tunnels. Them first days I gotta pay attention so I don't look like a bumpkin." Eddie grins his adorable grin and looks young and innocent, two qualities that can help or hurt him depending on whose path he crosses.

"Ask for help. People are willing to help if you ask."

"I got Gus Flannery," he says proudly, as if a pierced girl the size of a gnat is his golden ticket. "I showed her them stories I wrote for *Creekrise*. She said they was real good, both entertaining and educational. She thinks I might get to work for the school newspaper in a year or two. She's gonna show 'em to her mama."

"You'll do well, Eddie," I say and mean it. I'm pleased that his days won't be ruled by fear.

We arrive at the burned trailer, and Lydia, Gus, and Theresa are sitting on the stumps wearing a film of black dust. I'm grateful Rachel gave me an excuse to skip the dark. I point to the old crow on the low branch who gazes in the distance ignoring us. "Theresa, that's Birdie's crow. Used to ride on top of her head."

"He's silver. How old is he?"

"Very, very old," I say because I don't know.

Lydia glances at her watch. "We beat you by seventeen minutes."

"That much? And you came out in Birdie's room?"

Theresa interjects, "It's where Birdie made her books. There are stretchers for skins to make vellum, pots of ink, paint, and delicate brushes." She glances over at Granny C. "Now that Kate's here, may we three take a closer look at Birdie's chamber? It would help with the important work we're doing, and it doesn't make sense to come back another day when we're already here."

I want to say I don't need to go underground again, but Granny C says, "Y'all won't take nothin?"

I quickly say, "No, they won't. Not without your permission." I don't look at Lydia or Theresa when I make this promise. The things Granny C needs will stay.

I follow Theresa and Lydia down the stone steps but stay by the open trap door. Sadie has gone home, and Gus and Eddie wait at the trailer site, but Granny C brings her evil eye to watch us, leery we'll take something though I gave our word. The room is dominated by a chestnut table in the center. The four-foot-wide plank top is a single piece of chestnut from a mighty tree that used to be king of the forests. They could grow a hundred feet tall and eight feet thick. Birdie wrote that the white blossoms in the spring looked like snow on the mountain. Then a blight came and left hollowed-out carcasses in its wake.

There's a square opening in the center of that table. "I bet the manuscript box fits that opening. There's a rim inside to keep it from falling through," I say.

Theresa nods. "A place of honor, but if it belongs here, why was it in Birdie's trailer?"

"Maybe she moved it so we'd find it and turn curious," Lydia suggests.

Theresa adds in admiration, "She was a sneaky witch, wasn't she? And these are tools for making her books. Lime to soak the skin, a wooden beam and curved knife to scrape it, and a frame to keep the drying skin taut." She nods toward a barrel. "That's chalk. It leeches out fats and oils from the skin and makes the surface smooth. It takes a dozen steps to make the materials for a book. This crone knew bookmaking from A to Z."

How little I knew Birdie Rocas because I never bothered to ask. I saw a curmudgeon with a crow riding on her head. I didn't see her power and purpose.

Lydia's flashlight scans adjoining rooms where we can see more walls of shelves holding more books, and a line of canvas cots. Theresa states loud enough for Granny C to hear, "Didn't Birdie's note read *Books go to teacher*? Do you think she meant all her books, Kate?"

I groan.

# Chapter 46

## VOICES

**Lydia Brown**

We return from our expedition and bring Theresa back with us. She shouldn't leave without seeing the view at the bluff. Now she sits with Kate and me on the porch, and we're bathed in the golden light and revelations. We slip off dirty shoes and settle around the table. I pour Greek wine, and we munch on olives, miniature spinach pies, hummus, and pita bread I bought at the café. The unraveling of Birdie's hidden life is in full swing, and I add four more clue cards to the stack: *Birdie's bookmaking room*, *Waterfall tunnel to Birdie's writing chamber*, *Triangle sign for Keeper*, *Gaelic message on cave wall*. I spread all the cards on the table, and we move them like chess pieces into different groupings, looking for the pattern.

Theresa picks up *Birdie's writing chamber* and separates it from the rest. "This one best represents Birdie's expansive life." She pops another miniature pie in her mouth then rubs her tiny feet with their turquoise-painted toenails the size of buttons. "I think it holds the heart of the mystery."

"If that's true, it'll be like finding the proverbial needle in a haystack," I say. "The scope of that place is overwhelming.

We don't even know how many rooms there are or how the place is organized. Discovering that will be an overwhelming task, and my least favorite place is underground."

"Well, ladies, how I wish I could stay till the very end, but tomorrow I go home. After lunch I'll recount my findings with you, but for now, I need a shower and my soft bed. It has been a most excellent day."

She leaves Gus and Kate with the wave of a weary hand, and I drive her to the inn in unusual quiet. Theresa's all talked out. When I return, Kate still sits in the swing watching the remnants of the sunset. Since the curator arrived, we've had little time alone, and I finally get to ask, "What do you think about all this?"

"What am I thinking? How could I live in a place for ten years and know so little."

"Don't feel guilty. You saw what Birdie wanted you to see."

Kate stares into the wine she swirls in her glass. "Maybe," she says. "But I know she wanted me to be more inquisitive. To challenge my beliefs. Instead, I held tight to my narrow ways." Kate looks up with determination. "But I want to make one thing clear, Lydia. I will not be digging through the contents of that depressing chamber room. I will not spend one day underground."

I chuckle at her honesty. "I don't think Theresa was suggesting that. She was reminding Granny C that you were called to care for the books. But I will be the one to do that deed, not you."

"Because of the mark?"

"Maybe." I hold up my hand, like an Indian peace sign. "Maybe because I share this sign with Granny C and Birdie and two other witches."

"Two?"

"Loretty and my childhood friend Trula Freed. But the

primary reason I'll search Birdie's chamber room is because she asked me to."

It takes a moment for Kate to understand what I'm saying. "When did she ask you? The night you stayed in her yard?"

"No. Today."

"You heard her *today*."

"Yes. I don't expect you to understand, Kate, but Birdie spoke to me when I entered her chamber."

"What did she say?"

"*I been waiting on you, Lydia Brown. Bout time you come. You finally there.*"

"Did anybody else hear?"

"No. Not even Gus. Birdie spoke to me, but I knew who it was."

"And you're happy to have a ghost talking inside your head?" Kate begins to grin.

"I am thrilled."

It's Theresa's final day. She will leave us a bounty of information, and we are settled into our familiar spots at the top of the stairs when the curator calls out in a tremulous voice we've not heard before. "Lydia, Kate, you've got to see this."

She turns to face us with rapture on her face, like she won the lottery or found the Ark of the Covenant. The manuscript is open on a bookstand near the end, and the format has changed. It's no longer an image of a healing plant and a list of its qualities and recipes for cures. It's the cameo portrait of a woman.

"Who's that?" I ask.

"I'm scared to look away for fear she'll disappear." Theresa takes a deep breath then translates the lead paragraph.

"*In The Apothecary Book of Elcho Priory herein lie abbreviated biographies of skilled women whose contributions are recorded. May these pages mark their dutiful place in Scottish history.*"

I whisper in reverence, "Biographies. Of the women who created this masterpiece. Women who could have been lost from history."

Kate asks, "Ever seen anything like this?"

"No, no, no," Theresa replies. "Not this kind of testimony for and by women in medieval history. Certainly, there are articles about larger-than-life women like Joan of Arc and Pope Joan and Saint Hildegard of Bingen, but less than one percent of written history captures contributions by women. Their talents and gifts have been intentionally excluded throughout time. Virginia Woolf said it succinctly when she wrote in *A Room of One's Own*—and I quote: 'I would venture to guess that Anon, who wrote so many poems without signing them, was often a woman.' I believe that's true in all literary forms. Women chose anonymity in order to write. In the case of our manuscript, this proclamation is an audacious and brave claim that is extraordinary."

Kate and I study the first portrait of a thin-faced, benevolent woman who lived nearly five hundred years ago. Theresa reads,

"*Euphemia Leslie, prioress of Elcho, sought papal dispensation at age eighteen and was elevated to prioress. She was the spurious daughter of Walter Leslie, the parish priest of Kirkton of Menmuir and the daughter of John Stewart, Earl of Atholl. Her personal seal bore the arms of the houses of Leslie and Stewart of Atholl.*"

"*Spurious*?" I lean forward to see the word in Gaelic. "Doesn't that mean illegitimate?"

"Yes."

We look at Euphemia's portrait, her enigmatic smile that is reminiscent of the *Mona Lisa*. Was she responsible for this courageous addition? Her place at the start of this section is telling of her position.

I ask, "How many women are there?"

"Eleven, including our young Florie Leslie."

Theresa gently turns page after page to the last image—a woman with red hair.

I ask Kate, "Are these the ghosts you saw at Birdie's funeral?"

She has the strangest look on her face. The look when the impossible turns believable because facts can't be denied. The moment of enlightenment. "Yes, but how can that be? Ghosts aren't real. At least I don't believe in them."

"Maybe they believe in you," Theresa says, then continues. "We know from the journal that Florie is the illegitimate daughter of the prioress who was raped during a battle with the English. Eugenia became pregnant and chose to carry a bastard. That bravery gave Florie and her mother a special status. We already know that abortions were common during the Middle Ages, and that was due in part to the teachings of Aristotle."

"What did he say about the matter?" I ask.

"He proclaimed a fetus was *ensouled* not at conception but at a later date. He proposed that the soul infused the male fetus at forty days because of his hotter temperament but eighty days for a woman with the cooler disposition."

The three of us pause to contemplate this preposterous theory, and then we laugh at the influence of a clueless man twenty-four centuries ago. Kate speaks first. "How did he come up with that bizarre theory?"

"From studying fertilized chicken eggs."

Theresa lets that remark hang in the air, then adds, "It took two thousand years for his liberal view to be overturned by papal order. God bless the jury of men who guess dreadfully at the divine mystery."

The curator carefully turns the pages back to the beginning of the biographies and says, "Let me read these eleven names aloud. These brave women have been boxed in the dark for too long, haven't they? Against staggering odds, it's my pleasure to introduce the original Keepers of Truth."

We hear the names *Margaret Towers* the herbologist, and *Isabel Barclay*, skilled in obstetrics and aborticide. *Elinor Stewart*, *Christian Moncrief*, *Christine Rocas*, and *Kathryn Smith*, scribes, librarians, and herbalists, and *Christina Harker* the beekeeper. By the time Theresa speaks the last names *Isobel Wedderburn*, *Elizabeth Pollok*, and *Florie Leslie*, my hands are folded in prayer. It is the cherry-on-top moment we did not foresee in this unraveling of Birdie's secrets.

"Kate," I say. "Do you remember the directions we found from Romi to Birdie's place through the tunnels?"

"I do."

"Did I tell you Romi's last name is Harker? She is a medicine woman and beekeeper. Like the name in the book."

Kate says, "Then Christine Rocas is linked to Birdie."

"Yes. I believe she is."

Theresa's orange Volkswagen is packed and it's our final lunch before she leaves, and we celebrate with a meal on the patio at Little Switzerland Inn. Sandy brings a platter of succulent tomatoes, fresh mozzarella, and thinly sliced prosciutto beside pickled beets and corn salad. Dessert is lemon tarts topped with meringue. Between mouthfuls, Theresa asks the final question.

"Have you decided what will become of these treasures?"

I look to Kate for answers.

"They don't belong in a rich man's library," she says. "Birdie's books are teaching tools meant to inspire and educate."

"True, but generating a lot of money isn't a bad thing, is it? If they're auctioned, they'd bring a fortune. I know the Rare Book School would make a generous bid."

"But to what end?" Kate asks. "The money wouldn't be mine. It was Birdie's labors."

"But she's dead, Kate," Theresa says tenderly. "Figuring out what's next is up to you."

We signal for more iced tea, and I ask a question that's been nagging me.

"Where are the men?"

"What men?" Kate asks.

"Precisely. In all we've reviewed, there's no mention of men, yet for this lineage, generations of female babies were born—yet even witches and medicine women need sperm to conceive."

Theresa easily adds plausibility. "Witches and healers were commanding women. They could cast spells, so why not cast one over a convenient man when the time was right? We lesbians have found ways to become mothers that don't involve legal commitment, and we can't even cast spells."

This is Theresa's first admission that she is gay. It is the ease with which Theresa claims her identity that registers on Kate's bewildered face. "So, you're gay," she says, plopping back in her chair. "Without hesitation, you say it out loud." She glances around at diners within earshot.

"Of course. Being gay is like being born right-handed or left-handed. It's simply part of who I am, and I've never denied my reality. What about you?"

In that split second the professor turns the table on Kate, and there it sits. An easy declaration for one, and something that is a source of pain in the other. Kate squirms under Theresa's gaze.

"You don't understand," she begins.

"I probably do."

"It was Mother—"

"Ah...Mother."

# Chapter 47

## MOTHER

**KATE SHAW**

My defense against Mother while she was living and now dead is to ban her from my thoughts. Theresa Cotton is too confident to appreciate that childish option. Brazen to ask me to stand up against my greatest adversary, the one who never buckled or backed down in our battles. When I do, to this day I turn weak. The air around every experience where Mother-Daughter stood in the same space is spoiled like curdled milk. We never made a gentle memory.

The news of Mother's death four years back came in the mail in a padded envelope. I picked it up at the Rusty Nickel and guessed what it was from the return address of a law office. It held a check for one hundred thousand dollars—a mere snippet of her wealth—and a pearl necklace in a padded jewelry case. Could these be Mother's Mikimoto pearls? I remember how proud she was to own something so extraordinary. As if her status was elevated when she wore them. To me they were a noose.

I deposited the money in the bank in Burnsville, but in rebellion I took the pearls to the edge of my creek and broke the string. They scattered in the icy waters to lie with the slugs and slime. I may have had a smug look on my face, but Mother had the last stab.

Later, I saw one of the pearls lodged in the rocks. The outer shell was splitting to expose a plastic bead. Mother hadn't given me Mikimoto pearls or even cultured pearls. She gave me a strand of fake pearls. The remarkable thing was that her cruelty could still surprise me.

I don't know how she died, but at that moment, I hoped it had been a slow death. That she had lain helpless in her upholstered bed with walls papered in suffocating toile and heavy drapes snuffing out the light. That she discovered the clangor was missing in the substantial handbell that always sat on the bedside table. That its silence galled her to the point of apoplexy.

Maybe it was Peggy-the-Maid who tended Mother's needs who did the devious deed, because Peggy wasn't her real name. *Peggy* was what Mother called every hired woman who tended to her whims. I knew five Peggys who had never been called by their given name.

The true tragedy is that Mother's entitlement never sweetened her days. She was a parsimonious woman living a stingy life, a life that fell short of her vision of importance despite the obituary that took up three columns in the newspaper. The obituary photo she had chosen to show the world was taken thirty years before when she looked like a movie star ingenue. She thought she looked glamorous. I thought she looked desperate.

As her brainy, tall lesbian daughter, I embarrassed her and she embarrassed me. We never respected each other. How old do I have to be before I give that respect to myself? Can I see, at last, that Mother wasn't anything like her precious Mikimoto pearls, where a seed of mother-of-pearl was painstakingly introduced as an irritant in an oyster. Mother was merely the irritant. At her core, she was a common plastic bead.

I'm pulled from my toxic reverie feeling lighter, even liberated. I say, "Did I tell you she was dead?"

Theresa raises her glass of iced tea, and says, "Precisely."

# Chapter 48

## FAMILY

**Lydia Brown**

The veil over Birdie's mystery grows thin. What is coming to light are answers I feared I'd never find. That I have a rightful place in all this. That my lost years had purpose and that my destiny is being fulfilled.

In these remaining summer weeks, Kate and I follow a simple routine of transcribing Birdie's words, but there is no urgency. There is no deadline. Every Wednesday I go to the mountain to be with Granny C in the chamber room and Gus accompanies me. She tutors Eddie. School will start soon. They've become fast friends.

Recently, Granny and I discovered a gift growing in the ash where the crone's trailer had burned. Ginseng in mature abundance is rising up. Granny C believes a ginseng burial ground had been protected by Birdie's trailer and clearing until they were exposed to the elements. Today, a pound of dried ginseng root brings twenty to thirty dollars. Even beyond the grave, Birdie provides for her people.

More truths come forth from the chamber findings. Each woman from that forgotten Scottish priory begat a line of women who are scattered across southern Appalachia. Over the centuries, they've worked as healers, midwives, teachers, apothecaries, and librarians. They each birthed their generation of successors—except Birdie. She didn't birth her successor. The records show her babies were stillborn. She chose in her stead Granny C, Loretty, and me. Birdie was the coven's librarian, and as a Keeper, that job is mine. I will now oversee and protect the clan records.

That's my destiny. The elaborate plan included my curious birthmark, Trula Freed, my husband Jack, Romi Harker, Gus, and the skeptic Kate. Birdie laid down a trail of breadcrumbs and I followed. I was not being shunned. I was being pulled and pushed to where I needed to go.

Tomorrow, on Friday August 15, Gus goes home, so tonight on the porch, Kate, Professor Covey, and I celebrate her birthday. She turns fourteen on Sunday, and we baked her a chocolate sheet cake decorated with gold and silver icing that spells *HAPPY XIV BIRTHDAY GUS*—our edible version of an illuminated manuscript.

Kate's gift is a leather diary weathered to look like one of Birdie's books, complete with leather binding. It was made at Penland School of Craft. The key hangs from a silk cord and can lock her secrets inside.

Professor Covey gives Gus a first-edition Nancy Drew mystery book, *The Witch Tree Symbol*. The thirty-third book in her mother's favorite detective series. On the cover is an image of witches' broom fungus which changes the natural structure of a plant. It's a metaphor for Gus who is changing into her own. Maybe Lucy will read it and remember when she was a girl looking for mystery in her days.

My birthday gift is the Ouija board. Gus can recite the opening and closing prayers for safety, and she knows enough about the *other side* to be cautious. I resist saying she should hide it. All teenagers know that wisdom. Ouija is best kept hidden.

This final afternoon, Uncle sits on the bed watching Gus pack the duffel bag that's large enough to hold a body. Around her neck hangs a dull green stone wired to a thin strip of leather. It's a raw emerald Eddie found among the stones in the mushroom cave. The cuckoo clock strikes five, and she reaches under her bed and pulls out a scrapbook.

"What's this?" I had wondered when the project would surface.

"It's for you. From Uncle Jack."

"Uncle Jack? What do you mean?"

"He hid photos and poems for you in secret places around the cottage and I found them. Photos of the two of you, and new poems he wrote. He put dates on the back so I could figure out the order."

My hands tremble as I open the cover. The first is a photo of Jack and me on our wedding day. Not the one framed on my bedside table where we stand posed *just so*. In this one our faces are slightly out of focus because the sun is in the wrong place. It's behind us creating a misty aura. We look ethereal and hope-filled and achingly young. I never saw this photo.

"Where did you say you found these?" I ask, but Gus is silent.

The next page holds one of Jack's handwritten poems that he titled "Brimful of Grace." It starts *Grace falls into this / measured chalice, taunting us*. Seeing new words from Jack's brilliant mind makes me sob, and I grab tissues so I don't drip tears on the precious album. I turn page after page of wonder, and there is our history as I've never seen it before. Photos that weren't the first choice where we smiled in unison. These photos were the castoffs that didn't make the original cut, likely taken by an amateur cousin or aging uncle. But in hindsight they are the most precious. Eyes closed, mouth open in jest for my sister, Lucy, who the camera often catches that way. A close-up of an ear or missing the top of Jack's head but catching the scar on his cheek that I love. Some were taken so far away that we're specks in a wide panorama making us look like an afterthought or tiny humans in the big scheme of things.

Gus points, "And this poem tickled me, Aunt Liddy. *Mom went in there a / week ago. Smiling, she said / Kudzu was on sale, / and they have Green Stamps! She musta got lost in that / leafy verdant vale, / Dodging sprightly vines, / Snagging stamps, adrift on the / Cut-rate kudzu trail.* Did you know he could be funny like that?"

"I did. Every topic was fair game for that clever man." I pull my eyes away from the page and hug my niece. "I love every page," I say and squeeze harder. "They mean the world to me. Truly."

"I know," she says simply then adds, "Do you smell that?"

And I do. *Cherry pipe tobacco*, and it lingers as the final packing is finished and piled on the porch ready for transport.

"You gonna miss me?"

"With every breath I take."

"You gonna feed Uncle?"

"When she's here, but I won't worry if she goes off. She'll know when you're coming back."

My niece says, "You have four white cats in your wood now. They're spirit cats, Aunt Liddy. They hold the souls of those who love you. You've got Uncle Jack, your mama and daddy, and Trula Freed. They're powerful spirits on the other side, and they're coming close to your cottage to watch over you. That's a good thing."

What can I say to something so glorious? Since Birdie's ghost spoke to me in her chamber, my bridge to the spirit world has been rebuilt. The nightly visits are a comfort. But what a complex maze I've traveled to become part of this ancient, feminine history. The last decade has seen progress for my gender, but my fervent hope is that Gus's generation and every one that follows will have more choices and fewer barriers. May we lift each other up and let no one be left behind.

We sit in the swing with Uncle between us and rock slow while a flock of Canada geese heads south. We'll meet Lucy at six at the inn. "You ready to see your mama?"

"I guess."

"It'll be a good thing."

"How you figure that?" Her sullenness has returned.

"You're not the same girl who came in June. That girl was looking for a fight but didn't find one. When your mama was your age and determined to be called Lu, she tested boundaries and it got her into trouble, but that didn't stop her. You and your mama are more alike than different."

Gus hugs me fiercely and I close my eyes to feel her wiry strength, smell her vanilla scent with a hint of spicy pepper. I wait for her to let go and whisper, "I'm always here for you, a phone call away. Any time night or day, I will come when you call."

"I want to be your junior intern next summer."

"I'm counting on it."

I glance at the clock. "It's time."

We walk to the car and Uncle is in the lead, the duffel dragging the ground, marking the trail. The cat waits while Gus loads the bag then comes back and speaks parting words I can't hear. At Little Switzerland, our favorite waitress Sandy saved the best table for us on the patio. When we're seated, I say, "We'll take three burgers and fries," and surprise Gus.

"Three?"

"Your mama's joining us for dinner."

"Isn't she too busy?"

"Not tonight."

"Oh," Gus says.

And here comes Lucy right on time, looking younger, wearing jeans and a T-shirt like her daughter. Gus walks into her mother's open arms, and Lucy ruffles her daughter's blond pixie hair. It's a different meeting this August night from the one in June. We chatter about underground tunnels, hidden chambers, caves, and emeralds. About new friends and a white cat named Uncle and a mystery that started far away and spans five hundred years. Lucy is entranced, her elbow on the table, her chin cupped in her palm.

Then I tell the most wondrous news that came in a dream last night. I say, "You have a message from Mama."

"*Oh my stars*," she whispers and claps her hands like a little girl. "The spirit voices came back."

I nod and flush with joy.

"What'd she say?"

"*Write that book*."

"What book?"

"The one that's inside you. Mama wants to know how it ends."

"The one about a tobacco farmer who raises bees?"

"Could be. Or maybe the one about a witch who died and left a treasure of silver and gold. Gus can help with that one."

When we part after dinner, Lucy's hug is sincere. "Thank you—for everything."

And when Gus embraces me, she whispers, "Watch for Samuel. He'll be passing over soon."

# Chapter 49

## FARE WELL

**Kate Shaw**

Birdie's Books of Truth will not go to the Rare Book School. Or to the J. P. Morgan library in Manhattan, where they would feel out of sorts. They will not be auctioned to the highest bidder at Sotheby's to burnish a rich man's ego. All options are discarded but the logical one: the Books of Truth will stay close to their roots.

I follow Lydia's advice and accept the glorious offer for the Books of Truth from Appalachian State, where they will be studied under the tutelage of Dr. Cratis Williams. Dr. Williams's reputation grows as the Father of Appalachian Studies, and he is held in high esteem on an expanding stage. Born in Kentucky of Scots-Irish heritage, Williams understands folk speech and is dedicated to discovering and preserving the mysteries of this rich culture. He will pull from Birdie's books every truth and lesson. The sale of seventy-eight books generated a fortune. It is the pot of gold at the end of the rainbow only dreamers imagine, and I've become a dreamer.

To understand how this fortune will work for Baines Creek, Lydia and I visit an investor recommended by Professor Covey. Mr. Lourdes of Peyton and Lourdes exudes confidence in his three-piece suit, buffed nails, and groomed beard. He explains that the income will be wisely invested in blue-chip stock that has a large market cap, a sterling reputation, excellent financials, and many years of success in the business world. They will not gamble with Birdie's gift. The outcome could benefit the children of Baines Creek forever. In the future, it will pay for any educational endeavor they can imagine. It will help students fit in. There will be little standing between the students and success except their own aspirations and hesitations. This news will be delivered at church on Friday. It's my hope that *possibility* becomes a good thing for tomorrow and not a threat to their past. Baines Creek will fare well because of Birdie Rocas.

My name is openly tied to these discoveries as if I were the mastermind who brought these treasures to light. In the academic world I've become *interesting,* and I am amused by the attention, as if my ten years in a one-room schoolhouse had an overarching motive. But the truth is that all I did was wander and be found. Birdie would say the accolades were unbecoming to a woman honest about her limitations. She humbles me still, but now I find it reassuring, not degrading. I became a pawn in her plan, but a willing one.

Granny C told Lydia and me that the eleven clans meet in the meadow at Birdie's place every summer solstice. They met quietly this year to celebrate Birdie's life and to determine what was best for their manuscript and Florie's journal. They don't want them to remain hidden and be returned to the underground chamber. They will loan them to the Rare Book School in Charlottesville. There scholars can study them and visitors can bear witness to something extraordinary created centuries ago by women. Without trying, Birdie Rocas has become an international curiosity. An icon with a feral eye who smoked a corncob pipe and had a crow ride on her head. A truth seeker. A Keeper. My friend.

# Chapter 50

## FULL CIRCLE

**Lydia Brown**

Dusk is approaching when Granny C, Loretty, and I climb the worn stone steps from the book depository. We've spent this last Wednesday in August sorting blown-glass apothecary bottles of tincture and spices. Their faded labels are hard to decipher. Large magnifying glasses on stands help. There are hundreds more holding seeds and ointments and crushed flowers, but we've done enough today. When we exit the chamber, we hear it. A ruckus is building. A lamentation rising.

It's Samuel.

The past week the white crow has stayed near Birdie's burying place, and today is his dying day. In an instant I know this firmly, and my heart quickens. I want to remember every facet to tell Kate and Gus.

It starts with droves of crows flying to the meadow, pulled by something mighty that pulls the three of us to its rim. The beating of a thousand wings moves the air like ocean waves and makes the tall grass to lie down. In the center is exposed a round, dull green stone. Samuel, with all the living bleached out of him, lies on that stone. He watches crows fill high branches. Black feathers torn from chests rain down like ash.

I didn't know this united sorrow was possible for the passing of a crow. Then I remember the majestic crow embedded in the top of the ancient coffer. And the brilliance of crows referenced in Florie's journal. Samuel is linked to a powerful legacy as Birdie is linked to the heroes of Elcho Priory. The sun sinks below the rim and the dark lies soft across the land, and the keening continues. Samuel radiates with an inner light, and the harsh cries of the crows merge into *Om*.

Ten angel lights appear. They drift down and encircle the air above Samuel. Ghosts arrive one by one. Birdie and her sisters. Generations of witches and healers and Keepers of Truth. They raise their right hands, and Granny C, Loretty, and I raise ours, and amid the swirl of feathers the spirit of the silver crow ascends to Finally There. The home beyond.

Once out of sight, the meadow is empty yet feathers are everywhere and the silence is profound. I am washed in the truth that, at last, all the puzzle pieces of my life fit. All my wanderings have brought me to this pinprick on this planet to witness purpose and true altruism. Surrounded by testimony to a life well lived, I yearn for home. My earthly home, and that yearning is a reawakening.

Once upon a time, we Browns had the perfect simple life. When it shattered, we pretended the fragments were unimportant. But we were wrong, and it's not too late. I need to go home to be with my brothers and sisters. We need to tell old stories and hear new ones from the other side. We need to take our fractured pieces and make us whole.

# Chapter 51

## THE BEGINNING

### KATE SHAW

Today is a day of utter joy. After a final deed in Baines Creek, Rachel and I will be off to our new destination. Tomorrow we'll drive east on Route 40 across North Carolina, then north on Route 29 to Charlottesville. I've rented a carriage house behind a stately Victorian within walking distance to work. I will imbue that place with creature comforts that mean the most to me. Granny C gifted me one of Birdie's wind chimes, which will hang four hundred miles from its source. It will hang on my front porch between two rocking chairs. I hope there are days it will jingle even when the air is still.

Theresa Cotton hired me as her research assistant at the Rare Book School, and my head is dizzy with plans she's making. The first was for me to join the American Association of University Women. Founded in 1881 by a small band of college women in Boston, the AAUW is united to advocate for women's rights. A hundred years ago, their first battle was to fight bizarre myths such as the belief that higher education diminished a woman's fertility and that women's brains were less developed. Men argued that admitting women to college was a dangerous experiment that would upset the balance of things. Women had a valued place in the home that took their waking hours, and now they wanted to challenge their minds—where would they find the time?

Theresa is president of the organization that boasts 170,000 members. She writes important legislation exacting equal rights and opportunities for all people. Her voice is added to the growing army of women demanding our fair share. Requiring our contributions be recognized. When I thought my life had lost use of me, it has become vibrant.

Such as today.

Three months ago the community met in Eli's church at five o'clock on a Friday. They were given no warning about change coming before strangers in blue suits said school would close and not reopen. Ready or not, come September students would go to county schools. Fresh gravel and a bridge over the creek were pledged, and the county has done a mediocre job. A rudimentary bridge with framed sides and planked decking has been built, but it won't hold when big rains come. A better one will have to be built. That's what the old-timers say.

But at summer's end this story has a new chapter: Birdie Rocas died and left a startling legacy. With funding coming from one of their own and not do-gooders off the mountain, people may be inclined to accept help. Under Eli's supervision, Sadie Blue will meet with families to determine what the students need to succeed. They'll get new textbooks and tutors and encouragement to help them adjust. Every year each child will get new shoes and a warm winter coat. Birdie's gift will help them fit in. This will be a paying job for Sadie. She'll be good at it.

Lucy Flannery, Lydia's sister, has found expanded purpose teaching at Mountain Heritage. After Gus recounted Eddie's work to prepare for change, Lucy wants to help. She recommended he write for the school newspaper and create a unique column called "Creekrise." His words will bridge old mountain ways with town life. Lucy will meet weekly with the displaced children and be their sounding board. With guidance on both ends of the new road they travel, their chance for success goes up exponentially.

The summer solving puzzles ends differently than we imagined. The closing of the one-room schoolhouse could have meant a dead end, but the card EXPECT A MIRACLE continues to bestow blessings. Before leaving the area, I went to the school where the October Festival was held last fall. I was curious about the gypsy woman with the crystal ball in her tent of scarves. I wanted to tell her about the good things that had turned me into a believer. But the strangest thing happened.

Neither the principal nor his secretary remembered a gypsy booth at the festival. They said I must be thinking of a different carnival. I assured them it was only theirs that I'd attended. Then I asked Loretty if she recollected the gypsy reading my fortune. She looked puzzled and said she remembered bobbing for apples, the man on stilts, and Jimbo throwing up from eating too much candy. I'm left with only one conclusion: The gypsy with the card was a miracle for me, possibly conjured by Birdie.

Today is my final drive to Baines Creek, and it's bittersweet. I thought I came as penance and my expectations were simple. But I leave reborn and open to more. My Edsel holds my meager possessions, and I cross the new bridge and park beside Lydia's Jeep. Rachel with his graying muzzle walks beside me. It's the last Friday in August and the community has been told to come at five o'clock to hear good news. Long tables and folding chairs have been set up. Food will be delivered by Easy Street Homecooked Meals in Burnsville. Fried chicken, potato salad, coleslaw, corn on the cob, and baskets of angel rolls with creamery butter. There will be apple pies and peach pies, too, and homemade ice cream packed in ice and rock salt and cranked in steel cylinders.

I wave to Sadie Blue and her brood standing beside Granny C and Lydia Brown, and there's Gus and her mama laughing with Eli, Eddie, and his mama Jolene. These are the faces of support for the future. This is the moment I could not fathom when hope had dwindled to a grain of grit. Birdie gave us a puzzle to solve, and it led to this moment.

There's going to be standing room only in church.

It is the night that will change everything.

# ACKNOWLEDGMENTS

This book came to be because of generous, gifted people. My brilliant agent Rebecca Gradinger and co-agent Lily Dolin believed an early draft held a better story if I was willing to do major surgery, and I did. My extraordinary editor, Shana Drehs, and the Sourcebooks dream team asked provocative questions, cleared the final muddled parts, and launched the book into the literary world. Special thanks to Arthur Russell, who trudged through an abysmal first draft; to Frank Brown in Little Switzerland, who spent a day sharing local history; to Gene Hyde, archivist in Special Collections at UNC Asheville; and Ross Cooper in Special Collections at Appalachian State University in Boone, NC. There were early conversations with Fran Harker, Cameo Hoyle, Jenny Beirne, Janet Moore, and Phil Garmey that gave the developing story authenticity. There was the magical book club week with Muriel Hunter, Lisa Back, Sheila Peters, Shannon Brennan, Sally Santmyer, Dominique Gendrin-Magnuson, and Sue Ginter, where I read an advance reader's copy in a gorgeous beach setting. These friends were enthusiastic cheerleaders for the story's first public unveiling. When I was frustrated in the middle of the tiresome process, my creative son, Paul Clements, and his talented wife, Bea Gutierrez, inspired me to not give up, and my sister Glo Swann supported me at every rewrite. As always, my husband, Dave Harpster, was my gentle partner. His steady kindness helped me heal from difficult writing days.

# AUTHOR NOTES

The underground tunnels in this book were inspired by the Spruce Pine Mining District that claims more than seven hundred mines. Mica production and gold, silver, and gemstone mines were once prolific. Over a hundred commercial mineral mines are still active. Today, Emerald Village near Little Switzerland encompasses a hundred acres where you can pan for treasure and explore historic tunnels. Linville Caverns is a limestone show cave open to the public. Connecting the underground tunnels to chambers and a cave is fabricated.

The poems attributed to the character Jack Reynolds were written by Gene Hyde, writer, poet, photographer, editor of the *Appalachian Curator*, and retired Appalachian archivist. Gene became Jack's beating heart, and I am grateful he gave me permission to use his wonderful words. You can find more of his work at banteringbibliocrat.com.

There are numerous adjustments I made to the story's location and history. The Rare Book School (RBS) was founded at Columbia University in 1983 by Terry Belanger and moved to the University of Virginia in 1992. For the story's sake, I placed the RBS in Charlottesville in 1980. In 1980, the café in Little Switzerland, NC, was named the Sandwich Gallery, but I called it the Diamondback Café. Likewise, the delightful

Books and Beans bookstore in the same community didn't open until 1986, but I took the liberty to make it fit my timeline in 1980. Baines Creek and the haunted woods are fictional, as is *Appalachian Folklore* magazine, but the hollers of Appalachia are real. Hollers are defined as *a sheltered valley with a winding creek in a sparse, close-knit community*.

A major theme in the book is recognizing the value of women's contributions. Virginia Woolf's famous adapted quote belonged in this book and was originally found in her book *A Room of One's Own*. It reads: "For most of history, Anon was a woman." I chose to use the implied word *Anonymous* on the opening page. You can find Woolf's accurate quote referenced in chapter 46.

The icon Gloria Steinem plays an important role in the history of women's rights. Her book of personal essays, *Outrageous Acts and Everyday Rebellions*, came out in 1983, but I set it in 1980 to fit my story.

The eleven women who lived at Elcho Priory in sixteenth-century Scotland were a glorious discovery. I modified a few names and bios to fit my characters, but the bio of Euphemia Leslie is original in its entirety, including her being the *spurious* (illegitimate) daughter of Walter Leslie, the parish priest. I was surprised to find this fact preserved and accepted.

To tie the treasure more tightly to Scotland, I chose to have the secular illuminated manuscript and Florie's journal written in Gaelic instead of Latin.

And lastly, I want to reference two truths provided by Ross Cooper in Appalachian State's Special Collections. They became the compass for this book. First, a page from an ancient illuminated manuscript had been found in Appalachia. And second, an article revealed a gifted woman in the Middle Ages was also a creator of illuminated manuscripts: "The 900-Year-Old Nun with Blue Teeth." (Look it up. It's an interesting read.)

# READING GROUP GUIDE

1. The book opens with the closing of the one-room schoolhouse. What are some benefits to that kind of education? Can any of those benefits translate to modern education?

2. Kate believes she failed her students. Do you think she did a good job? If so, why?

3. Why do you think Birdie wrote the Books of Truth?

4. Why did Birdie leave the Books of Truth to Kate, and what did she expect Kate to do with them?

5. In what ways are Kate Shaw and Lydia Brown alike? How are they different? How does Birdie change them?

6. How has the fight for women's equal rights changed since 1980?

7. *The bridge to the other side* is Lydia's constant quest. Do you or anyone you know have psychic gifts or spirit dreams?

8. How would you feel if someone had a dream message for you? Would you be skeptical or intrigued?

9. Do you have a favorite scene in the book?

10. What resonates most for you in this Appalachian story?

11. How do you think the next unwritten chapters would read?

# A CONVERSATION WITH THE AUTHOR

**Where did the idea come from for this book?**

The idea came from readers. At speaking engagements and book clubs, I was often told that my characters and their stories were unforgettable, and readers wondered what happened next. I wondered too. So I decided to write a story told by a character from each of my first two books and ground it in surprising truths, with mysterious Appalachia and the powerful witch Birdie at its heart. I chose the teacher Kate Shaw from *If the Creek Don't Rise* and the psychic child Lydia Brown from *All the Little Hopes* to solve a puzzle with an extraordinary outcome.

**What kind of research did you do for this book?**

The tedious but wondrous kind, for I wander and collect bits and pieces for years to find the whole story. I worked with Ross Cooper at Appalachian State's Special Collections, and he helped me discover two intriguing Appalachian truths that fit my premise and became my story's springboard. I spent time in Special Collections at UNC Asheville with archivist Gene Hyde and visited the campus at Penland School of Craft outside Spruce Pine, NC. I read a daunting stack of books that included *Hollow Folk* by Mandel Sherman and Thomas R. Henry, *Roaming the Mountains with John Parris* by John Parris, *Gift from the Hills* by Lucy Morgan and LeGette Blythe, and *Appalachia on the Table* by Erica Abrams Locklear. As always, the internet provided rabbit holes to follow and amazing facts to uncover.

**What is your writing process like?**

I have never taken a writing course other than the weeklong summer writing workshops at Wildacres Retreat and Conference Center near Little Switzerland, so I'm not trained in the academic steps to follow. I don't use digital writing tools. The few times I've tried to create an outline, the characters refused to follow it. Later in the process, I create an overview table of chapters, and the columns hold title, page numbers, highlights, key characters, problems, and timeline. It's the only way I can maneuver and find the gaps or redundancy and judge the pacing. In the end, no matter the tools, there are no shortcuts to writing a good book but to sit and write and cut and write and cut. Twice in this book I eliminated a hundred pages that held subplots that hurt rather than helped the storyline, then I wrote more intentional ones.

**What do you hope readers will take away?**

May they find *The Creek, the Crone, and the Crow* a natural extension of my first two books, which were conceived and written long before there was a hint they could be intertwined. I hope they are drawn to empowerment, redemption, and healing, and are captivated by fantastical possibilities. I hope they appreciate the humble Appalachian way of life. And may the ending be as satisfying for them to read as it was for me to discover.

# ABOUT THE AUTHOR

PHOTO © MYERS PHOTOGRAPHY

Leah Weiss is a bestselling Southern author born in North Carolina and raised in the foothills of the Blue Ridge Mountains of Virginia. Her debut novel, *If the Creek Don't Rise*, was released in 2017, followed by *All the Little Hopes* in 2021 and *The Creek, the Crone, and the Crow* in 2026. Her short stories have been published in *The Simple Life* magazine, *Every Day Fiction*, and *Deep South* magazine. You can contact her at leahweiss.com.

READ ON FOR A LOOK
AT *ALL THE LITTLE HOPES*
BY LEAH WEISS

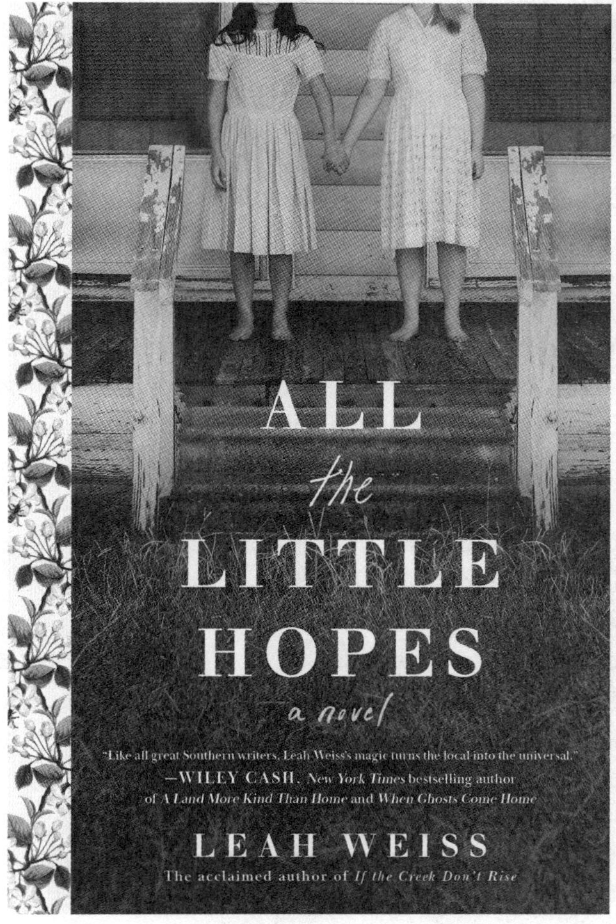


**Available now from Sourcebooks Landmark**

# Chapter 1

## LUCY: BITTERSWEET

The gray car with the faded white star slows at our mailbox, deliberates, then lumbers down our rutted road, raising dust. It interrupts my reading of *The Hidden Staircase* when Nancy Drew discovers rickety stairs leading to dark tunnels beneath mansions. I slip the bookmark in place and watch the arrival from the hayloft, curious.

The car stops under the oak tree whose leaves are limp from summer heat. The driver turns off the motor, and the cooling engine ticks like a clock marking odd time. He sits wide and tall in the seat and hasn't seen me studying him from on high, with my bare legs dangling over the edge of the loft. He checks his teeth in the mirror, flattens a cowlick with spit, and opens the door. The hinge creaks as he rolls out. If it's grave news this government man brings, news that is going to alter our family tree, I thought it would be delivered with more decorum. My belly turns sour.

At the coming of the car, Mama steps on the porch, wiping her hands on her apron. The screen door slaps behind, and she jumps. These days she stays wound as tight as Oma's cuckoo clock because of our men gone to war. *The not knowing is the hard part,* Mama says—like my thirteen-year-old self doesn't know that by now.

The government man is corpulent with flushed cheeks. He carries a battered briefcase and takes two steps while studying a scrap of paper. “I’m looking for David Brown,” he calls out with a voice abnormally high for a heavy man.

“Is it Everett Brown or Wade Sully?” Mama’s voice pinches, saying the names of my oldest brother and my sister Helen’s husband.

“Oh, Lordy, ma’am.” He clears his throat. “I’m sorry I scared you thinking that way, seeing this government car and all. No, ma’am. I bring good news.”

Mama’s body softens, and I turn curiouser.

She rings the dinner bell to call Daddy in from the tobacco field where the crop is already stunted from a dry spell this year. I come down from the loft, tuck Nancy Drew between hay bales, slip on my bee suit like I was supposed to when I wanted to read instead. I tie my sneakers and walk out of the barn in time to see the tractor chug this way on high. Grady stands on the frame, his shirt billowing in the air. When they get close, Daddy cuts the motor, and they jump down and move at a fast clip. Mama yells, “It’s not our boys,” so they don’t race their hearts.

Daddy walks up to the stranger, sticks out his right hand mannerly, and slides his toothpick to the corner of his mouth. “I’m David Brown. My son, Grady.”

Juggling the briefcase in his left arm, the good-news man wipes his right hand on his trousers before he shakes Daddy’s hand, then Grady’s. “I’m John T. Booker, sir, representing the United States government. Mind me asking how many hives you got there?” He nods toward the white boxes beyond the barn.

“Beehives?” Daddy was thinking bad news and is confused. He glances at me holding my bee hat in one hand and the unlit smoker in the other when it should be smoldering. I can’t help that I love books with a passion and they can interrupt tending bees, but Daddy's forgiving. His eyes settle back on the fat man. "Bout a hundred, last count."

"Whew. That's a nice operation. Does that come to about a thousand pounds of beeswax and eight thousand pounds of honey a year?" Mr. Booker throws out figures I've never heard before.

"Thereabouts..." Daddy answers, but he doesn't elaborate on how often a hive absconds when the temperatures change, or the queen dies and throws the hive into a quandary, or their food source dries up in a drought like we had two summers back. It's rare to have all our hives in working order.

"I'm here to talk bee business with you, Mr. Brown."

"You want my honey?" Daddy frowns because with the war on and sugar scarce, honey is a prized commodity.

"It's mostly beeswax we need, sir. Is there somewhere we can talk? I've got a proposition for you."

Daddy nods to the table under the oak tree, where dinner is served at noon to field hands. "Here'll do."

Mr. John T. Booker brushes off twigs and leaves, sits on the bench, and plops his bulging briefcase on the table. Grady leans against the tree, chews on his toothpick, and adroitly rolls three glass marbles between his fingers. Mama sits between my little sisters, Lydia and Cora, shy on each side. I sit, too, unzipping the bee suit for ventilation. Unexpected company takes precedence over chores. My older sister, Irene, is at her newspaper job in town, but she's going to be sorry to hear a proposition secondhand. And my oldest sister, Helen, stays inside the house like she's prone to do. Mama says it's melancholy that's taken hold of Helen since she got in the family way and her husband, Wade, is fighting in the Pacific. Even a stranger coming and sitting at our table won't bring her outside.

Mr. Booker looks nervous with so many eyes aimed at him. He is a rumpled mess, rifling through his muddled papers. He pulls out a wrinkled pamphlet, irons it out with his palm, and gives it to Daddy.

"This here will explain what I come to talk about." He uses his index finger to wipe sweat off his upper lip, leans toward Mama, and speaks low. "Ma'am, can I bother you for some water? I'm mighty parched." With a tilt of her head, she sends Cora to the well to fetch a cup. Mr. Booker stares after the pale and frail of my sister who has often been mistaken for an apparition. He takes the cup from her, but his hand trembles. Still, he drinks the water and nods his thanks.

Daddy reads aloud, "Honeybees and Wartime," then studies the brochure while we study the government man. Mr. Booker wears a shirt straining at the buttons and a skinny black tie, like an encyclopedia salesman peddling knowledge a month at a time. His belt is brown, but his shoes are black with scuffed tips that have never seen a lick of polish. He has surprisingly tiny feet that don't look able to keep him upright when the wind blows. He squirms at the silence and starts talking before Daddy's done.

"It pretty much says *Worker Bees, Uncle Sam Needs You*," and he grins like he told a funny. He adds weakly, "We could use your help, sir," then studies his chewed fingernails for somewhere to lay his eyes.

I've been holding back questions, so in the lull, I let loose in a polite way. "You a military man, Mr. Booker?" I say. I've never seen an unkempt military man.

"No, I can't be a soldier cause I got flat feet," he says and nods toward his briefcase. "I do paper stuff."

"Where you from?"

"Greenville," he says but not which Greenville.

"Did you know there are fifteen states that have towns called Greenville? Unless you're from Greeneville, Tennessee. That's different from all the others because of the extra *e* smack-dab in the middle. Which one are you?"

Mr. Booker mumbles, "North Carolina" without a crumb of interest in the insight I shared. He didn't even want to know the names of the Greenville states I can list alphabetically. I change course.

"Do you know rubbing beeswax on a fishing line makes it float?"

"No, I do not," he says.

"Do you like to fish?"

"No, I do not."

"Who's your favorite author? I love Carolyn Keene. She wrote the Nancy Drew books about a girl like me who solves mysteries and knows a lot about a lot of things. Do you like mystery books?"

Mama says quietly, "Enough, Lucy," and cuts off my litany of questions. "Leave Mr. Booker alone."

I comply, but I already know he's a dolt who's pitiful at conversation.

Daddy passes the brochure over to Mama and says, "Let me get this straight," and shifts his toothpick to the other corner of his mouth, and Grady does the same. "You want some of my honey and all my beeswax."

"Yes, sir, and we'll pay good money for it."

"And if we sell you beeswax, you'll give us barrels of cane sugar so we can supplement the hives with sugar syrup and sugar cakes. All the sugar I need, no ration coupon needed."

"Yes, sir."

"Say again what it's used for?"

"The war effort uses a million pounds of beeswax a year to waterproof canvas tents and lubricate ammunition, drill bits, and cables, stuff like that."

"You think it'll last much longer?" Daddy asks.

"Beeswax, sir?"

"The war."

"Don't rightly know, but we gotta be ready for what comes."

Daddy leans back on the chair legs. "Says on that piece of paper my boys won't have to enlist if they work the hives."

"Yes, sir… I mean, no, sir. They'll be doing war duty working bees. We know making sugar water to keep bees making wax will take a lot of man-hours. A hundred hives might need twenty-five gallons of sugar water a day. We'll give you the sugar, the scale, boxes, paper dividers, cutting tools—everything you need, even the postage to ship the wax—and send you a check."

"Is my son-in-law exempt, too?"

"Yes, sir. That release option applies to all the men tied to your family. Well, those who want to stay home, that is. It's kind of a sweet deal, don't you think?"

Daddy looks at Mama.

Our bees sign up.

# READ ON FOR A LOOK AT *IF THE CREEK DON'T RISE* BY LEAH WEISS

**Available now from Sourcebooks Landmark**

# Sadie Blue

I struggle to my feet, straighten my back, lift my chin, then he hits me again. This time I fall down and stay down while he counts, "…eight, nine, ten." He walks out the trailer door and slams it hard. The latch don't catch, and the door pops open. I lay on the floor and watch Roy Tupkin cross the dirt yard and disappear into the woods.

My world's gone sideways again.

"Sadie girl." Daddy's spirit voice comes soft from behind my open eyes. "You got yourself in a pickle this time. No two ways about it. That husband of yours won't stop till you and your baby draw your last breath. You don't even look like yourself no more. He broke bout every piece of sweet in you. You gonna let him break your spirit, too? You gonna do nothing?"

*I'm tired, Daddy. Wore out. Roy Tupkin don't just beat me, he beats me down. Let me rest a spell. I don't know if I can lift my head just yet.*

Now Daddy's voice comes from the yard where a lone wind rattles late-summer oak leaves and sounds like hollow bones. "If I could follow the bastard and kill him for you, I would, sweet girl, but it don't work like that." His voice drifts toward the rusty red truck up on blocks. "Don't lay there too long, Sadie. You don't need rest." His words fade. "You need…"

*What, Daddy? What do I need?* I listen but he's gone.

Percy scampers in from the hunt with a dead chipmunk. He drops his gift by my hand. When I don't move, he nudges it close till I raise a finger and touch fur that's still warm. Then he crawls on the rise of my belly and curls up. Purrs vibrate clean through to my spine.

*I gotta get away, Percy, but don't know how. Gotta be careful.*

Percy listens good but he's short on advice. I can't think what to do right off with my brain muddled from this morning's beating, so I gather strength to move. Shadows grow longer, and cold air glides across the doorjamb, giving me goose bumps. I roll over gentle to my side, scattering pieces of the green plastic radio I got working at Mooney's Rusty Nickel. Little Percy slides off without complaint. I put my palms on the floor and push to my knees. My arms tremble. My heart pounds in my ears. A bloody smear on the floor marks where my head landed. I brush sticky hair off my temple, hold on to the counter, and pull up, dizzy, one hand on my baby bump. I don't know I'm crying salty tears till they sting the cut on my cheek.

"You know what you gotta do." Daddy's voice is back burrowing inside my ear.

*I do? Tell me and I'll do it.*

"You'll figure it out. You got smarts you don't even know bout yet."

Daddy loves me better in death than he ever did in life. In life, when I was ten, with my hair in crooked braids, me sitting on a overturned bucket in a corner of the kitchen, watching the men round the table gamble, he throwed a night with me in the poker pot instead of five dollars he don't have. Granny and Aunt Marris never heard what he done, and I don't say cause they'd take a belt to him and take me away from him when he needs me. Daddy won the hand. Said he counted on it. But he woulda made good on his bet if he'd lost. He won't go back on his word.

Daddy hung bones on the walls inside our house like some folks hang giveaway calendars or pictures of Jesus. They was mostly bleached-out skulls he found hunting or tending the still. He ran twine through their empty eyes and wound the twine on a tenpenny nail high on the wall. He had the skulls of a fox, bear, bobcat, and panther, and the rib cage of a bear. Daddy even had a man's skull in the lot. Found it in a cave near a rockslide that pinned the poor soul down till he wasted away. Said it was likely a miner and a dreamer looking for rubies and stones. At night, under moonlight streaming through the front window, those bones glowed like pieces of ghosts.

Granny won't set foot in our house cause of Daddy's bones. Said it was a heathen thing to do. Said it won't natural. I asked Daddy why he brought such things inside when nobody else did. He grinned and said, "One time these bones was wrapped in flesh and muscle and brains. They mighta fought a good fight to the end. But in the end, even the smart ones is just bones with all the fight gone out. Looking at em makes me think different bout power and petty things."

I hear he don't start hanging bones on the wall till Mama left.

Some folks say Daddy was a peculiar soul. Some say he was a thinking man. He was funny, gentle, and always a pinch of sad the years I knew him, cause the pitiful truth is he got nothing from loving Mama cept me left behind.

I think it was a broke heart that killed him, mostly cause Mama left him with a baby girl who lately looked too much like her. I don't remember her face cept from a faded picture in a dresser drawer in a back room at Granny's. Mama had hair the color of mine, and she was built thin like me. Aunt Marris said she had gumption in her eyes and a slice of selfish that won't pretty.

That night Daddy ended up dead, he stumbled in my room on wobbly legs and fell on top of me sleeping in my iron bed. "Carly, my Carly Blue." He cried out Mama's name next to my ear, slobbering like a sorry fool. I never liked it when Daddy don't know me cause he tried things. So I pulled up my knees and pushed, and he fell off me and hit his head on the edge of the bed with a thud. I jumped over his body and run into the woods, wearing a thin nightgown that snagged on brambles that scratched my arms, a ghost girl on bare feet. I hid under the weeping willow at the creek, shivering till the moon went away and morning come shy on the mountain.

When I walked through the door, I saw death claimed Daddy. His body lay on the floor where I had left him. The color was drained, and his skin was like ash in a fire gone cold. His eyes stayed open, and a fly crawled on his cheek. He puked like drunks do, and it dried in his beard and over his ear and puddled at his neck. Daddy died cause I won't there to turn him over.

I wanted to stay at Daddy and my place on Bentwood Mountain, down the road from Granny and Aunt Marris, but Preacher Eli said to move in with Granny so she could help me through a sad time. Granny don't do my heart any good, but when the roof on Daddy's house caved in the next big winter snow, I was glad to be outta the rubble. Then that summer, vines started to crawl up the sides and through the broke windows, and over and around those pointy teeth and skulls on the wall. Nowadays, five years since, the vines claim it all.